M000214985

PRAISE FOR *YULE ISLAND*

'Remember her name. Novel after novel, Johana Gustawsson has become a leading figure in French crime fiction. *Yule Island* is impossible to put down' *Le Monde*

'Johana Gustawsson brilliantly illuminates the depths of the human heart' *Le Figaro*

'Since the publication of her first novel, *Block 46*, Johana Gustawsson has become the French queen of the thriller genre' *Le Point*

'Gustawsson has no equal when it comes to hooking us with stunning twists' *Les Echos*

'A thriller that manages to astonish us ... with a plot as complicated (and brilliant) as a four-cushion billiard shot' *L'Indépendant*

'Gustawsson enjoys taking her audience for a ride ... She always finds a way to surprise her readers' *La Provence*

'Spellbinding. Ethereal, romantic and as cold as death ... a cruel and thrilling Nordic tale' *La Fringale culturelle*

'A captivating story that grips you from the very first page and keeps you on the edge of your seat until the very end' *Nous Deux*

'This highly effective novel, set against a backdrop of Norse mythology, takes the reader on a journey inspired by the urban legends of the real island of Storholmen' *Télé 2 semaines*

'A breathless, spellbinding thriller' *L'Écho d'Ancenis*

PRAISE FOR JOHANA GUSTAWSSON

SHORTLISTED for the CWA International Dagger
WINNER of the Balai de la Découverte
WINNER of the Nouvelle Plume d'Argent Award
WINNER of the Cultura Ligue de l'Imaginaire Award

'A wonderfully dark and intricately woven historical thriller spanning three generations, *The Bleeding* will have you hooked from the very first page' B.A. Paris

'Gustawsson's writing is so vivid, it's electrifying. Utterly compelling' Peter James

'Cleverly plotted, simply excellent' Ragnar Jónasson

'This novel is a whirlpool that draws you irresistibly into levels of darkness so much deeper than you can possibly be ready for' Ambrose Parry

'Wonderfully dark and creepy, with a superb twist in its tail!' James Oswald

'*The Bleeding* begins with a truly macabre and ritualistic crime that leads back to mysteries in Belle Époque Paris and 1949 Post-War Quebec. Intriguingly dark and vivid, and so cleverly told through three different time frames' Essie Fox

'I was hooked from the first page – a stunning and beautifully written gothic thriller full of atmosphere, intrigue and delight' Alexandra Benedict

'A dark world of elegance and grotesque … mesmeric' Matt Wesolowski

'What a brilliant, brilliant book … the last chapters knocked me sideways, and it's a long time since that's happened' Lisa Hall

'Harrowing, compelling, haunting, vivid, twisty and shocking!' Noelle Holten

'A dark tale of magic and murder, of witches and women – and an otherworldly tale you will not forget' B.S. Casey

'A real page-turner, I loved it' Martina Cole

'Bold and audacious' R.J. Ellory

'A gripping story of murder and black magic ...Gustawsson slowly weaves together three seemingly disparate strands of her narrative with a skill that shows why she is such an admired crime writer in her native France' *The Times* BOOK OF THE MONTH

'Bewitching and wonderfully gothic'
Sunday Express BOOK OF THE YEAR

'Assured telling of a complex story' *Sunday Times*

'Dark, oppressive and bloody, but it's also thought-provoking, compelling and very moving' *Metro*

'A bold and intelligent read' *Guardian*

'Utterly compelling' *Woman's Own*

'A must-read' *Daily Express*

'A relentless heart-stopping masterpiece, filled with nightmarish situations that will keep you awake long into the dark nights of winter' *New York Journal of Books*

Also by Johana Gustawsson and available from Orenda Books

ABOUT THE AUTHOR

Born in Marseille, France, and with a degree in political science, Johana Gustawsson has worked as a journalist for the French and Spanish press and television. Her critically acclaimed Roy & Castells series, including *Block 46, Keeper* and *Blood Song*, has won the Plume d'Argent, Balai de la découverte, Balai d'Or and Prix Marseillais du Polar awards, and is now published in nineteen countries. A TV adaptation is currently under way in a French, Swedish and UK co-production. Johana's gothic historical thriller *The Bleeding* was a number-one bestseller in France and worldwide, shortlisting for the CWA Crime Fiction in Translation Dagger in the UK. *Yule Island* – the first in the Lidingö Mysteries series, and based on a true story – has followed suit, winning the prestigious Cultura Ligue de l'Imaginaire Award, the Gujan Thrillers Festival Readers' Prize (Crime Novel of the Year) and Crime Novel of the Year at the Saint-Laurent-du-Var Polar Festival, hitting number one on the bestseller list, and reprinting five times in the first two months after publication. Johana lives in Sweden with her Swedish husband and their three sons. Follow her on Twitter @JoGustawsson, Instagram @johanagustawsson and facebook.com/johana.gustawsson.

ABOUT THE TRANSLATOR

David Warriner grew up in deepest Yorkshire, has lived in France and Quebec, and now calls British Columbia home. He has translated Johanna Gustawsson's *Blood Song* and *The Bleeding* and Roxanne Bouchard's Detective Moralès series for Orenda Books. His translation of Roxanne's *We Were the Salt of the Sea* was runner-up for the 2019 Scott Moncrieff Prize for French-English translation. Follow David on Twitter @givemeawave and on his website: wtranslation.ca.

YULE ISLAND

JOHANA GUSTAWSSON

Translated from the French by David Warriner

J. Gustawss (signature)

**ORENDA
BOOKS**

Orenda Books
16 Carson Road
West Dulwich
London SE21 8HU
www.orendabooks.co.uk

First published in the United Kingdom by Orenda Books 2023
Originally published in French as *L'Île de Yule* by Calmann-Lévy 2023
Copyright © Calmann-Lévy 2023
English translation © David Warriner 2023
Poem on page vi from *Seachanger: Wave Weaver* by Sussi Louise Smith,
© Sussi Louise Smith, 2021

A catalogue record for this book is available from the British Library.

Hardback ISBN 978-1-914585-97-5
Paperback ISBN 978-1-914585-90-6
eISBN 978-1-914585-91-3

Typeset in Garamond by typesetter.org.uk

Printed and bound by CPI Group (UK) Ltd, Croydon CR0 4YY

For sales and distribution, please contact info@orendabooks.co.uk

For Lilas,
My writing fairy godmother

And so it begins
with a moonrise
kissing the edges of the eastern sea
harvest sized

Red horizon seeking me
I am right here,
as ever.
Open arms.

Ready for the first rush of night

This is how it always begins
with a moonrise,
by a sea
and my open heart

—'And So It Begins' from *Seachanger: Wave Weaver*
by Sussi Louise Smith

Author's Note

Storholmen is a car-free island in the Stockholm Archipelago in Sweden. A manor house was built there at the turn of the twentieth century, and rumour has it, it's haunted. It's a five-minute boat ride away from my home, and I'm about to take you there.

Are you ready?

Wrap up warm. It's cold outside.

1
Karl

29 December 2012

This morning I opened my eyes to the nape of my wife's neck and a tangle of strands. My nose fumbled its way to the heart of the messy matter. I parted her curls with my breath to find her skin. And with just the tips of my lips, I kissed her. Again and again, until she quivered. I paused to savour the morning lushness of her mouth, that dewy sound it makes. Then I started all over again.

An hour and twenty minutes later, I'm here on the island of Storholmen, on the other side of the bay. A majestic evergreen towers proudly in front of me, sprinkled with frost like something out of a Christmas story.

The nape of the neck I'm looking at now hangs from the branches.

The icy air burns the back of my throat like a shot of *snaps*.

I free my boots from the grip of the compacted snow with a struggle and move in for a closer look. The rope has lifted her blonde hair up to her cheeks. It looks like there are two clownish tufts sprouting from her ears. She's dangling from a low branch, practically right up against the trunk of the tree, her feet hovering thirty centimetres off the ground.

I place my thumb and index finger on her shoulder. The latex of my gloves sticks to her frozen skin and, for a few dilated seconds, all I see is the mauve of my fingers, a glaring blemish on an immaculate backdrop. Cautiously, I rotate the body towards me. The rope creaks on the branch.

Her eyes are wide open.

I close mine for a moment. She's young. Good God, she's so young. A child. Fourteen, fifteen years old at most. Under the tangle of hair and the rope, there's a leather cord. Attached to it, like an oversized pendant, is a pair of open scissors; one of the tips has nicked her bare breast – the one on the same side as her heart. A great deal of blood has flowed from the gaping cuts on her inner thighs, right at the femoral arteries. The lines are clean and smooth, sliced with seemingly surgical precision.

I crouch down to look at her feet. What I had mistaken earlier for a twig caught between her toes is in fact a black thread, binding her big toes together in a symbol of infinity that twists and turns as the body sways in the wind.

They have to cut her down now. They have to stop this child from hanging there. They have to lay her down on the ground and cover her up.

A crime-scene technician pokes his head out from the skirt of tree branches. He doesn't bother to get up, just motions for me to join him. What else – what worse thing – could be lurking there for us to find beneath this tree?

I nod, gulp, and clear the dry air from my throat with a cough, then I get down on my hands and knees and follow him under the tree's skirt.

It suddenly occurs to me that, since I got here, I've heard nothing around me other than the swishing of our coveralls and the crunching of our boots in the snow. A hushed, ominous soundtrack playing in the background. No one says a word. No one dares to. Something about this island unsettles me deeply. I feel like I have to mute the sound of my movements. And my thoughts. It's like I'm advancing in enemy territory, finger poised on the trigger of my gun.

Storholmen has imposed a silence on the muted crowd that surrounds me. A crowd that stands here listening to that silence, as to the calm before a storm.

2
Emma

I pull the patchwork shawl I sewed for myself at Christmas over my shoulders and duck through the kitchen window with a steaming mug in my hand. My minuscule balcony – more of an alcove in the building's roof, really – is just big enough for me to sit out on and enjoy my morning coffee or sip a French 75 with a friend.

I barely slept a wink. The fear, trepidation and doubt all kept me awake. But also, I have to admit, the giddiness about these few weeks I'll be spending on Storholmen. I don't know if I'm up to the task I've been given. I honestly don't.

I swaddle my legs in wool and as I take a first scorching sip, I look down at the old city, which didn't get much sleep either. Stortorget Square buzzes day and night, like it's echoing with the steps of the conquerors who've crossed it over the ages. Down there, five centuries ago, eighty-two heads chopped off by a Danish tyrant sparked the Swedish resistance and ultimately heralded our independence. The imprint of time is everywhere, from the vivid heritage façades that were built to be as narrow as possible to outsmart the taxman, to the cobblestones polished by horses' hooves and the blood of the defeated. I revel in this living museum – when I get out of bed in the morning and when I get home from work at night.

Suddenly, my phone sparks to life, its light spoiling my ritual.

I glance at the screen and instinctively close my eyes.

I know I shouldn't pick up. But still, I answer the call.

'It's five in the morning, Mum.'

Silence, then a clucking of her pasty tongue against her palate and a smooching as she parts her lips.

'I have to get going soon, Mum. I—'

A dull thud makes me flinch. She must have had a fall.

Then I hear her mucousy cackle on the other end of the line.

'Swee … tie,' she drawls drunkenly.

'I've got a hard day ahead of me, Mum.'

'*Ha … ppy … bir… thday … to … you…*'

She's singing.

I feel sick to my stomach.

'*Ha … ppy … bir… thday … dear … Em … ma…*'

I cough to keep my tears at bay.

'You've got the date wrong, Mum,' I mutter.

I hang up and duck back inside the kitchen window, then I dash to the bathroom and give in to the nausea.

✄

'Mild out, isn't it?' says the water-taxi driver, sweeping away the white strands the wind keeps blowing across her face.

My reply is drowned out by an infant's cry so shrill it makes me squint, as if my optic nerve were directly connected to my eardrums. On the other side of the cabin, a teenager with headphones in his ears is oblivious to this assault on the senses.

The woman at the helm – Lotta, her badge says – erupts with a hearty laugh that smothers the baby's laments and sets the dad at ease. Any more and he'd be ready to throw the kid overboard.

'It is,' I reply as a matter of course. Making small talk about the weather is our national sport. There's a hint of blue sky amidst the grey. It's warm for November, almost a springlike morning. 'Nine degrees – that's pretty much a summer's day!' my boss at Von Dardel's would smirk, with a soupçon of a French accent. Charlotte von Dardel's directness is refreshing. It makes a change from the convoluted Swedish politeness. Every 'no' is buried beneath so many layers of 'maybe', it takes a lot of digging to get there.

My career owes everything to Charlotte. All the women I've worked for before were so hung up on masculine ideals of success, they wore themselves out trying to prove they had the biggest proverbial you-know-what to swing around. But there's nothing misogynistic at all about the way Charlotte coaxes me up the ladder. There's rarely any parity or sisterhood in the world of work. Always enemies, never allies, the women I've encountered have been the first to pull up the drawbridge to protect whatever little ground they've fought tooth and nail to gain. In Charlotte von Dardel's eyes, sex – the stronger, the weaker or whatever – doesn't matter. Personality and competence are what really count. She judges people on the strength of their work, or how hard they hit, as she puts it, and their 'adaptability'.

A few weeks ago Charlotte offered me a 'fabulous opportunity', the kind you can't refuse at my age. And I don't want to seem ungrateful – it really is fabulous – but this springboard of an assignment is also a test. A personal and a professional one. The Gussman family, whose collection I've been asked to appraise, is the fourth wealthiest in Sweden. From what I've heard, their heirlooms could fill a museum. The thing is, this 'fabulous opportunity' means that I have to go Storholmen. To the manor house. Where the 'hanging girl', as people called her, was found.

'You look like you've seen a ghost,' Lotta exclaims, nipping my ruminations in the bud. 'We're only doing six knots, so it can't be my sporty driving making you feel queasy!'

Her gaze falls to my bag and the laptop case. Her mouth forms an 'O' of surprise.

'Ah ... You must be the expert who's coming to appraise the Gussmans' treasures. I forgot you'd be here this morning. This centennial is quite the event for us, you know. Especially because we're getting loads of grants to update the wharves and make a big celebration of it all.'

She marks a pause, unscrews the cap from a bottle of Ramlösa and takes a sip of the sparkling water.

'Although, I wouldn't be too keen about doing that particular job. Rather you than me,' she goes on, wiping her mouth with the back of her hand. 'Those Gussmans are a piece of work. If that Niklas could have his family coat of arms tattooed on his balls, he would.'

The dad glares at her. As if that kid of his, who's not walking yet and can barely babble, could even understand that kind of language. Honestly, parents these days. They get so hung up about all their standards, rules and restrictions, which they'll only end up dropping when they push out a second kid after giving the whole bloody world grief with the first one.

I laugh to show her whose side I'm on, and Lotta joins in, making me forget for a second about the silhouette of the island that's emerging ahead of us.

'You been here before?' Now we've broken the ice, Lotta's talking to me like we know each other.

I shake my head.

'You must be the only one. Since the murder of the hanging girl, I reckon all of Sweden's come here to see the place for themselves. We even had to bring in a booking system and set opening hours for off-islanders. The hordes of tourists were getting unbearable. People move to Storholmen to get some peace and quiet, not to be invaded. That's why there are no cars on the island. There's not even a corner shop. All we've got is Anneli's café, Ett Glas, and in the summer she only opens in the morning. It's a good thing we don't have a hotel, otherwise it'd be hell on earth. That's put some people off coming, but not enough, if you ask me. Sometimes, we get a few late in the season, before Halloween, but not this last couple of years, thanks to Covid. Honestly, too many people out there are voyeurs. Either that, or they're bloody masochists. If you're that afraid of death, why would you want to be around?'

I swallow to get rid of the lump that's swelling in my dry throat.

Personally, I have no desire to be at the scene of the ... the murder. And even less to be rubbing shoulders, potentially, with a killer who's still on the loose.

Lotta manoeuvres the water taxi up to the dock and pulls a lever with a hand as wrinkled as it is agile. The gangway reaches out to the landing area like a metal tongue.

'I wish you the best of luck, sweetheart. Coming here, you'd better not be afraid of ghosts.'

3
Emma

Twenty or so passengers are waiting on the south dock, in that early-morning kind of silence that extends the sleepy remnants of the night. This stream of islanders is ready to flow to work in Stockholm or on Lidingö – the big island next door that's connected to the capital by a bridge. Some will be picking up their cars in Mor Anna, the small harbour on the north side of Lidingö, where the water taxi docks. What a rigmarole to put yourself through just for a bit of peace and quiet. They must really need it if they're prepared to do all this travel, day in, day out.

The memory of another ferry boat suddenly sparks in my mind, this time in Marseille, aboard the age-old *César*: the short hop between City Hall and Place aux Huiles only took a few minutes, but it always brightened my day. They might have had sleep written all over their faces, but the people down there always had a spring in their step. There's a fire that thrives in the Mediterranean spirit. Up here, we Scandinavians throw a blanket over ours to put it out. That's if it even sparks in the first place. These dark nights will suck the life out of anything. Today, a little bit of that lively French atmosphere would really help me put one foot in front of the other. Literally, I tell myself, raising a hand in response to the old man waiting for me at the end of the gangway.

I give Lotta another smile and step off the boat behind the exhausted dad, whose kid has finally fallen asleep.

'Emma Lindahl,' the old man greets me, as if it's written on my forehead.

He's staring at me. Wild, snowy eyebrows perch like mountain summits atop his grey eyes. His mid-length hair is combed back from a broad face furrowed by wrinkles that lend him the presence of a warrior – which is somehow both reassuring and intimidating.

'Björn Petterson. You ready?' With a quick hand he smooths his beard, the tip of it tickling the collar of his parka.

'Yes, I'm ready,' I assert, thrusting my chin forward, adopting a tone and posture worthy of my title as a representative of the great Von Dardel's auction house.

'Off we go, then. Can I carry that for you?' he offers, pointing to my bag.

'I'm all right, thanks. It's not heavy.'

'As you wish,' he says, clasping his hands behind his back and striding off up the hill towards the manor so briskly, it's a stretch for my legs to keep pace. 'It's not that hard,' he adds a moment later without looking up from the rocky path, 'to get to the manor. From the south dock. Where are you from?'

'I live in Stockholm.'

'Ah,' he replies flatly. 'Lotta must have told you there's nothing on the island besides Ett Glas if you want a bite to eat. I'll let Anneli know you're here, because Gussman's not known for his hospitality, and something tells me you're not the type to cart a Thermos and a lunch box around with you.'

I'm about to protest when my heels and blood-red lipstick draw a smile out of me. If I were him, I'd make the same assumption.

'Thanks, that's very kind of you.'

He mumbles something unintelligible in reply and quickens his step. I let him go on ahead, figuring we share the same desire for solitude.

A few minutes later, I'm adjusting the strap of my bag on my shoulder when I realise there's not a single sound to be heard on the narrow path that runs alongside these charming, unassuming houses. No engines throbbing, no dogs barking, no children crying, singing, playing or yelling, not even the slightest hint of a hushed conversation. Nothing. Only the clicking of my heels and the clunking of Björn's boots on the rocky surface. The silence makes me want to raise my voice just to breathe some life into the eerie emptiness.

'Here we are,' Björn announces without warning. He points to a little gate to the side of the path.

I stop, and my heart leaps into my mouth. I can feel it pounding.

The lower portion of the grounds, to the rear of the manor house, are home to an English country garden where nature abounds exuberantly, unbridled by human hands. Björn opens the gate and enters the estate. I follow him, reluctant to tear my eyes away from the trees. I'm looking for one in particular. The hanging girl's tree.

Grandiose, yet completely out of place on this understated island, the building towers like the stronghold of a ruler surrounded by the shantytown of his underlings. A double flight of four stone steps leads up to the main entrance, which sits beneath a semi-circular portico flanked by ivy-clad columns. Two lion-shaped knockers adorn the austere wooden front door.

Björn reaches through the vegetation to press a hidden doorbell, and we wait. After a few minutes, the door opens to reveal a man in his early forties.

This must be Niklas Gussman. The very picture of an heir to the family fortune, only too proud to show off his coat of arms, just like Lotta joked. Fair hair slicked back and greying at the temples, subtle wrinkles, white shirt with sleeves rolled up to his elbows to show off his tan and the timepiece that leaves no doubt about the depth of his inherited pockets.

'Splendid,' he purrs, his face devoid of all expression.

Björn gives him a gruff nod and disappears.

'Follow me,' the man says, his voice as gravelly as the stuff crunching beneath Björn's retreating boots, leaving me to shut the door behind myself.

I do as he says. I slip off my shoes, and he leads the way across an entrance hall that's tiled like a chess board.

I'm dying for this man to look at me and introduce himself. I want to ask him not to treat me like his subject. It's like he's in a different century. The inappropriateness of some clients can be shocking. Keeping my mouth shut is what takes the greatest toll on me in my line of work. Managing to bite my tongue and not speak my mind.

Niklas Gussman ushers me into a drawing room that looks out onto a French formal garden punctuated by majestic trees. Two pools, which must be fifty metres long, flanked by tunnels of greenery, draw the eye seaward. My host plucks a cardboard folder from a sleek writing desk and hands it to me without inviting me to sit. I wait politely for him to invite me to open it, but he remains tight-lipped and looks at me inquisitively.

There's nothing intrusive or provocative about his gaze. Rather, Niklas Gussman seems to be examining me, as if he were the appraiser here, and I were one of the objects being appraised.

'So you're the one Christie's has to thank for the 450-million-dollar sale of their *Salvator Mundi* in 2017,' he says abruptly.

'That is correct, sir,' I reply, regaining some composure.

'You were still in your twenties at the time. A stroke of luck, perhaps?'

I smile to keep the sarcasm on the tip of my tongue. 'Like Thomas Jefferson, I'm a great believer in luck, and I too find that the more I work, the more I have of it.'

'Why leave Christie's for Von Dardel's on the heels of such a triumph?'

'Von Dardel's is twice as historic an institution, and by far the most prestigious auction and appraisal house in the Nordic countries. Not to mention that Ms von Dardel doubled my salary and offered me an obscene signing bonus.'

His eyes are still on me. It's impossible to decipher the message they're sending. For a second I even wonder if Gussman is going to tell me to leave. His next words make me instantly regret my boldness. My arrogance.

'This document sets out the schedule for your visits to the manor and the order in which you are to proceed. You will also find a map showing the layout of the premises.'

Niklas Gussman moves to the doorway, clearly to see me out.

'Your time at work here begins this afternoon at two-thirty. Knock twice to make yourself known before you enter. If you have a question, write it down on a piece of paper and leave it on the dresser in the hall. I shall leave my answer for you the next day.'

The smile I give him is certainly more curt and less amenable than politeness would require, but I'm at my wit's end.

As soon as I'm alone, out by the front steps, I open the folder and glance at its contents. It gives me a sinking feeling: the time slots are six hours at the most, and some are split in two. Bloody hell. I've worked with eccentric clients before, but none as controlling as this. There must be hundreds of heirlooms here for me to appraise. I'm nowhere near even scratching the surface of my assignment. Let alone being able to leave this wretched curse of an island.

4
Emma

Still five more hours to wait.

I'm more astounded than annoyed.

I thought I'd be able to access the manor house at my convenience, but here I am, twiddling my thumbs for half a day. I have no information to work with yet. Nothing with which I can make a start on the job. And there's no point leaving the island and going home, or even dropping into the office for an hour or so.

So, I've taken Björn's advice and retreated to Ett Glas, the only place for non-islanders to go. The café sits right on Storholmen's south dock. It boasts a spectacular view across the water to the shores of Djursholm, which is Stockholm's, and Sweden's, swankiest and most exclusive suburb. It's where most of my colleagues are bringing up their children.

I'm sitting in the bay window, the closest spot to the sea – and to the sun, which is always too eager to make itself scarce in the autumn. There's a work of art on the wall across from me. It's captivating. It looks like something Séraphine de Senlis might have painted. She was a housekeeper whose immense talent was discovered only by chance. She used to hide away and paint by candlelight, and would often etch her signature on her works with a knife. She ended up alone, like her contemporary Camille Claudel, descending into delusion and eating grass and all kinds of rubbish.

'What do you think?'

The waitress is beside me. I didn't hear her coming. She digs her hands into the pockets of her embroidered apron and joins me in contemplating the painting. There's something both sad and powerful about it. The leaves on the painted tree look like they're having one last dance in the wind before dying.

'It's magnificent.'

'Really?' She gives a bashful little laugh that creases the corners of her bright eyes and brings out her dimples.

'Ah, you painted it,' I smile, touched by her coyness.

She slowly nods, keeping her eyes trained on the painting. Then she turns to me. 'Are you ready to order? Or should I give you a few more minutes?' She gives me a smile that's more genuine than businesslike and sweeps a lock of red hair behind her ear.

'I'll have a latte, please.'

'Anything to nibble on?'

'Maybe later, thanks. I'm going to hog this table for a while, if you don't mind.'

'Not at all.'

She draws a sharp breath, as if to add something, or voice a thought, perhaps. But she thinks better of it and gives me another smile instead, a briefer one this time, before returning behind the bar. The espresso machine starts hissing. There's a clinking of porcelain on the counter. And a comforting waft of freshly baked bread that makes me wish I'd ordered more than just coffee.

I can see Lotta, now, at the helm of her water taxi, pulling up to the dock. In that same moment, a portcullis of sunbeams descends onto my table, bringing the grain of the wood alive and revealing the scars of time. I wonder what treasures are hiding in the collection the Gussmans have neglected for the last century.

'Here you go.' I'm almost startled to find a frothy latte in front of me, as well as a golden-brown bun sprinkled with pearl sugar.

'I couldn't resist bringing you a *saffransbulle*,' says the waitress, her eyes sparkling hungrily. 'They're fresh from the oven. It'd be a sin not to try one.'

I'm about to thank her when she carries on.

'You ... you're here to appraise the collection at the manor, if

I'm not mistaken? News travels fast. There are fewer than three hundred of us on the island, you see.'

She slaps herself on the forehead, sweeping back a cascade of red locks as she does so, before they fall gently back on her shoulders.

'Sorry, I'm forgetting all my manners. I haven't even introduced myself. Anneli Lund. I own the café. Björn told me you were coming. I should have led with that, shouldn't I?'

We exchange a smile. This woman is as radiant as Niklas Gussman is impenetrable.

'I should have introduced myself too. Emma Lindahl. And yes, I'm the lucky one who gets to venture into Ali Baba's cave.'

'What a fabulous, unique experience that's going to be for you – all alone, surrounded by the treasures of Niklas's great-grandfather. The manor's only been standing for a century – but what a century! Gustav Gussman was an insatiable collector, you know. And he moved in many of the artists' circles in the Roaring Twenties. People compare him to the Great Gatsby, what with his panache and his penchant for extravagances. I bet you'll find some incredible heirlooms – priceless ones too, probably.'

Her gaze drifts out to sea.

'The centenary of the manor is next year. Everyone here's hoping that it will make people forget about...' She shakes her head, like she's looking for the right words '... the tragedies that have haunted this place.'

I nod in silence and take another sip of my latte.

'Did Niklas Gussman mention the story about his great-grandfather?' she continues, on something of a lighter note.

I want to reply that he's not the type to make conversation, but I settle for a shake of the head.

'Apparently, Lenin was desperate for foreign currency to fill the Revolution's coffers with. So Old Man Gussman seized the opportunity, as the story goes. Something about chartering a ship and moving priceless treasures out of Russia. He even used to tell people how the Bolsheviks came after him when he left Saint Petersburg! So it might be a bit of a headache tracing the provenance of some of those works. I don't mean to put you off, though.'

✂

It's a quarter past two when I leave the café and make my way back up to the manor house. The weather has freshened, a sign that the sun will soon be taking its leave. Legs numbed and face reddened by the cold, I walk faster to try and warm myself up.

As I enter the estate, I try to think about the work ahead of me, keen to create a buffer against the drama that played out here.

I give two raps of the knocker, as Niklas Gussman asked me to, and push open the front door.

While I'm removing my shoes, I go over the floorplan again in my mind. Through the hall to the doors that lead to the French formal garden, turn left, down the corridor to the central staircase, up two floors, turn right. And then the room I've been given access to for the next three hours is behind the fourth door on the right.

The marble stairs are covered in a red tongue of a carpet that warms my feet after the chill of the chessboard tiles in the hall. Upstairs, I'm surprised: the ceiling can't be much more than seven feet high. That seems very low to me, compared to the ground floor.

I'm just about to open the fourth door on the right when there's a bloodcurdling scream, followed by a crash.

5
Viktoria

The scream makes me jump, and a few pieces of the silverware that I've arranged meticulously on the tray tumble to the floor with a crash that makes me close my eyes and clench my teeth.

För helvete. For God's sake.

With my luck, 'Madam' as she insists I call her, is going to lecture me for an hour now. And she'll be right to. These screams come out of nowhere, and I always let them catch me by surprise. They're never like one of those arguments that's clearly getting heated, the kind of thing you can hear coming so you make yourself scarce. No, these screams erupt suddenly, like claps of thunder.

I set the tray down at my feet and inspect each piece of cutlery one by one to make sure nothing is damaged. I'm going to have to polish them again. What else can I do? I can't put them away as if nothing happened, knowing some have fallen on the floor. Not the silverware engraved with the initials of the great Gussman family. I'm sure Madam wouldn't notice a thing, but I like to do a job well.

I carry the tray to the solid oak table in the kitchen and set about the task once more, in front of the big picture window.

What an amazing view this is. With its formal French garden reaching seawards and its wooded grounds to the rear, the Gussman manor house truly has nothing to envy the Grand Hôtel in Stockholm. It's just as imposing. Not to mention the treasures this place holds. Obviously, I'm respectful and I try not to go snooping around where I shouldn't. But the temptation is huge. This house is like a museum. Someone's supposed to be coming to appraise all these treasures, but I haven't seen anyone yet.

Last year, when my colleague at the Grand Hôtel told me the owners of the manor were looking for a live-in housekeeper, it piqued my curiosity, so to speak. The pay was enticing, as was the room and board in the servants' quarters, which came with two bedrooms, a shower and a kitchenette. I was hesitant, though. There was no guarantee that Pontus would let us leave. He's been very generous to my daughter and me, but he only thinks with what's between his legs. This job was the perfect opportunity to keep my daughter out of his claws. I finally made up my mind when I got home one night to find Josephine in tears. The hand of God was guiding me. I had to leave without delay.

My references were impeccable. I'd worked for more than fifteen years in the royal palaces in Copenhagen and Stockholm. So Madam couldn't help but take me on. I'm used to clients and their eccentricities. And I excel at making nothing of their whims. The nice thing here is that there's only one family's worth of those to deal with. At the Grand Hôtel, we had to place slippers at the end of the bed, just so, for some, fold hand towels in the shape of a flower for others, be sure to only let a tiny sliver of daylight find its way into some rooms and make sure others were bathed in sunshine. Not to mention the clients who insisted on only the finest Egyptian cotton or refused to drink anything but Evian.

Here, there's only the 'Duke', as I call him, with his air of self-righteousness that comes with being from nobility, I suppose – it certainly makes me feel we're cut from a different cloth. And then there's Madam and their son.

The Duke is often away, and when he is here, he shuts himself in his study. He does nothing to care for his kid, or his wife. And so it falls upon Madam to raise the heir to his fortune. Some of the time she's a mother hen; the rest of it, it's like she's just not there. I'm talking about their son as if he's a five-year-old, but he's a skinny teenager with a rebellious glint in his eye who wanders all over the place as soon as his mother turns her back. He sometimes reacts to things a little … unexpectedly, dare I say, as if he's in a world of his own. But he doesn't have a bad bone in his body.

Oh, how we all complain about the sleepless nights when our kids are little. But when the monsters under the bed turn out to be real, we're the ones who have nightmares.

I inspect the silverware one last time. Satisfied, I place every piece back in the box. I run a finger over the leather I polished earlier. It's as shiny as the day it was first opened, or so I like to imagine. I'd love to have been here that very first day, between the two world wars, although it must have been hellishly cold in the servants' quarters back then.

Now I'm going to give the oil lamps in the salon the once-over. It's quite the collection that's been left to moulder. Later, I'll move on to the tarnished silver brushes I noticed upstairs. Being surrounded by beautiful things and taking care of them gives me great pleasure. It gives me the illusion of riches and grandeur, and that's enough for me. Personally, I'd struggle to let anyone else touch my things. No, the idleness that goes hand in hand with opulence, that's not for me. I find it so hard to just sit and do nothing. And Pontus would never allow it anyway. He'd always be pestering me to come and pander to his needs.

Not having to cater to my husband's 'needs' in the evening is one of my little pleasures here. Before I go to bed, I open the window in my room and enjoy my cup of tea with the fragrance of the night my sole companion. That was how I caught Madam in the act the first time, when I opened the window for a breath of air. I saw her walk across the garden in the inky night and vanish into the trees.

6
Emma

Waiting for the water taxi in Ropsten this morning I'm chilled to the bone. I did a couple of two-hour sessions at the manor house yesterday, plus one three-hour stint, and I came home exhausted. Still, it was dawn by the time I fell asleep, only to get up three hours later.

I've been going over to Storholmen to photograph, label and study the Gussman family's treasures nearly every day for six weeks now. Six weeks of research and investigation, and amazement too, as I've feasted my eyes on huge slices of history. As well as a series of objects in pristine condition, I've laid my hands on a Botticelli that would fetch more than five hundred million kronor and a Ming Dynasty porcelain bowl that wouldn't go for less than seven million. And I've only been through three rooms so far. Today I'm going upstairs. I wonder what riches I'll come across there.

At last, the boat with the number 80 on the front comes into sight. In the thirteenth century, travellers wanting to go to Storholmen or Lidingö from Ropsten, the easternmost point of the Stockholm mainland, had to shout for a boat or a barge to come and pick them up. This custom and a large rock in the water here gave the place its name, which translates to 'the shout stone'. Hopping on the spot to warm myself up, I'm thankful for the times I live in.

As I duck inside the water taxi, Lotta leads with, 'What's got into you, lovey? You look like you've aged ten years overnight.'

That's exactly how I feel.

'I've turned the heat up full blast. Let's thaw those icy bones of yours.'

I've only just sat down when I notice Björn holding two steaming cups. He sits next to me and hands me one.

'Here you go. The wife's orders.'

I smile and thank him for the coffee.

'Anneli told us you're working on New Year's Eve.'

'Yes, I'll be at the manor from nine to noon, then from two to four.'

'Stay and have dinner with us.'

'That's very kind of you, Björn, but I haven't celebrated the New Year for ages.'

'It's just a meal.'

'To *not* celebrate the New Year?' I tease him.

He smiles beneath his avalanche of a beard, clicks his tongue against his palate and skips away to join Lotta in the wheelhouse.

I'm still feeling the damp and cold when we get to Storholmen. I disembark at the south dock and hurry straight to Ett Glas to join Anneli for our morning coffee.

As I take off my parka, she places my avocado toast and scrambled eggs on the table next to my latte and her black coffee, then sits down across from me. We hear the creaking of the gangway and turn our gaze to the dock, where Lotta is about to continue on her way to Lidingö.

We savour our coffees in peace, buoyed by the aroma of the buns rising and browning in the oven. I think about the screams I hear sometimes at the manor house. The arguments – or rather reprimands, because all I hear is a woman shouting – that shatter the silence. Anneli knows very little about the Gussmans. Niklas travels a lot, and apparently his wife and son rarely go anywhere. They must have a live-in housekeeper too, I imagine. The Gussmans travel exclusively by private boat from the dock on their property and no one on the island ever sees them.

'I've been thinking about something that might make your journeys easier,' Anneli says, tearing her eyes away from the grey sea.

I've taken to meeting her here between my two daily work sessions, with Lotta and Björn. They've already suggested that on days when I'm working late, I could drive out to the port at Mor Anna and leave my car there. That way it's only a three-minute crossing to Storholmen and I'll be warm and dry in the evening instead of waiting for the metro or the bus in Ropsten and then walking home.

'When you finish at silly o'clock, you could always stay here,' Anneli says. 'In the spare room.' She smiles, then turns towards her painting. A lock of red hair falls over her arm, across her breast. Anneli sweeps it back over her shoulder. Our conversations are often left open, as if she has all the time in the world or doesn't want to put a full stop at the end of them.

'You don't need to let me know ahead of time. The bed's made. Just stay if you feel like staying.'

She stands up, strokes my cheek and goes to busy herself behind the counter. I close my eyes to let the feeling of her palm linger on my skin. It's been too long since anyone touched me. Not even a handshake, let alone a hug, a kiss or a one-night stand.

I finish my breakfast staring at my computer, gathering information about a collection of five imperial Russian Easter eggs dating from the late nineteenth century, which I've valued at seven hundred thousand kronor.

A few minutes before nine, I collect my things, wrap my coat around me and sneak behind the counter to give Anneli a kiss on the cheek.

'Thank you,' I whisper.

'As you like,' she replies with no hint of resentment, understanding that my 'thank you' is really a 'no, thank you'. I need to go home every day. I need to get out of this Storholmen bubble. I need to ground myself in the real world again. I don't like the relationship this island is drawing me into, this place I was terrified of until I set foot here. I feel like it's cast a spell on me and is making me forget everything.

✄

After two raps of the knocker, I open the door and enter the manor house. The room I'm going through today, and for the next few days until I've catalogued everything, is the only one I'm allowed access to on this floor. It must be because the other ones are lived in.

As I open the door, I wonder if this is going to be another box room with shelves full of paintings by the masters and priceless objects. But I find myself in a room with furniture covered in big white sheets. Two windows, one on the wall to the left and the other across from the door, cast light on these ghostly forms, which look like they're floating on the dark oak floor. The windows offer sweeping views over the manor's grounds, all the way to the sea.

The French formal garden snakes its way to the shoreline, and it's calling me. I slide my way behind the dresser in front of the window on the left wall. Sunbeams pierce the clouds here and there, like torchlight in the night. Some thirty metres from the shore, there's a mound with a crown of evergreens.

I press my face to the window.

That's the place.

Where they found the hanging girl.

Where she was dragged. Bound. And strung up naked.

I can feel a lump in my throat. A tightness in my chest. Suddenly, I can't breathe. I stagger backwards and bump into the dresser behind me. It throws me off balance and I reach out to steady myself. The dresser wobbles, sending ripples through its sheet. I grab at it blindly, trying to stabilise it, and a cascade of clinking metal breaks the silence. I wince in spite of myself, realising what's happening.

I open my eyes and see a series of brushes on the floor. One is a hairbrush; the other two are for clothes. The silver casing of the round brush has cracked open, like a shell. I'm mortified.

Helvete. Helvete. Helvete. Bloody hell.

What have I done?

I hurry to pick up the pieces and take a closer look. The two rectangular brushes don't seem to have been damaged in the fall. I breathe a little slower and put them back on the dresser. Then I reach for the third and pick it up like a wounded bird. Trying to reattach the part that's come off the handle, I notice there's a piece of paper folded up inside.

My reflex is to pull it out.

It's a note.

The words I read are enough to cover me in goosebumps:

HELP ME I'M TRAPPED

7
Emma

I push open the door to Ett Glas. I just need to sit down.

'*Hej*,' Anneli smiles.

Then her face falls. She cups my cheek with a gentle palm.

'Emma, what's wrong?'

I look up at her, shell shocked. I don't remember walking here from the manor house. I don't even remember leaving the room.

'Are you feeling all right? Are you hurt?'

I shake my head, trying to find the words, but my heart is racing. I can feel it pounding in my throat, at my temples.

One hand on my shoulder, the other on my arm, Anneli leads me into the back kitchen, where she sits me down on a stool in an alcove by the pantry and strips me of my laptop case, sliding the strap off my shoulder cautiously, as if my arm is battered and bruised. Suddenly I realise that I don't even recall gathering my things or putting on my coat and shoes.

Anneli goes over to the bar and returns a moment later with a shot glass filled with an amber liquid. I down it in one. I'm pretty sure it's whisky. I can feel the alcohol burning in my throat, then my chest, bringing me back to my senses.

Anneli kneels before me and places her palms on my thighs.

'Oh, Emma, what is it?' There's something reassuring in the way she looks at me. I find it comforting. There's a softness to her gaze, something I've always sought in my mother's.

I reach into the pocket of my jacket and hand her the note. It's still folded in half, exactly as I found it. She opens it and frowns, then sits back on her heels to read it.

A few seconds later, she looks up at me. 'What is this? Where did you find it?'

I try to gather my thoughts and recall the chain of events. I tell her how I staggered and then knocked the brushes to the floor.

Anneli listens. She doesn't take her eyes off the scrap of paper.

Suddenly, she gets up and hurries over to a cupboard, where she pulls out a box of freezer bags and slips the note inside one of them.

I close my eyes.

How stupid have I been?

How many times did I fold and unfold that piece of paper without thinking about my fingerprints? I must have spoiled, maybe even erased, any prints that were there before mine.

'Have you called the police?' she asks, sitting down in front of me again.

There it is again, that lump in my throat.

'No ... I ... I mean, I will,' I say, choking on my own words.

'Did you show Niklas Gussman the piece of paper you found? Have you told him anything about it?'

'No,' I whisper, staring at my fingers, which I'm clasping like a child caught doing something I shouldn't.

Anneli smooths the paper flat inside the plastic bag and focuses on the capital letters written in pencil.

'Help me I'm trapped,' she reads out loud, with a quick shake of her head. 'Is the brush you found this in ... an antique?'

I can picture the hallmark on the silver casing, the patina of the metal.

'Yes, I'm sure it is. But I didn't have the chance to look at it long enough to tell you how old it is.'

'The paper doesn't look that old though, does it?'

I nod. It's far too smooth and the grain is too consistent for it to date back as far as the brush.

The bell on the café door rings twice.

'You have to go to the police,' Anneli says as she gets up and hands me the bag. 'And you shouldn't go back to the manor house. Maybe the Gussmans ... I don't know ... I don't think it's a good idea. The water taxi will be here in six or seven minutes.' She glances at her watch.

I get up from the stool. Grab my bag. 'I'm going to get some fresh air.'

She opens her mouth, about to object, then thinks better of it. 'I'm here if you need anything. Anything at all. Keep me posted.'

We walk out of the back kitchen together. Anneli forces a smile as she goes to greet her customers.

I clutch my bag close to my body as I leave the café, compensating for the hug I so desperately need. And I make my way down the wharf, drawing in deep breaths of icy air to calm my nerves and silence the thoughts that are turning my stomach.

In the distance I can see the water taxi making a beeline for the dock, and I wonder what kind of a mess I must have left behind at the manor. I can't remember a thing. I don't have a clear picture in my mind of how I got out of there.

I think about the brush that's broken.

About the furniture shrouded in those huge white sheets. And whatever else I might find in there.

I sigh and feel a burning in my chest like the whisky I had earlier. Then I decide to turn around and retrace my steps.

I walk back along the wharf, past the café, where I can see Anneli is busy serving customers. And I make my way back up the rocky path.

8
Emma

I don't bother knocking because I'm still within the two-hour work window they've given me this morning. I hurry up the stairs.

The door to the room is ajar. I push it open slowly until it nudges the doorstop. I'm worried that someone might have been in here since I left. I can see that two of the brushes are still on the dresser I bumped into. The third lies broken on the floor. The room looks empty, but my mind won't be at ease until I've checked under the sheets.

I shut the door behind me and start with the dresser by the window. Mindful not to damage anything else, I pull the sheet away carefully and leave it in a heap at my feet. I'll take the time to fold it later.

It's not a dresser, it's a dressing table. The wood is painted almond green with pale-pink roses. The top is covered in a dark-green fabric embroidered with lilies and sits beneath a protective sheet of glass. An oval mirror is positioned above the table. A rectangular stool upholstered in the same fabric is tucked beneath it.

I pick up the broken brush and grab the others too, then pull out the stool and sit down to examine them. The casings are stamped with initials that look like an H and a G. Perhaps these belonged to Harriet Gussman, who was married to Niklas's great-grandfather, Gustav. That means they're probably from the 1920s, which fits with the style of the dressing table. After I manage to click the casing back into place, I try – and fail – to prise the casings of the other brushes apart. The dressing table has five drawers: two shallow ones under the mirror and a stack of three on one side. I open them one by one, feeling for any hiding places, false bottoms or buttons that might open a secret compartment. But I find nothing. I inspect the back of the mirror, then the legs and the underside of the table and the stool. Nothing there, either.

I sigh.

I don't even know what I'm looking for. Another note? That seems unlikely. What, then? I don't know, but I feel an urge to search the room from top to bottom. To make sure I don't miss anything. To leave nothing to chance.

I stand up and decide to pull all the other sheets off the furniture to get a better sense of the space and the vintage of the pieces.

I start with what must be a four-poster bed, judging by the size of it. It's as high as the ceiling. As it falls, the sheet reveals an olive-green velvet canopy and matching curtains tied back at their middles with gold-coloured ropes, as well as an ornate bed frame in very good condition, it too painted almond green and adorned with roses. The otherwise bare mattress is topped with a gold-tasselled bedspread that matches the dressing table and the stool.

Next, I turn to my left and liberate a nightstand and a bedside lamp with a delicate blown-glass shade that looks like a flower on the verge of blooming. Beside it, by the window, a large white-and-blue Limoges vase stands on a pedestal painted the same pastel tones as the rest of the room. It's only now that I notice four charcoal drawings, hanging in the shape of a cross on the wall. The one at the top is a sketch of a green statue. The three others are portraits of children.

I take a few steps back to stand in the doorway. Now I'm sure this must have been Harriet Gussman's room. And perhaps other women in the family called it their own after her. It has been cleaned regularly, judging by the lack of dust on the floor and surfaces.

I'm startled by a sudden thundering of footsteps. Everything echoes in the manor house, so there's no telling where the sound is coming from.

'That's enough! Do you hear me?' I hear a woman shouting. It's the same screeching voice I've heard before. I'm frozen to the spot, waiting for what comes next, when the door flies open and slams into the doorstop.

A blonde woman stands in the doorway, hands on her hips. The angry look on her angular face softens to one of surprise.

'Are you still here?'

I realise I've forgotten to check my watch and have lost all sense of time.

'I'm sorry, madam, er, Mrs...'

'Madam will do,' she retorts, smoothing the corner of her lips with her little finger.

She glares at me, making it clear that it's time for me to leave.

'I do apologise, *madam*,' I say, intentionally stressing the word. 'Please forgive me,' I add, as I grab my bag. I can feel her eyes on me as I leave the room, like claws digging into my back.

9
Viktoria

Someone needs to show that woman how to speak without shouting.

Her patience seems to wear thin more and more quickly. Or maybe I've just lost all of mine. I'm getting tired of hearing her yell at that poor child. I do wonder what she finds so offensive. The kid's a typical teenager, with a face as long as a wet weekend sometimes and a brain that seems to have offloaded everything it's learned since birth. But is that really any reason for her to lose her temper every time they speak to each other? Who knows, maybe she didn't want to have the kid in the first place? Still, here in Sweden, we have eighteen weeks to figure that out and do something about it.

A series of short knocks jolts me from my thoughts. I turn around and see Pontus at the kitchen window, pressing his nose to the glass.

I stiffen.

I open the window for my smiling husband and a blast of icy air enters the room uninvited. I reach for the cardigan on the back of my chair and pull it on quickly.

'*Hej* there, lady of the manor.'

'What the hell are you doing here, Pontus? I've told you not to drop by unannounced, for God's sake.'

'Your schedule's too complicated to keep track of.'

'There's nothing complicated about it. You just like to be awkward, and you're as stubborn as a mule.'

'What, so you're not allowed to have visitors?'

'Stop it. You know this isn't my home to invite people into. Are you trying to get me fired?'

'Oh, come on, loosen up a bit. Where's Josephine?'

'She's playing video games with Thor.'

'Oh, is that what they call it these days?'

'You sicken me, you know that? She's still a child, Pontus.'

He shakes his head and rolls his eyes. 'You have no sense of humour.'

'How much do you want?'

'Aren't you going to give me a guided tour first?'

I snort.

'At least give me a kiss. You're really turning me on. I can see your nipples through your cardigan.'

I tell him to keep his voice down. 'Stop it. You've got a one-track mind.'

'I miss you, that's all.'

'How much do you want?' I ask again.

'Five thousand kronor.'

'How big are the holes in your pockets? I thought you found a job.'

'I did.'

'What happened this time?'

'Turns out my boss was a woman.'

I step into the back kitchen for a second to get my purse. He's still droning on.

'As soon as a woman gets into a position of power, she lets the whole bloody world know it. All those career women are just sexually frustrated, if you ask me.'

'Give it a rest, Pontus. If anyone's sexually frustrated, it's you.'

'Tell me about it. You *could* come and see me when you have a day off, you know.'

I take a few notes from my purse and thrust my hand towards him. 'If you come here again without an invitation, this is the last you'll get from me.'

He snatches the money and, before I have time to react, he reaches his other hand through the window and pinches my nipple.

'Understood,' he says with a wink as I shut the window.

I watch him disappear into the night and wonder, not for the first time, why I tolerate this man's presence in my life.

10
Emma

I'm waiting on the balcony with my shawl wrapped around my shoulders. Looking down at the crowds in Stortorget Square, trying to trick my mind into losing its way. I love flitting from one silhouette to another, musing about all the different here-and-nows and relationships sparking to life or fizzling out.

From out of nowhere, I see Lulu crossing the square in his belted three-quarter-length coat, which lends him more of a banker's air than a papyrologist's. There's something in my friend's stride, a confidence I've always envied, that makes me think of the conquerors who trod the same path. Lulu knows where he's going, and he's determined to get there.

He looks up at my building, the Schantzka house as people call it. Its tall, red façade is punctuated with dozens of white stones, in tribute to the souls that perished in the square at the hands of the Danish invaders during Stockholm's notorious sixteenth-century bloodbath. I duck back into the kitchen and go down the hallway to open my front door.

'So, how's my queen?' Lulu calls from the last flight of stairs.

He takes off his shoes and opens his arms so I can snuggle in for a hug. For the first time all day, I manage to draw a breath deep enough to release the pressure in my chest.

When we go through to the lounge, he squeals with joy and changes the energy in the room in an instant.

'Oh my God, Emma!' he cries, making a beeline for the dress I finished sewing last night. 'This one's a killer. Those magic fingers of yours are wasted at that manor house.'

I smile and take the dress off the wooden mannequin.

'Now hurry up and get over your allergy to New Year's Eve, because you simply must join us at Natti this year,' Lulu insists as he strips to his underwear. 'The show's going to be wild. You can't miss it.'

Gingerly, he slips into my creation. The skirt is embroidered with blue diamante flames and the white-feathered bodice is a thing of beauty.

'Ooh la la! The layering in the lace. You've blown my mind. Oh, sweetie,' he gushes, 'you've really outdone yourself this time.'

He draws me into a hug and kisses my hair, purring with pleasure. But his warmth stings like a burn. It reminds me of everything I've so desperately missed and somehow keep searching for in the people who always seem to be just passing through. People I build up into something they've never asked for and, most importantly, don't deserve.

'Oh, Emma, what is it, queen?'

Bloody hell. I'm crying.

Lulu releases me from his embrace so I have no choice but to look at him.

'Sorry. Shitty day,' I sniff, and wipe my face with the back of my hand.

'A bit more than that, perhaps? I've rarely seen you like this.'

He pauses and leads me to the sofa. His dress ripples in sync with his movements.

'What's going on?'

I clear my throat, but my voice is still drowning in tears. 'Today, when I was going through the Gussmans' things, I came across some sort of SOS.'

Lulu frowns.

I open my laptop bag and pull out the freezer bag containing the note. 'Here, see for yourself.'

He peers at it for a few seconds, then looks up at me.

'There might be nothing sinister to this, Em. Kids messing around, or playing detectives. Hang on.'

He gets up, rummages in his bag by the door, then dashes to the bathroom and comes back and stands in front of me.

'Follow me,' he says and heads for the kitchen. 'And bring your phone.'

I don't ask any questions, just do as he says.

Acting like he owns the place, Lulu opens the cupboard under the sink and grabs a roll of cling film. He tears off a sheet and lays it on the table next to my tweezers. Then he plucks his phone out of his bodice, picks up the tweezers and sits down.

He unzips the plastic bag and extracts the note with the tweezers, then places it on the cling film with great care.

'To think that this all began with some philosophical texts on papyrus scrolls that were carbonised and buried in the ash of Vesuvius in 79 AD. All roads lead to papyrology, my dear. Now give me some light from your phone, will you?'

As I switch on the torch function, he picks up his own phone and opens a magnifying-glass app. He carefully examines each letter of the note before moving to the next and comparing them. Then he turns the note over and meticulously inspects the other side.

'Well, the paper isn't from the Roaring Twenties. The grain is regular, which tells us it was mass-produced. But you must have seen that already. The form of the letters, though – now that's interesting. See these little dots by the E in "HELP" and the first P in "TRAPPED"? The person who wrote this paused at those points. This has nothing to do with personal writing style. Look, here, and there, the pencil only leaves the paper to form the middle stroke of the E. I'm not a graphologist, but if you want my opinion, in the circumstances and based on so few words, in capital letters to boot, it would be very difficult to tell who wrote this.'

I nod and follow the movement of the magnifying glass with my eyes to the word 'HELP'.

'See the L here? There's a slight break at the bottom of the letter. And there's bit of an indent on the M in "ME" here. These tell me the paper was moved to a different surface, as if suddenly, the person writing those words had to use something soft to put the paper on instead, maybe her leg.'

The look on Lulu's face has gone from cheerful and confident to worried.

'Oh my God, Em, I was wrong,' he says. 'I really don't think this thing was written by kids, for a treasure hunt or a murder-mystery party or something ... Definitely not.'

I pocket my phone and finish my breakfast standing at the kitchen counter. I wash the last two bites of my flatbread and cheese down with a swig of lukewarm coffee, then pour a fresh cup for my wife and leave it on the table.

The cold seizes me the second I step out onto the porch. Sheets of ice line the foreshore like the cheeks of a sea with a beard of snow. My frost-covered kayak is ready and waiting for me on the jetty, but I probably won't have time before the sun sets at around three to get out there and paddle until the pain erases everything.

My wife and I share this need to be at one with the water every day. Freyja swims daily, and even at night. How many times have I seen her shivering body swallowed up by the black water before returning to me as if risen from a casket?

With a loud yawn, and stepping around the icy puddles, I walk across the garden to the narrow steps that lead to the jetty where our little runabout is tied up, covered with a sprinkling of snow. The boat's engine sputters to life, and I sound just like it as I clear the burning-cold air from my throat.

A few hundred metres of inshore waters are all that separate Djursholm, where I live, from Rödstuguviken, where I'm expected – a bay in the small community of Sticklinge, at the north end of the island of Lidingö. The crossing only takes a few minutes, and soon I'm tying the boat up by the red wooden cottage that gives the cove its name.

The area has already been cordoned off to keep the rubberneckers at bay. There's more of them than I'd have thought, given the early hour. Not to mention those scoping out the scene from their balconies or from behind their windows. And it's quite the scene.

'*Hej.*' Alvid's there to greet me. He's the head of the NFC – the crime-scene team. He's wearing his trademark white coveralls. 'I figured we had no choice but to call you in for this one,' he says by way of apology, pursing his lips.

I give him a friendly pat on the shoulder and walk with him down the jetty to the tent the NFC has erected on the small beach, a few metres up from the frozen water's edge.

'I'll be with you in a second. I'm just going to have a word with these ladies first,' I say, leaving him to go into the tent alone.

I walk over to a trio of seniors who are standing around chatting on the road by the red cottage.

One of them has a stripy beanie on her head. 'Are you Detective Inspector Rosén?' she asks me.

I nod.

'See, Ilse, I told you it was him,' she says to the woman to her left, who's wearing a fur hat.

'They told us we could put our clothes back on,' the woman continues, turning back to me. 'But I do wonder if that was the right thing to do.'

I look at her, uncomprehending.

'The problem, Inspector,' her friend Ilse explains, 'is that the rest of your team here are still wet around the ears. Just look at them.' She points to my officers, who are all hard at work. 'I really don't know if we should have listened to them. I mean, shouldn't they have taken our ... oh, my brain is getting so old, I don't know ... our fingerprints, that's it!'

'Assuming you didn't touch the body, then no,' I reply, only half joking.

'Of course we didn't. Heaven forbid!' the third woman chimes in, pressing her palms to her chest.

'And that wouldn't have been an easy thing to do, obviously,' Ilse adds. 'She was trapped in the ice.'

I nod, appreciating the logic of her comment. 'Can you tell me how you found the body?'

'We were getting ready to go for a dip around eight, as usual, just the kind of thing to smooth out the wrinkles and wake up the heart,' the third woman explains. 'We swim here every day. There's a few more of us on the weekend, but during the week it's just the three of us besties from Braxenvägen. That's the street just behind the house with the turret up there, see?' She points to a building painted green and Falu-copper red. 'Normally, we go into the water from the beach, where you've pitched your tent. But when the sea's frozen over like it is today, we go in by the jetty, where you've moored your boat. Sometimes we have to poke a hole in the ice, or if it isn't that thick, we just slide into it. It's not that hard.'

The two other women nod.

'And that was when we saw her.'

'But we didn't think it was – how should I put it? – a woman,' Ilse continues. 'We thought it must have been a mannequin or something. You know, the things you see in shop windows. With her pale skin, those glassy eyes, that dull blonde hair and those long slim legs of hers – and stark naked too. So we stood there looking at her for a while through the ice, cursing the hooligans who'd throw such a thing in the sea. We wondered how the heck we were going to get it out of the water.'

'What did you do when you realised it was a ... a body,' I ask, making sure to soften my words.

'Ilse thought we should try to get her out of the water,' says the swimmer with the stripy hat, 'but I told her there was no point. She looked dead enough to me, so I said we'd better call the police.'

I nod robotically, quite surprised by their composure.

'Did you see anyone else in the area?'

'Of course. Everyone's on their way to work or school at that time.'

'Did you notice anyone you didn't recognise?'

They shake their heads in unison.

'Thank you, ladies. You're almost free to go. An officer will take a quick statement from you and a psychologist will be in touch.'

They turn and stare at me, their eyes like dinner plates.

'A psychologist? Whatever for?' Ilse asks.

'To help you, er ... to talk to you about the shock of what you found.'

'Don't you worry, Inspector, we'll talk about it among ourselves. And with our swimming club friends this weekend. If there's one thing you can be sure of, it's that we're going to talk about this!'

'I don't suppose we can go for a swim now?' one of the other women pipes up.

'You can, just not here in Rödstuguviken,' I reply, thinking this intrepid trio and their nerves of steel would put many of the recruits on the force to shame.

I thank them again and duck back under the crime-scene tape to pull on the coveralls that one of my sergeants has ready for me. Then I enter the tent where the NFC officers are working in a silence broken only by the swishing of their protective gear.

The victim is lying on a stretcher.

'Fifteen, maybe sixteen years old,' Alvin says, joining me beside the body.

I shake my head.

I don't have kids, and I probably never will. Still, nothing wrenches my heart more than the death of a child. The parents always die with them. It's like they're uprooted by their loss. The grief drains the life from them, even if they have other kids to support. And it's not just the mothers who suffer. Sometimes the fathers are the first to lose their grip. They let themselves go and forget about the others who have also been left behind – those cursed to go on living in the wake of a sister or brother who's never seemed more alive than in death.

'She wasn't in the water for long,' Alvid explains.

It certainly doesn't look like the sea and its creatures have had enough time to make a mess of the body. It's frozen and blue from the cold – the temperature went down to minus eleven last night – which makes this death a little easier on the eye, at least for now. Her hair is soaking in a puddle around her head. It strikes me that the ladies who found her were right – to look at her, there's nothing really human left. Rather, there's something ethereal and intangible about her, as if I'm in the presence of one of Tolkien's elves.

My gaze lands on the wounds on the insides of her thighs. Sealed and solidified by the cold, they look like two big claw marks.

'Like I said,' Alvid sighs. 'We really needed you here.'

'I know.'

'Are you going to be all right?' he asks, not daring to look at me.

'I'll be all right.'

Alvid nods and points to the pair of scissors attached to a leather cord around the victim's neck. They're now resting on the stretcher above her shoulder.

'So, did those grannies see anything?' he asks.

'No, nothing at all. Believe me, if they had, they would have said something.'

I see wrinkles forming in the corners of my friend's eyes, and I can picture his dry smile beneath his mask.

'When we fished her out, her hair was caught in the cord and the scissors were hanging down her back. If those three grannies didn't see them, we'd better keep all this to ourselves for now.'

I move down to her feet and see the thread looped around her big toes.

Now, the hanging girl of Storholmen is not alone. And she's come back to haunt me.

12
Emma

I push open the door and walk into Ett Glas along with a blast of icy air. It always affects my mood when Lotta has a day off, and this morning when the taxi dropped me at Mor Anna there was a guy named Jonas at the helm of the boat with the number 80 on the front.

I find Lotta sitting at a table by the emergency exit with Anneli and Björn. She has a serious look on her face. I don't want to interrupt, but she looks up and invites me to join them. Björn grabs a chair for me and slots it in between his and Anneli's.

'I had a call from Ilse in the swimming club,' Lotta says, giving me a pat on the hand. 'She and her friends found a body at Rödstuguviken this morning.'

'On Lidingö,' Björn explains.

'A young woman. Can you believe it? A young woman!'

Anneli gives me a long look.

The note.

HELP ME I'M TRAPPED.

Oh my God. The note. What if it was written by that young woman?

A wave of nausea washes over me.

The Gussmans. Could this have something to do with them? Maybe not all of them … just Niklas, perhaps? But why give me access to the manor house if he has something to hide? It would explain his intransigence and the schedules he imposes on me though.

Björn and Lotta get up, damming the flood of questions in my mind.

'Apparently, the detective on the case is the same one who investigated the murder of the hanging girl,' says Lotta, pulling on her coat. 'Anyway, Ilse and the ladies will keep me abreast of things. Right, we'll be off, then. We have to go into town. Emma, I hope you'll change your mind for New Year's Eve. We'd love to have you. I'm counting on you to twist her arm, Anneli.'

She gives me a wink and disappears, followed by Björn.

Anneli gets up in turn to start serving customers again.

'If you haven't called the police yet,' she whispers in my ear, 'then now's the time.'

Detective Inspector Rosén is sitting across from me at Anneli's place, upstairs from the café. With his never-ending arms and legs folded into an orange armchair that's too low for him, he looks like a spider crab stuck in the sand.

I've just given him the note, and he inspects it through the plastic bag as I explain how I found it. When he looks up at me, there's something unsettling about his piercing gaze. Perhaps he doesn't believe me and he's searching for the crack in my story. Or maybe he's trying to intimidate me.

'Why didn't you contact us earlier?' he asks in a hoarse voice.

He clears his throat and starts again.

'You've had this note since yesterday morning. Why wait twenty-four hours to call the police?'

I glance down, not wanting to look him in the eye, and notice that I'm repeatedly clasping and unclasping my hands. I place my palms flat on my thighs, hoping that will calm my nerves.

'I wasn't sure how recent it was. I told you, I found it in a disused room. All the furniture was under dust sheets. If I'd thought someone was in danger, I would have reached out to you immediately.'

'It's not up to you to draw conclusions, Miss Lindahl. That's my job.'

His tone is cordial, his voice calm, but his words chill me to the bone.

'You only have one duty in this kind of situation: to call the police. Not after your day at work or dinner in town. Right away.'

I close my eyes.

He's right. I only thought about myself. Me and my own fears. And I blanked out an entire world of possibilities.

'Who else knows about this note, besides you and Anneli Lund?'

'Lucas Blix, a friend. He teaches at Stockholm University. He's a papyrologist.'

The detective's eyes widen. 'Did you really think the paper was that old?'

He seems amused and the hint of sarcasm I detect in his tone irritates me.

'Not at all, I...'

I pause to fight the nausea that's resurfacing. I'm battling my mother's words and her inebriated voice singing 'Happy Birthday'. Scorning my absence.

I'm fighting the nine years of pain inside me. But I haven't escaped the detective's inquisitive gaze.

My heart starts pounding as if I'm running, and that's what I feel like doing right now – running away. The way I have for the last nine years.

But this time I have to stay. And speak.

'I thought ... at first I thought those words were written by my sister.'

13
Karl

It's gone eleven by the time I get home tonight.

After three decades on the force and fifteen years of living with a wife who turns in early and has the hearing of a great grey owl, I'm no stranger to tiptoeing around, mindful of every creaking floorboard, like a parent fearful of waking a sleeping child,.

Making myself a bite to eat, I recall how I surprised Freyja on our crystal wedding anniversary this year – and how it backfired. Like an idiot, and a selfish one at that, I'd planned a weekend away golfing with my mates. It's always a headache trying to find a date for us to all get away and the only possible time this year was the weekend of our anniversary. Freyja persuaded me to go all the same, reassuring me that it was just a date on the calendar, after all. I agreed, thrilled to be going away with the boys. But when I got to the airport, I found a card from Freyja in my bag, wishing me a fun weekend. I felt so guilty at letting her down on our special day without so much as a card, a bunch of flowers, or even a plan to make it up to her at a fancy restaurant the following week, I left my friends high and dry and went straight home. My darling Freyja was in her office, sitting at her computer, snuggled up in her old dressing gown with her headphones on. I could barely contain my glee as I tiptoed right up to her. Let's just say she got the surprise of her life. She screamed like a bad actress in a B-movie.

My phone beeps, interrupting the flow of my thoughts.

It's Alvid, offering to pick me up in the morning when he drops his son off at the British school near my place.

I text him back to say yes, and my mind immediately turns to Emma Lindahl. As soon as I set eyes on her in that café on

Storholmen, I sensed that our paths had crossed before. As our interview went on, that feeling kept growing stronger.

There's no such thing as coincidence.

It turns out that Emma Lindahl is the sister of Sofia Axelsson, 'the hanging girl of Storholmen', as the press dubbed her. At the time, Emma was living abroad and our only contact had been by phone. The funeral ended up being an intimate affair, but I had a family photo and even though Emma had changed, straight away my subconscious told me I recognised her.

Her mother had said that the two sisters were very close, and I'd hoped that Emma could shed some light on how Sofia liked to spend her time and who she spent it with – a new acquaintance, a change in behaviour, anything that might give me something to go on. Emma had answered my questions in a toneless voice, punctuated by long pauses as she attempted to contain her grief. Her sister often went through 'rough patches', she told me, phases of depression during which she tended to withdraw, but the last time she'd heard from her, ten days before her death, she had found her mood light and cheerful. However, when Emma had texted Sofia again – several times – she'd received no reply. Worried, Emma called her mother, who then set her mind at ease. Four days after that, though, Sofia was found dead.

Emma had spoken about her sister with much love. They were eight years apart in age and each had grown up without her father. Emma's dad died of an overdose not long after she was born, and Sofia's walked out on their mother while she was pregnant. Emma loved her sister like her own daughter. She'd basically raised her.

I understood a lot of things when I met their mother. The mother who hadn't reported her teenage daughter missing, because she was sure the kid was 'just at it again', or so she told me, rolling her eyes and waving her cigarette in front of her face. The mother who sold photos of her dead daughter and auctioned off her belongings online. It was no wonder that Emma Lindahl had left the continent to get away from her.

It's been nine years now, and her sister's murder remains unsolved. I have nothing new to share with her, nothing to offer her, and I'm sorry about it.

But the note she found might just change all that.

14
Emma

I've hardly moved from the sofa since Detective Inspector Rosén left around noon.

As soon as the door closed behind the grey-haired giant I could feel the energy draining from my body. I dozed off and woke with a start two hours later to find my jumper so drenched in sweat, I worried I might have a fever.

I got up and had a shower and changed into some clothes Anneli lent me, then returned to sit on the sofa, where I spent the rest of the afternoon working instead of going to the Gussmans'. Before he left, the detective asked me not to go back to the manor house until after the family has been interviewed. That might take a while, because their lawyers will probably oppose any kind of formal questioning. The police will have to take the brush the note was in to the lab for testing. I've let Charlotte von Dardel know about all this, and she was very understanding.

It's nearly six in the evening now.

The last boat back to Ropsten has already left Storholmen, and Anneli has just come up to join me.

Despite being busy in the café all day, she's looked after me, taking the time to poke her head in at regular intervals and check how I'm doing. Lulu is the only other person in my life who would do this for me. I just let the hours go by, not finding the strength either to go home or make up my mind to stay on the island tonight. But for once, I have no desire to be alone. Lulu's at the cabaret. Plus, I don't exactly get the impression that I'm bothering Anneli.

'Are you hungry?'

Anneli's question speaks to the rumbling in my belly. Still, I can't stomach the thought of eating a thing.

'Sofia Axelsson,' I say, 'the hanging girl. She was my sister.'

It's only when I open my eyes that I realise they were closed as I confided in her. I've blindly taken the plunge, dropped this bombshell like I was desperate to let go of it.

Anneli nods grimly and comes closer to me. 'All right,' she says, stroking my cheek, 'if you're not hungry, then let's have a drink.'

That draws a smile out of me. She smiles too and steps away.

'I have a bottle of Chablis or some Carlsberg,' she calls from the kitchen.

'Chablis!'

I hear the squeak of a cupboard door, the cushioned *thunk* of the fridge, the clink of a bottle, the hollow smooch of a cork, then the tinkling of crystal.

My friend returns and sets two stemmed glasses on the coffee table, pours us each a generous measure and hands mine to me. Then she sits down cross-legged with her back to a beige velvet cushion on the opposite end of the sofa to me, balancing her glass on her knee.

'So that's the sadness you've been carrying around,' she murmurs, before tasting the wine.

'My baggage, you mean.'

She puckers her lips in mock disbelief. 'I'm sure your baggage isn't that cumbersome. You strike me as someone who travels in style and carries herself gracefully in a long, flowing coat.'

I take a sip of wine and try to wrap my head around that image.

'You have no idea what it's taken for me to set foot on this island and walk through the grounds of that manor house.'

In my mind's eye I can see the tree where my sister was tied up. I have to blink it away, like I have so many times before.

'My mother kept telling me Sofia was all right. My sister wasn't replying to my messages, but Mum kept giving me the usual spiel about me abandoning them, saying they were doing just fine without me and at least my being away meant that she got some love and attention from her youngest daughter. I don't think she meant to lie to me, you know. I think it was the alcohol talking. She would often get her days mixed up, so she probably thought she had heard from Sofia.'

'Were you living far away at the time?'

'New York. I was working for Christie's and I travelled a lot. Once, I bought a ticket for Sofia to come and see me in Marseille. We spent a long weekend in Provence together.'

I remember her smiling on the harbour ferry, wincing when the first taste of pastis touched her lips. Squealing in delight when we went skinny-dipping in the 'piss-warm' water of the *calanques*. Tickling her taste buds with the urchins in the Baie des Singes.

'What was the last thing she saw, I wonder, before she was strung up in that tree?'

I take a long swig from my glass, forgetting that it's wine in there. The alcohol stings all the way to my ears.

'We've never found out where she was for those nine days before she died. When I discovered that cry for help inside the brush, I couldn't help but think she was the one who wrote it.'

Anneli is sitting there, listening to me, her head cocked to one side. And for a second, I relish how good it feels to be with her. What a saving grace she, Björn and Lotta have been for me.

'My mother destroyed Sofia. To be fair, she drags down anyone she comes into contact with.'

'What about you? Did you run away to escape your mother?'

It wasn't like that, I'm about to tell her. The opportunity to work for the world's greatest auction house was what led me to move away. But I know that's a lie.

'Moving away was what saved me, yes. But it sealed my sister's fate too. It's like she was the price to pay for my freedom. A sacrifice I made willingly.'

I take another swig of Chablis to drown all thoughts of my mother.

Anneli unfolds her legs, reaches for the bottle and tops up my glass.

Outside, the sea merges with the night sky, the rolling of the waves with the wind.

'My mother phones me every year to remind me that I'm the one to blame for Sofia's death. Never on the same date, because she can't remember exactly when it was, but still she calls me. And she lets the phone ring as long as it takes for me to answer. Then she sings me "Happy Birthday" until I muster the strength to hang up on her.'

Anneli raises her glass. I respond with a bitter laugh.

'What are we drinking to? Toxic mothers or the stolen sisters?'

'To the survivors, Emma. To you and me.'

15
Viktoria

I'm about to finish work for the night when I hear Josephine's voice coming from the living room. The door is ajar, so I tiptoe over as quietly as I can, and listen.

'Is that why you only wanted Thor to have one present at Christmas?'

She can only be talking to Madam, because the Duke is away. I keep telling my daughter she's not to bother my employer's family. And she's especially not to question their education choices.

A tense silence fills the room, and I freeze, wondering how Madam is going to react. If I open the door and intervene right now, she'll know I've been eavesdropping.

I decide to stay put and just move a little closer so I can peek into the room, grateful for the fact that the ground floor of the manor house is tiled. A wooden floor would creak and give me away.

Josephine and Thor are sitting on the Persian rug at Madam's feet.

'I think a little enlightenment is in order, Josephine. Do you know what we celebrate at Christmas?'

'The birth of Jesus Christ.'

'No. Christmas has its origins in Yule, and that's a celebration of the winter solstice. It was a key date on the calendar of our Viking ancestors.'

'The twenty-first of December,' says Thor, in his soft voice.

'That's right,' his mother says. 'The twenty-first of December, when the days start growing longer at last, after giving way to the night. Our ancestors would herald the return of the sun, but they would stay indoors. They were terrified of going outside on the night of the Wild Hunt.'

'The Wild Hunt,' Thor explains, 'is when Odin ... do you know who Odin is?'

My daughter tips her chin sharply to say she does. 'The god who rules over Asgard,' she replies with a wink.

'Exactly. So, the Wild Hunt is when Odin gallops across the sky to gather the souls of the dead, isn't it, Mum?'

I'm watching my daughter, who's in awe, lapping up his every word. The boy has never been so effusive. It's like his words make sense all of a sudden. Perhaps because, for once, everyone else is speaking his language.

At first, Madam doesn't reply. She's staring out into the night.

'Some people think that Yule means "feast" and others think it means "wheel"', she eventually says, eyes still deep in the shadows.

'And what do you think?' my daughter has the gall to ask.

'That both things are true. In the Celtic tradition, Yule represents the point on the Wheel of the Year when the Holly King, who personifies the darkness at the end of the year, is defeated by the Oak King, who symbolises the return of the light and the advent of spring. Legend has it that they fought over the throne to see who would reign the longest. At Yule, the Oak King finally manages to cut off his brother's head and takes his place until Litha – the summer solstice on the twenty-first of June.'

'That's why we put holly wreaths – or crowns – on our doors,' Thor continues. 'To celebrate the return and the power of the sun.'

Josephine's hugging her knees with her thin arms. With her head tilted back to look up at Thor, her long hair touches the floor.

'But still, why just the one present?'

'I haven't finished, Josephine.'

'We haven't talked about the feast yet,' her friend adds. 'To celebrate Yule, the whole village would gather for a grand feast, where animals would be sacrificed. People would dip twigs into the animals' blood and splash it on each other to bring them protection and plenty in the year to come.'

Thor's eyes are sparkling with an excitement I find unsettling.

'Sacrificing the beasts in winter made it easier to preserve the meat, and it also meant they didn't have to feed them during the harsh, cold months'.

'That sounds like the story of the Christmas turkey, just not as civilised!' my daughter jokes.

Thor bursts out laughing. Josephine gives him a contented smile.

'Have you heard of the god Heimdall?' Madam continues with a poker face.

My daughter shakes her head.

'He had quite the family tree. He was the son of nine different mothers.'

'Nine mothers? How is that possible?'

'It's a myth, Jo...'

'Heimdall watched over the bridge that connected—'

'That bridge, in fact,' Thor cuts in, 'was a rainbow. Bifröst, it was called. It connected the kingdom of Asgard with the sky and the earth.'

'And so, at the end of every year,' Madam continues, 'Heimdall, the guardian of that bridge, would come and visit his children to celebrate Yuletide. For children who had been well behaved, he would leave a gift in their stocking, and for those who hadn't, he would leave ashes.'

'It all sounds a lot like *Lord of the Rings*, doesn't it?' Thor says. 'Have you read it?'

Embarrassed, my daughter shakes her head.

'Tolkien was a professor of medieval English, and he was very much influenced by Norse mythology,' his mother explains.

'Were there human sacrifices during Yule?' Josephine suddenly asks.

This conversation has gone on for long enough. I knock on the door and enter without waiting for an invitation.

'Josephine, it's time for bed. Sorry to disturb you, madam,' I add with a polite smile.

Begrudgingly my daughter gets up and makes a show of dragging her heels. When I close the living-room door behind us, Thor has already picked up the conversation again. But Madam is fixated on the shadows once more, and it doesn't look like she's listening to a word he's saying.

16
Karl

'Where's my coffee?' Paola, the medical examiner barks as we step into her lair.

'It's polite to say hello first,' Alvid replies, placing a steaming cup on his wife's desk before planting a kiss on the cap covering her hair. 'This is why our son grunts instead of speaking. He learns at the feet of an expert.'

'He only opens his mouth to eat or ask for money,' Paola quips after a first scorching sip. 'How lucky we are to be parents. You have no idea what you're missing out on, Karl.'

I smile and try to ignore the twinge I feel in my heart.

'I honestly don't know how much more of that kid's mumbling I can take,' Paola moans as she slips on a pair of latex gloves. 'It's like he's got a potato in his mouth that won't let him pronounce anything that isn't monosyllabic. Pff! Mmmh! Grrr! Argh!'

Alvid bursts out laughing at her little pantomime.

'So.' She reins herself in and approaches our victim, who's lying on the stainless-steel table. 'This smacks a little of déjà vu, doesn't it?'

'More than a little,' I sigh.

'As you can see, the body is intact. More specifically, the fish didn't have time to nibble her away to beyond the point of recognition. The temperature of the water was 2.6 degrees on average yesterday, so that will have slowed down the decomposition process too.'

'Have you been able to determine the time of death?'

'Oh, yes. And I guarantee that my adorable husband's jaw's going to hit the floor.'

'*Now*, I'm adorable, eh? You've stopped barking at me, then?'

'Woof!' she replies. 'Right, listen up, boys. Thanks to my fabulous colleagues in Japanese and British forensic medicine, there are now two elements – well, two major scientific discoveries and a litany of elements, if you really want to know – that provide us with a basis from which we can estimate the time of death when a body has been immersed in water,' she tells us with growing enthusiasm. 'Yes, I know, I have a terribly exciting life.'

'I didn't say a word,' Alvid replies with a cheeky smile.

'Let me explain, and I promise I'll be quick,' Paola goes on, raising her hands to quell our impatience. 'First of all, a protein found in muscles – fructose-bisphosphate aldolase A if you want to be intimately acquainted with it – declines as immersion in water persists. Next, tooth analysis, or more precisely, tooth enamel – get this – can be as revealing as a set of fingerprints. As it happens, a bunch of unicellular microalgae that go by the delightful name of diatoms – sounds like the name of a Greek goddess, don't you think? – latch on to the enamel and degrade the calcium and phosphorus in it. Doesn't that blow your mind, darling? All of this tells us that – drum roll please – death occurred between twenty-four and thirty-six hours ago.'

Alvid proudly applauds his wife.

'What's up, Rosén, you're not happy?' Paola's quick to add.

'After that kind of performance, I was expecting a time of death, give or take a quarter of an hour.'

'This isn't Netflix, Rosén, it's real life.'

'With unicellular microalgae.'

'Precisely. And there's more. A body in which the gastrointestinal tract *isn't* completely filled with decomposition gases – we have the Australians to thank for this discovery, by the way – won't float all the way to the surface, and most of the time it'll stay in the area where it went into the water. In other words, with normal sea conditions, it remains within a radius of one and a half times the depth of the water. So with a depth of a hundred metres, for example, that body is likely to be found within a hundred and fifty metres of where it sank.'

'How deep do you think it is around Sticklinge?' I ask Alvid.

'In the Baltic Sea, the depth varies from fifty to four hundred and sixty metres or so. Here, I'd say we're looking at the lower end of that.'

'Our victim was found within about seventy-five metres of where she went into the water, then.'

Alvid nods.

'To get back to that déjà vu thing,' Paola continues. 'This body has the same semi-circular incisions as Sofia Axelsson's nine years ago. Here, and here.' She points a gloved index finger at the inside of the thighs, near the femoral arteries. 'You know what an arterial wound does to someone, Rosén. It squirts jets of blood with every beat of their heart and they bleed out fast. Which means that the killer wasn't able to do a clean job. Especially since the victim was severely dehydrated. I'll get back to that, but I wanted to mention it because, in spite of the drop in blood volume, and unlike what you might think, dehydration accelerates the heart rate. So that's the cause of death. Not a drowning. A full-on exsanguination.'

'What are these marks?' I ask, pointing to some fine white scratches in the victim's groin area.

'Old scars. The water and the cold have made them look puffy. They're older than these ones around the iliac spine.' Paola uses her thumb and index finger to show me two wounds on the hip. 'Here,' she continues, moving to the end of the table, 'there are similar scars below the left talus – the bone that sticks out on the outside of the ankle. See?'

She twists the foot to the inside for the benefit of her demonstration, further dehumanising the body of this child, who now looks like a disjointed puppet.

'Your victim was self-harming. Based on the look of these injuries and the scarring, I'd say she'd been doing it for several years. Often, more recent cuts tend to be longer and deeper, because the subject gets used to the pain and keeps pushing their limits. It's tragic.'

She purses her lips and closes her eyes, as if to hold back her tears.

I've known this woman almost as long as Freyja, but I'm always surprised by the things that move her. Paola stays as cool as a cucumber when she's examining the body of a young woman who's bled to death, but she gets choked up at the thought of her being in psychological distress.

'There are burn marks on her wrists and ankles, and wounds consistent with friction from a cord,' she carries on after clearing her throat. 'Obviously, the water has washed away any fibres, otherwise we might have been able to compare them with those found on Sofia Axelsson's body.'

'Nothing to suggest that she was tortured or abused, or had any sexual activity?' I ask.

Paola shakes her head. 'No, nothing. Like Sofia. But her stomach had been empty for more than seventy-two hours when she died. Her skin and organs – her kidneys, for example – show obvious signs of dehydration. It wouldn't have been obvious when you fished her out of the water, but her lips must have cracked and bled.'

'What about the blood work? Any traces of drugs or pre-scription medication?'

'No drugs and nothing to suggest she was sick. Just high levels of uric acid and creatinine, and those are explained by the advanced stage of dehydration, if you ask me. So we're dealing with a lunatic who keeps their victims tied up for days and watches them waste away. And we still don't know who this little lady is.'

'She's a child.' My words come out sounding more scathing than I intended.

'You're right, Karl, she's a child,' Paola repeats. She glances at Alvid, but he's averted his eyes.

'What else can you tell me about the body?' I say, feeling a bit uncomfortable now.

'I didn't find any tattoos, braces or implants,' she replies very matter-of-factly. 'So assuming there are no missing-persons reports that match her description, you'll probably be calling this kid Jane Doe.'

17
Karl

'Come in!' Siv snaps.

My nostrils are assaulted by a heady waft of fish as soon as I open the door.

'Yeah, I know it reeks. Sorry,' my superintendent says, plunging her spoon into a can of tuna. Suddenly Arnold, her old Great Dane (aka Arnie, because of his size), pokes his head out from under the desk.

'And he's the other reason for the smell. I took him for a walk on the beach this morning. I haven't had time to give him a wash.'

Siv slips her navy-blue suit jacket over the biceps she sculpts every fibre of, every day. Then she gives her shaker bottle a jiggle and downs a long draught of the brownish mixture inside with a grimace.

'Bloody hell, Siv.'

'You don't get anything for nothing, Rosén. Spirulina, avocado, spinach and matcha. Not the most appetising to look at, but not that gross, really. You should try some.'

She puts down the vile drink, smooths her white quiff distractedly and sits down at her desk with a deep sigh of satisfaction.

'Lunch of champions. Anyway, how are you doing?' she asks, tossing a piece of gum into her mouth.

Arnold limps his way around the side of the desk.

'You know, nobody was expecting you to come back so quickly after your wife drowned,' Siv says. Her dog yawns odorously and flops his head down on my thigh. 'But I suppose you couldn't really avoid getting roped in on this one.'

'You're not looking so hot these days, Arnie,' I say, giving the pooch a scratch behind his huge ears.

'He's got rheumatism. Go on, I'm waiting.'

'We're looking at the same victim profile. Unidentified teenage female with psychiatric issues, maybe some sort of personality disorder – she was self-harming but stopped short of suicide. Likely a bit of an outsider, and chances are she was estranged from her family too. She was held captive for at least three days, and no one's reported her missing, which could mean she was out of touch with her parents or they're used to her running away. The killer has left the same signature as we saw with Sofia Axelsson: a pair of scissors on a cord around her neck and big toes bound together with black sewing thread. Same MO as well. Our Jane Doe was tied up and starved, then exsanguinated. Again, by deep cuts to the femoral arteries.'

'What's the murder weapon? A scalpel again?'

I nod as Arnold gets up with a whimper to find comfort at his owner's feet.

'That said, even if we're more than likely looking at the same predator, it's quite the change from the hanging last time, with all the staging that involved, to just dumping the body in the bay.'

'It doesn't stick,' Siv says, giving her dog a pat on the back. 'Why go to all that trouble, then stop short of the grand theatrics?'

She opens a desk drawer and scrabbles at what must be the bottom of a metal box, judging by the obnoxious grating of her nails. Arnold can't contain his excitement.

'Maybe our perp isn't as strong as before?' Siv suggests, feeding him one dog biscuit after another. 'What do you think? I mean, hoisting up a body that weighs...'

'Fifty-three kilos.'

'Fifty-three kilos. It can't have been easy to hoist a dead weight like that up into a tree.'

'Carrying one that weighs in at fifty-seven kilos is no mean feat either, even just to dump it in the sea. The branch Sofia was hanging from wasn't that high, remember. Her feet were only about thirty centimetres off the ground. If you ask me, strength isn't the problem.'

'Opportunity, then? Aren't you just the cutest, my big boy,' she smiles, wiping drool from her jacket. 'I mean, could the killer have been interrupted? Moving away from the hanging, changing the signature – that's huge.'

Arnold limps over to me and drops a soggy biscuit at my feet. I give him a good head-scratching, and he goes back to Siv.

'Nine years ago, the manor house wasn't a permanent residence like it is today. The Gussman family only went there on occasion. So the property would have been a lot more accessible back then.'

'Where were Niklas Gussman and his family at the time?'

'New York. Niklas Gussman was managing the American arm of the family empire. He came back to Sweden with his wife and son three years ago, when his father died, to take the helm. They only moved into the manor house earlier this year.'

'What do you make of the SOS Axelsson's sister found? Her name's Emma, isn't it? It's a go for the brush, by the way. The lawyers are sending it to us.'

'Emma Lindahl. That's not a married name. She had a different father to Sofia. Alvid's having the note examined this morning. That piece of paper has been through so many hands, I doubt we'll get any usable prints off it. Not to mention that the paper itself and the pencil that was used to write on it could be decades old. I don't think those will give us many clues. If we get some prints, though, at least we can compare those to Sofia's and Jane Doe's. If we do a comparative handwriting analysis, we could use that to try and get a warrant to search the manor house. And I do mean *try*, because the Gussmans' lawyers will probably shoot that down in a matter of seconds. I wouldn't put it past them to bring in an expert of their own to prove the exact opposite of our findings. To be honest, that note could just as easily have been written as a joke, as part of some sort of murder-mystery party, you know...'

Siv leans back in her chair and crosses her ankles and apple-green Nikes on her desk. 'So the brush is about a hundred years old, you say? And we don't know exactly how it got into the manor house.'

I nod.

'In other words, that note could have been written by anyone. I don't see how we can connect it with Axelsson or Jane Doe. Neither of them set foot in there, to our knowledge. Or am I mistaken? We found no trace of Axelsson inside the house, as I recall. Other than that, where are you at with the door-to-door enquiries?'

'Getting nowhere fast. By Paola's calculations, the body could have been dumped in the water at sea or from the shoreline. We've asked the local newspaper and the community associations in Lidingö, and even the museum, to put out a call for witnesses to come forward. Someone might have seen something on the twenty-ninth of December, or during the night of the twenty-ninth to the thirtieth. Obviously, if the killer dumped the body at sea, the boat could have come from anywhere. The link is clear enough between Sofia and our new victim, so I've decided to extend the neighbourhood canvassing to Storholmen too.'

'But not to your neck of the woods as well? Djursholm is just across the water.'

'I don't see any point in that at the moment. Djursholm is a world away. It's more connected to Stockholm than it is to the islands, and there's nothing to suggest right now that the killer has any connection to the swanky suburbs.'

Siv nods and taps her thighs as if they're a drum set. Then she springs to her feet.

Arnold does the same, certain this must mean it's time for his sacrosanct walk.

'Listen,' she says, 'this is all a good start. But I'm going to say the same thing I did nine years ago: I want to know where Axelsson and Jane Doe were drained of their blood. Find the answer to that question, and I'm sure you'll find a lot more too.'

18
Emma

'So, what's this "French 75" of yours, then?' Björn asks me, propping up the bar.

'Champagne, gin, lemon and sugar,' I reply, garnishing the last glass with a slice of lemon. 'Two measures of champers to one gin. Mix the gin, lemon and sugar in a cocktail shaker, then top it off with champagne – or another sparkling wine, like this local Särtshöga blanc de blancs. It's divine, you'll see.'

With a dubious air, Björn puts down his beer and takes the glass I hand to him. The sound of Anneli's and Lotta's laughter drifts through from the kitchen.

'It was invented in the 1920s and named after an artillery cannon.'

He winces.

'I know, with a name as hot as that, you think it's going to have a bit more of a kick. But it's a refreshing change to see the French not getting too carried away for once.'

'Aaaah, Emma's famous French 75!' Lotta exclaims, placing a tray on the counter. 'How do the French say seventy-five? 'Cos they do like to go overboard with what they call numbers. It's like every single one is an exercise in mental arithmetic. Talk about making things complicated. Listen to this, Björn: ninety-nine isn't just ninety plus nine, it's four times twenty, plus ten, plus nine. The Belgians and the Swiss keep things simple and follow the same structure as the English and the Swedes. But the Frenchies do like to be special. Unbelievable!'

'The French aren't convoluted, they're sophisticated,' I argue with a wink.

Anneli comes through to join us, accompanied by a tempting aroma of cream, garlic and butter, and grabs one of the canapés that I made this afternoon – salmon with whipped cream, dill and lime.

'*Skål! Gott Nytt År!*' she toasts.

'Happy New Year!'

We all take our first sips of the cocktails and the murmurings of approval from my friends make me smile.

'All right, I take back everything I ever said about the French,' Lotta sighs, licking her lips.

We carry our glasses and the canapés over to the big round table in the bay window and our eyes are drawn out to sea by a ray of moonlight reflected in the black water. There's a special word in Swedish for this very scene: *mångata* – the road to the moon.

Suddenly, the silence we share seems as rich and nuanced as a conversation. There's nothing awkward about it. Quite the opposite. It's as if we're cloaked in its warm embrace, just listening to one another.

'The silence on this island is…' I'm trying to find the right word for it. 'At first I found it a bit impenetrable. Intimidating.'

'But when you live here, it's like a cocoon,' Anneli smiles.

'When you come to Storholmen for the first time,' Lotta adds, her voice barely more than a whisper, 'you wonder how people can possibly live here, especially if you're from the big city.' She gives me a wink.

'But what do people do when they run out of pasta, or nappies, or paracetamol tablets when the last boat of the day has left?' I wonder. 'Or worse, if someone has a bad fall or a heart attack? Even if they have a boat of their own, it can't be that easy. They'd have to go down to the dock, get on board, get off again on the other side of the water and get into their car, right? Come to think of it, though, how many Stockholmers have to walk to the metro, tramway or bus stop to get to work? It's not that much harder to start your day with a boat trip, I suppose.'

There's something serene about the way Anneli is looking at us all right now. She exudes an air of blissful calm that I find soothing.

'Trust me,' Lotta adds, 'no one on Storholmen ever died because they couldn't make it to the hospital on time. The real question is what you actually need to live, materially speaking. What you need to live comfortably.'

She's drawing huge circles with her hands in front of her face. She reminds me of Isadora Duncan, the American dancer whose free-flowing movements were inspired by the harmony of nature.

I give her a smile.

'I mean, I'm not trying to say we should all go back to living off the land. I'm really not. But surely an abundance of everything, like you have in the city, creates its own needs, don't you think? All that focus on *having* instead of *being* isn't exactly conducive to moments of introspection. Or even building social connections, right? Here, though, if you're a parent and find yourself short on nappies, you reach out to your neighbour and they'll bring them right to your door. The community life on Storholmen is not a myth. It comes with a Scandinavian twist, of course. We know we can count on one another, but we make sure we respect everyone's privacy.'

I think about my apartment in Old Stockholm, up in the eaves, and how I don't know any of my neighbours. I'd barely even recognise them. Maybe Lotta has a point.

In one graceful movement, Anneli gets up and goes to fetch the champagne bucket from the counter. She gives the bottle a wipe and tops up our glasses.

'You have no idea how happy children are here,' Lotta adds, raising her glass to us all. 'There's no traffic, so kids can run around, ride their bikes, play with Lego and even go sledging in the street. Parents know they're safe, so they give them more freedom. The kids grow up to be more independent and responsible, and the adults get to enjoy a quiet life. It's a virtuous circle that benefits the whole family. Maybe that's why Niklas Gussman decided to move to the island. To get away from the whirlwind of city life.'

'Or to get away from something else,' Björn says.

'What are you on about?' Lotta tuts. 'Can you give it a rest with these ridiculous theories of yours? I really don't know what you have against him. Granted, he's not half the man his great-grandfather was, but surely he's not that bad. Anyone would think you have an inferiority complex.'

'I'm just saying what I see,' her husband shrugs. 'That man is running away from something. What, I don't know, but I'll bet it's not a love for the island or that big house that's brought him here.'

19
Karl

I left the house before daybreak. I couldn't breathe.

Several times in the night, I went out onto our bedroom balcony. A breath of icy air was the slap in the face I needed to calm my feverish mind. The biting cold was the wall of pain I needed to hit so I wouldn't have to think about anything else. There was something satisfying about that pain, something delightful even – because it was something I had chosen. I hate being forced into things. I hate being a victim.

I went out in my kayak for that all-too brief moment when the sun drags itself out of its winter slumber, only to fade wearily away in the early afternoon even though there's still so much to do, so much darkness to keep at bay. When I reached the open sea, the sky turned into an incandescent wave. The clouds blending in with the spray, it stretched lazily, bathing the horizon in orangey hues.

I paddled until the cramps crippled me. I returned to shore with my chest and my throat on fire, throbbing with a life-saving pain. My limbs numbed, torpefied by the cold, I found relief at last from the chaos of my thoughts and memories.

I light the fire pit outside around three in the afternoon. The sun's about to disappear when I see Alvid coming down our driveway. My friend gets out of his car with a pack of beer in one hand. He waves to me with the other and walks towards me on the garden path.

I greet him with a hug, and he makes it last.

We sink our first beer in silence, eyes glued to the dying light of the day. The only sounds are our lips on the bottle necks and the crackling of the flames.

'The tests on the note found by Emma Lindahl came back inconclusive,' Alvid tells me as he pops the cap off his second Höganäs. 'There are partial prints all over the paper in various layers, and none of them are usable. And I can assure you, we tried everything. We started with 1,2-Indanedione – that's a pretty new technique that develops latent fingermarks under laser light. You have to be sure the paper's dry, though, otherwise you've no chance. Then I ran the sample through Oil Red O as well. It was my buddy in Quebec, Alex Beaudoin, who invented that. That didn't get us any further though, unfortunately. We also checked for indentation, in case the person who wrote the note, or their captor, or anyone else, had got the paper from a notepad and there'd been any direct or indirect traces of other handwriting on there. In other words, if there was anything to find, I'd have found it. I tried ESDA too – that uses a bronze plate with polyester film. Just add some toner and *bam!* you get an electrostatic image and there's no danger of any damage to your document either.'

He takes another sip of beer and wipes his lips on the neck of the bottle, the way he always does.

'I mean, it was always going to be a long shot, but you know me, the eternal optimist, I had my hopes. Same thing with the brush. Whoever dusts and polishes the furniture in that place must have given that the once-over too. The only complete prints we found on it were Emma Lindahl's.'

I give him a curt nod.

I know my friend isn't really here to talk shop. The quicker he gets to the point, the sooner he'll leave.

'Siv told me they've called off the search.' His voice is almost a whisper.

My gaze is drawn out to sea – the mistress both Freyja and I have shared.

I realise I've left my kayak precisely where she used to leave her clothes. Otherwise so orderly and organised, she would just leave them in a pile on the dock. She's never liked the robe I gave her to warm her up when she came out of the water. She's always preferred to rub herself raw with a towel instead and get dressed quickly, then dash inside out of the cold.

That night, as was her habit, the pile of clothes was in the same place, like a beacon to guide my wife back onto terra firma. I called Siv right away, then Alvid. Shaken and shivering, I stayed beside Freyja's things until they got here. I explained to them how, when I came home after having dinner with Alvid, Freyja was neither in our room nor her office. I'd gone outside thinking she'd be waiting for me by the fire pit, and then found her things.

'Freyja didn't come back from her swim,' I kept repeating, before throwing up the anxiety that was tying my stomach in knots.

For the last week, Siv's been sending divers out to scour the shoreline and the open water, anywhere the currents could have carried her. But they haven't found anything.

My wife is now officially a missing person. And even though no one will say the word for a while, she's presumed dead.

I close my eyes and hiccup, suddenly overwhelmed by grief.

I can't handle any more waves of sadness.

They're exhausting.

They make me want to jump into the sea and let myself go under.

Alvid places a hand between my shoulder blades. It starts out as a friendly pat, then turns into a gentle rub. Like he's spreading his sadness onto me, giving me a double helping.

I open my eyes and see Storholmen, just across the water from us.

The island's presence reminds me that it's not just my pain that matters. That my duty, at the very least, is to ease the pain of the forgotten – those who remain, paralysed by memory and absence. The least I can do is bring them answers. Help them close a chapter of their life, and do it properly.

'I made her a cup of coffee and left it on the kitchen counter,' I admit, all of a sudden. 'The other day, before heading over to Storholmen. I forgot to ... I forgot, and it was cold when I got home.'

'You should come and spend some time at our place,' Alvid suggests, toying with his bottle.

He knows it's an empty invitation. Grief is not something we share.

Wherever I go, I'll carry the memory of Freyja with me. My wife is everywhere – in my morning coffee and my beer at the end of the day, in the silence of the night. I loved her in what she said was a feminine way. I loved being the shadow to her light. She thought it was romantic. It made her laugh.

Freyja is my rock. I carry her everywhere, clinging to the sole of my shoes. She follows me, whether I like it or not.

20
Emma

I sip my coffee and eat my toast and slices of *herrgårdsost* cheese in the café as I watch Anneli painting on the deck outside. I can't remember the last time I slept so well. I was surprised to see it was past noon when I opened my eyes to a pure sky and a landscape so immaculate and white it was almost blinding. Waking up to this scene made me feel like a little kid again. It gave me the urge to go outside and hear the fresh snow crunching beneath my boots.

The brash beauty of the panorama reminds me why my heart will always belong in the great north, in spite of everything. The sun seems to have risen much higher in the sky than usual. The snow that fell in the night has blanketed the muddy ground and clothed the bare trees and bushes. It's masked the brutal bleakness of winter, making it suddenly as radiant as summer.

Björn and Lotta left around one, after we'd laughed ourselves silly re-enacting a Spanish tradition Lulu introduced me to that involves swallowing a grape seed and making a wish on every stroke of midnight. I wonder if Lulu enjoyed wearing my dress. I wonder how it moved and caught the light. He messaged me in the early hours with a sublime photo of himself on stage. He was eager to hear if I'd finally let my hair down and done something wild and physical. I told him that drinking champagne and sleeping for more than ten hours straight was exactly the kind of pleasure I needed.

The sun's shining in her eyes now, so Anneli gets up and moves her chair to face a different way. She sees me and waves.

After a quick shower, I dress warmly and join her outside.

'*Hej*,' she says, turning away from her canvas for a moment.

There's a melancholy in her face I haven't seen before. Perhaps painting connects her with her pain. And the brush strokes bring it back.

She's playing with daylight, blending pink into yellow on the top part of the canvas. She's brushed a line of green just below. Maybe that's the bay across the water at Djursholm, studded with conifers. Pale-blue streaks, or tears, run through the dense forest to the virgin space beneath.

Suddenly, and without a word, Anneli stops what she's doing.

'Am I bothering you?' I ask, bashfully.

'Are you kidding? I'm just pottering, really,' she smiles.

'It's amazing how much your technique has evolved.'

'Are you thinking about that painting in the café?'

'The one in the loo, actually. The half-mountain, half-woman painting.'

'Goodness me, I all but forgot that one's there. I used to be into diptychs. Honestly, what was I thinking?' She winces and bites a nail. 'It pains me to think of an expert like you seeing a monstrosity like that.'

I shake my head and laugh. 'Why do you keep playing down your art?'

'The only people who've ever bought my "art", as you put it, live on this island. And if you ask me, that says more about their friendship than their taste. I haven't picked up a brush in months,' she carries on, subtly changing the subject. 'But when I got up this morning, I felt like painting the first day of the new year. Isn't it glorious?'

Her gaze drifts to the jigsaw puzzle of ice that's holding the boats along the shoreline at bay.

'Do you feel like a stroll?' she asks. 'We've got time to make it around the whole island before sunset. We could even go for a dip!'

'Ooh, I'd love to. I haven't done that in years.'

'We don't have to decide right away. And I've got towels and some cider in the sauna. I'll get it going when we set off, in case you feel like it when we get back.'

'The sauna? What sauna?' I ask, mentally scanning the island.

'Down there, in that grey hut beside the dock.'

'I must have walked past that a hundred times. I thought it was just a shed.'

Anneli tilts her head to one side and winks at me. 'Just let me tidy this away and then we'll get going, if you're ready.'

I give her a silent nod and help her carry her easel and brushes into the storage room at the back of the café. Then we set off on our walk.

Storholmen's beauty this afternoon is astounding. It always has been, but I must've been too preoccupied by the manor house to really notice. Now that I've shared my fears, they seem easier to bear and I feel much more able to let my hair down. The island is bathed in a silence so deep, it's easy to forget that people live here. The only signs of human activity I see are the smoking chimneys and the first lamps blinking to life in windows. Even the occasional cries of joy of children out sledging make the silence seem more profound.

As we walk, I reel off memories of my New York years and I tell the story of how I met Lulu, one night at a gallery that was hosting an exhibition of a mutual friend's work. Often I leave my words hanging, struck by the splendour of the view. As the sea darkens in time with the sky, the bushes and their blossoms of snow stand out on the landscape. They look like cotton plants. The thick branches of a shrub frosted in white make me think of a bride in a veil, tousled by a gust of wind or a burst of passion.

Anneli has the discretion to respect my moments of silence and the sense of complicity to join me in my excitable impulses. Everything about this walk is so harmonious. It's perfect.

We make it back to the dock as the sun sinks beneath the sea. The darkness is descending and the temptation to dive into the icy water is impossible to resist.

Anneli opens up the hut. The sauna has had plenty of time to get up to temperature. Inside, to the left, is the sauna itself, behind a glass door. To the right is a narrow changing room fitted with benches. It's simply decorated and looks like it's been frozen in time, with an old oil lamp hanging from the ceiling, a rusty mirror on the wall and a shelf with an enamel basin and pitcher. The only other thing on the wall is a poster from the inter-war years with a moustachioed man in a bathing suit demonstrating the breast-stroke.

We undress, at ease with our nudity, as is customary for Swedes, yank open the door that leads to the sea and draw a sharp breath as the cold bites into our bodies. Without further ado, we run laughing across the frozen sand and launch ourselves into the darkness. The frigid air stings my skin and snatches my breath, readying me for the blast of the waves.

I scream as I enter the water. Then in one swift movement, I immerse myself to my shoulders, paddling like a dog to fight the cold.

Anneli prefers to take her time.

I swim a few bracing strokes to remind myself I still have Viking blood running through my veins, then I dart out of the water, thinking of the warmth of the sauna and the cider waiting mere metres away. But it seems to take an eternity to cover that short stretch of frozen ground.

'You'd forgotten how good that feels, hadn't you?' Anneli teases, following me up the beach.

We enter the sauna with a sigh of relief. The temperature difference is so great, I can't tell what's burning my skin the most – the remnants of the cold or the heat from the coals.

The dim light from the pendant is an invitation to relax.

I take a deep breath in, another out, savouring this delicious sensation. My body is buzzing with a curious combination of intense vivacity and numbness.

Anneli gets up, her full buttocks striped by the slats of the bench, and steps out for a moment to fetch two bottles of cider from a box by the entrance. We unscrew the caps almost in unison, a gesture that speaks to our familiarity.

I close my eyes and revel in the first sip. I open them again and look at my friend and her pale, naked body. Her head's resting on the upper bench, hair spread out behind her. Her legs stretch to the floor. Pearls of sweat and saltwater roll down her chest.

She turns to look at me.

Then comes a silence, tense and drawn-out like the screeching of a bow on a violin string.

I know there's a question mark in the air between us. A question I don't know the answer to – not in this instant.

Anneli comes closer and, with the gentlest of touches, she draws a line down my thigh to the crease of my knee.

I quiver.

She moistens her lips, then leans down and places the palm of her hand on my nipple.

She kisses me.

I close my eyes.

She tastes of cider. Her mouth is warm, her skin is slick and scorching. I feel her fingers caressing my nipple, the swelling of her breast touching my side, the moistness between her legs pressing against my hip.

I gasp and open my eyes to the curves of her hips. They look coppery in the yellow light. Her damp hair ripples over the pale wood like tentacles. I lick her lips, tasting her tongue. Then I reach for her breasts and they fill my hands like wine overflowing from a cup as her fingers find their way between my thighs, part my folds and slide inside me.

21
Viktoria

I'm crossing the hall when I see Josephine and Thor stretched out on the living-room rug, their legs up on an armchair, in a position that looks far from comfortable to me.

They have their backs turned to me, and my daughter's feet are dancing on the seat as she listens to Thor reading out loud. I'm thrilled to see Josephine enjoying a story, because she's never been one for books. That probably has a lot to do with me. I'm not a big reader, myself. I've read to her since she was little, but I've always been too tired to concentrate for long. My mind keeps skipping ahead to things like shopping lists and dentist's appointments, and I lose track. I do a bit better with TV – when I'm watching there always comes a point where I manage to unwind – but that's as far as it goes.

'So, a *draugr* is like a zombie,' my daughter sums up.

'Yep. A revenant,' Thor confirms in his crystalline voice, placing the open book on his chest. 'Monsters that come out of the ground to spread death.'

'And how do they appear? Where exactly do they ... come out of?'

'Dunno. I'll ask my mum. I bet she'll know.'

Josephine smooths her long hair. It's fanned out like sunbeams on the rug.

'It must be hard to have a name like Thor.'

'Tell me about it. It wouldn't be so bad if I had the physique to go with it, but just look at me, that's not happening anytime soon,' he jokes, gesturing to his slender frame.

My daughter puts a foot on Thor's leg. He reaches for a strand of her hair and twirls it around his finger.

'I can't get over it,' she says.

'What?'

'What you read to me earlier.'

'About the *blót*?'

Josephine nods and turns to him. 'Killing those animals—'

'It's called sacrificing,' he corrects her.

'Sacrificing animals I can understand, but men?'

I stiffen. Is this another one of those bloodthirsty Norse myths?

'In the time of the Vikings, boys became men much earlier than they do today,' he explains. 'When they were about twelve or thirteen years old, I think. There was a purpose to the sacrifices, too. To ensure an abundant harvest or victory in combat. Or to breed male children. Sons who could stand up and be fighters. Because everyone knows, girls are good for nothing!'

He turns to Josephine and gives her a couple of playful punches. She bursts out laughing.

I smile. I've never seen my daughter so ... free. Back in Stockholm, she was climbing the walls. She seemed gawky, like she was trapped inside a body that was too small for her. Here, she's flourishing. She's finding her place. It's good to see. There's a certain beauty to it. Thor, too, seems like he's had a weight lifted off his shoulders. It's as if, suddenly, he's not afraid to express himself. He's not afraid to *be* himself.

'But when you think about it,' he goes on, 'sacrifices are a part of life, aren't they? You can't make progress without making sacrifices. Sometimes, a sacrifice is like a blessing.'

He looks Josephine in the eye and smiles tenderly.

And suddenly I realise how wrong I've been about this boy. It's not mythology that's sparked the passion in him and made him so effusive. It's my daughter. Josephine is showing him who he really is.

22
Emma

I set foot on the Gussmans' property with a knot in my stomach. Walking in the footsteps of my sister's murderer, past the very place where the killer carried her body, is terrifying.

I woke with a start in the middle of the night, thinking of the shift I had to do at the manor house this morning. After trying in vain to get back to sleep, I tiptoed silently to the guest room so as not to disturb Anneli. Seeing her snuggled up close to me when I opened my eyes earlier filled my heart with joy.

Making love with a woman is liberating.

It's not so much about the pleasure as the balance of our bodies, I feel. I don't worry what I look like, or wonder whether I live up to my partner's aesthetic expectations at a time when my pleasure should be leading the way. There's no male ego to flatter, either – you don't have to pretend to like something that doesn't float your boat. In the arms of a woman, my confidence is complete and I can let myself go.

No sooner have I climbed the four stone steps to the front door than apprehension sweeps aside the memory of my night with Anneli.

I rap twice with the knocker, then push open the door, take my shoes off and walk across the hall.

'Miss Lindahl?' It's Niklas's voice.

Oh, how I hate the way he calls me 'miss'. As if my age were a sign of inexperience. I was hoping I wouldn't run into him.

Fearful that having Charlotte intervene would undermine what little authority I still had in connection with the Gussmans, after the incident I insisted on writing an official apology on behalf of

Von Dardel's myself. In my letter, I laid the honesty on thick –
even revealing my personal connection to the hanging girl, in the
hope that Niklas, knowing this, might be more inclined to
understand why an expert of my calibre had been unsettled by the
sight of a tree. I pointed out that the brush was not broken or
blemished and hadn't lost any of its value. The note inside added
a certain mystique, I stated, and was the perfect way to drive
auction prices higher. And I also reminded him that Detective
Inspector Rosén had asked me to wait for the green light before
returning to the manor.

The Gussmans' lawyer wrote back to me, stating that his client
understood and agreed with the decision made by Von Dardel's.
His response was cordial, but the fact that he deferred to the
authority of the auction house I represent rather than acknowledging my apology made me feel insignificant, invisible.

In light of this, the acidity of Niklas Gussman's tone comes as
a bit of a surprise.

'Hello, Mr Gussman. *Gott Nytt År.*'

'Yes, ah, Happy New Year,' he replies, caught off guard. 'The
police see no issue in you continuing to work in the bedroom
upstairs.'

It's hard not to smile. I already know this. It's the very reason
why I came back to work this morning. The family lawyers must
have argued that there's nothing to suggest the note has sinister
implications, and the police probably couldn't provide the
evidence to prove otherwise.

One question is niggling at me though. It's nothing offensive
or inappropriate, so I go for it:

'That bedroom was your great-grandmother, Harriet
Gussman's, wasn't it?'

'If you say so. You're the expert. Don't expect me to do your
work for you.'

I have to bite my tongue to stop myself snapping at him. I
remind myself that the client is king. The client. Is. King.

'Not at all, sir.'

With this, he turns on his heels and vanishes into the drawing room where he greeted me the first time.

I climb the stairs with a growing sense of unease.

The bedroom door is closed.

Obviously, I tell myself to calm my nerves. Niklas Gussman, or I don't know who else, must have come in here to pick up the brush and give it to the police. And any normal person would close the door behind them.

I take a deep breath and work up the courage to open it.

The sheets that were draped over the furniture, the ones I left in a pile on the floor, are now laid out on the bed. They cover the gold-tasselled bedspread almost completely. The flower-shaped bedside lamp has been moved to the pedestal by the window, beside the Limoges vase. Three frames have been taken off the wall and placed face down on the dressing table. Only one of them remains on the wall – the sketch of a Greek statue.

Then something peculiar jumps out at me: someone has wrapped a sheet tightly around the mirror on the dressing table, like a bandage on a head wound.

'Apparently that's how they get in.'

I yelp in surprise and whirl around.

A skinny boy with feminine features is standing in the doorway. A teenager.

'Through the mirror,' he explains, with an air of apology.

I smile back at him, not understanding what he's getting at.

'The people in the drawings. The revenants. They come through the mirror.'

The penny drops as I follow his gaze to the pedestal.

'Are you talking about the portraits of those children?'

He nods.

'Is that why you took the frames off the wall?'

His Adam's apple moves lower on his slender neck. It reminds me of one of those dimmer light switches.

He nods once more.

'I closed the door as well. *Their* door.'

He pauses for a moment and shifts his weight from one foot to the other, then purses his lips as if regretting sharing a secret.

'You're the one who put the sheets on the bed, then.'

'Yes. I slept in here to keep an eye on them. I wanted to make sure that blocking the way would be enough to stop them coming back. They keep talking to me. All the time.'

He scans the room anxiously.

'I didn't think you'd come back and work in this room, otherwise I'd have put everything back in its place.' He tugs at the neck of his wool sweater. 'I'm not allowed to be in here,' he adds, lowering his voice. 'Dad told me it's off limits. I'm not allowed in any of the rooms you're working in, actually.'

I try to reassure him with a gentle voice. 'I promise you, I won't say a word.'

'Really?'

'Of course. You can trust me. I won't say a thing.'

'Thanks,' he murmurs with a tear in his eye, before vanishing without a sound.

I turn to the dressing table and the blindfolded mirror, telling myself that Lulu may well have have been right – and wrong. This boy could have written the note I thought my sister had penned. So maybe this is just a child's game. A game that's real for him, but not for me.

23
Karl

I feel frozen through. With a shiver and a grimace I get up to close the window I left open when I went to bed. The wardrobe door, with the hinge I've neglected to fix, swings silently to and fro in the icy wind that's blowing into the bedroom.

I close the window and am about to do the same with the wardrobe when I notice a piece of pink silk sticking out like a tired dog's tongue.

Just one tease of a dress of Freyja's is enough to make me need to sit down. I remember seeing her grab hold of this trailing flounce that was getting in her way and tucking it into her wedding ring so she could keep on dancing without getting it caught in her heels. I remember her warm skin on the palm of my hand and the feel of the cool silk on my fingers.

The memory fuels a surge of desire in me, mixed with a suffocating rage.

Do I have to rewrite everything I've learned by her side – retell the history of how I became the man that I am? Shackled to a reality that no longer exists, I have to cope without her, even though she's ever present.

I turn away and allow my gaze to wander to her bedside table. I can see Freyja now, going through her bedtime ritual – putting her watch in the blue bowl in front of the postcard-sized naïve-style painting that sits on a tiny easel, lighting a candle and leaning over to give me a kiss, putting her glasses on and reading a few pages before sleep. With a yawn, she blows out her candle and falls asleep in an instant before even putting her book down or taking off her glasses.

I can feel a tightness in my chest. I miss those moments so much.

I need a deep breath of cold air, but all I manage are a few short gasps.

I bend forward and hold my head in my hands.

For the first time since that night, I submit to my sadness. And now that I'm letting it in, it surges through me in waves. My heavy tears well up from somewhere deep in my belly, rising up to catch in my throat and shaking me to the core.

I let them flow until the very last hiccup. The last shiver. Then I force myself to step into the shower.

✂

I pay a quick visit to the police station, so it's mid-morning by the time I get to Storholmen. I'm meeting Emma Lindahl at the café.

Anneli Lund is busying herself behind the counter. Emma is on her laptop at the table in the bay window. She gives me a warm smile and asks if I'd like a coffee.

As I sit down she gets up to make one for me.

The sky has turned grey once more and it's started snowing again. Flakes are falling on the window, where they melt and drip down like tears.

Emma puts my coffee on the table in front of me and sits down to sip the froth that's overflowing from her own cup.

The resemblance to her sister is striking. Every time I see her, it's like Sofia's dead body is right there talking to me. The centre parting in her blonde hair, the thin, arched brows framing eyes such a pale shade of blue they look bleached.

I get straight to the point. 'We were only able to collect partial prints from the note you gave me. They didn't show enough reference points for comparison with Sofia's, so unfortunately, they're unusable.'

Emma winces and clenches her jaw.

I recall a father whose only son died by suicide after being bullied at school. He couldn't bear to hear his son's name in public. As if hearing it come from strangers' mouths diluted his pain and his grief. As if his child were sinking into the collective memory of others.

'The paper and the pencil have been mass-produced for decades, so it would be difficult to glean anything from those.'

'I'm sorry,' she says, looking me straight in the eye. 'I should have been more careful.'

'Emma,' I hasten to add, 'you have nothing to blame yourself for. Under such intense stress, only a few people would have been mindful of preserving fingerprints, and those people would have been my colleagues. At least that call for help is in our hands now, and not still inside a forgotten brush, waiting for someone to discover it. Instead of beating yourself up, you should be happy to have found a message in a bottle, so to speak.'

I take a sip of my too-black coffee.

'I'm waiting for the results of the handwriting analysis, though I'm not pinning too much hope on that. No matter what conclusions you draw, there's always an expert who'll stand up and say the exact opposite. In other words, I only trust that kind of analysis if it confirms and adds to an existing stack of evidence. That said, we're having a graphologist compare the note to your sister's diary, so we'll see what comes of that.'

Emma opens her eyes wide in disbelief. 'You kept her diary?'

'The case was never closed, so it's still evidence.'

A slow tip of her chin tells me she understands.

'I met the Gussmans' son at the manor house yesterday,' she says. 'Well, he didn't introduce himself ... I just assumed it was him. I was in the room where I found the brush when he came in and startled me. He seems to have some ... psychological issues. He thinks ghosts travel through mirrors.'

'The Gussmans' son?' I echo, in my mind riffling through what I know about the family.

Niklas, the heir, is married to the heiress of a more recent fortune, which stems from Bizair, an airline that only operates business-class flights. Their son, who's fourteen if I remember rightly, isn't in school. He does some kind of distance learning because he has a hyperactivity disorder. It's a bit of a stretch to go from that to seeing ghosts, though. Maybe he was just winding Emma up.

'I thought he might have written that note to … I don't know what.'

She sighs and turns towards the dock.

She looks back at me after a moment and says, 'It sounds like you're telling me you won't go and see what's going on with the Gussmans.'

I shake my head. 'We don't have anything to warrant gaining access to the property.'

'So who do you think wrote that note?' Emma asks me.

'I don't know. And I don't think this "clue" is really what we should be focusing on.'

'So, what's your next move?'

'We have a number of leads, but there's nothing I can share with you.'

Emma doesn't seem to hear me.

'How old was that girl you found at Sticklinge the other morning – the thirtieth?' she asks.

'Somewhere between fifteen and seventeen, we think.'

'Had she been dead for a long time?'

I interlace my fingers and put my hands on the table. 'Why?' I ask, a little too unkindly. Because I know very well where she's going with this.

'Did she die on the twenty-ninth?' Emma presses me.

'Probably, yes,' I have to admit.

'She was the same age as Sofia. She was killed on the twenty-ninth of December, like Sofia. And her body was found not far from here. Not far at all. Sounds to me like you *have* figured out your next move.'

'I need some air,' I say to Anneli as I slip outside a few minutes after Karl drives away in his boat.

I pull up the hood of my parka and set off along the path behind the café. On my way past the sauna and the little sandy beach, I notice the dark silhouette of a swimmer in a wetsuit emerging from the water onto the frozen bathing platform.

I walk and listen to the sound of Storholmen breathing. In front of pretty much every house, there's a sledge. In the winter, the locals use these like bikes to carry shopping back from town, and tired kids back home. Anneli was right. The silence is surrounding me like a cocoon. And it doesn't feel scary anymore. Maybe these last few days have tamed my inner turmoil – enough for me to tolerate such a deep calm.

I'm not far from the grounds below the manor house now.

Everything about Detective Inspector Rosén's reaction suggests there's a connection between Sofia's murder and the death of the girl whose body they found in Sticklinge Bay. But the fact that two girls of the same age were killed on the same day of the year in approximately the same place isn't enough to connect these cases. The deciding factor has to be the way in which they were killed.

I stop and massage my temples in an attempt to shut down the horror movie that's started playing in my mind. Every violent image that flashes before my eyes I flip over, like I'm playing a game of Solitaire, so I see Sofia's smiling face instead.

I keep going, towards the sea, and pick up the pace. From this angle, stripped bare in the cold and under a blanket of snow, the tiers of the French formal garden, with its two rectangular pools and fountain, look like the layers of a cake draped in white icing. The place looks unscathed by the ravages of winter, and it must be glorious in the scintillating light of summer.

I'm at the tip of the island now, where the Gussmans' property runs down to an inlet, hidden from me, behind a chain of evergreens. If you're looking out from the manor, I realise, these trees must also block the view of the wharf where the water taxi docks.

I notice the swimmer I saw earlier coming my way along the narrow path. The warrior's gait tells me who it is.

'*Hej*,' I call.

Björn gives me a friendly wave. His longish hair is sticking out from under his woolly hat. The water's made it a bit frizzy.

'I was just about to have a coffee at my *båtstuga* by the water when I saw you,' he says. 'Would you like to join me?'

'With pleasure,' I reply, invigorated by the mere thought of a hot drink. Björn beckons for me to follow him down to a pebble beach, his worn boots squeaking with every step.

He goes into the wooden hut to get changed and comes out a few minutes later with a Thermos flask and two mugs. He's wearing a thick wool sweater, corduroy trousers and a different hat. This one's dry, and he's pulled it down to the top of his bushy eyebrows.

'This place used to be my dad's,' he explains, pouring the coffee. 'Take a pew,' he adds, gesturing to a plastic chair.

'Was it a fishing hut?'

He groans and sits down on a rock that's been polished smooth by the waves.

'My dad would come here mostly to get away from my mum. He hated fishing. A lazy man's sport, he called it. He couldn't stand waiting around for the fish to bite.'

'Is that why you come here, too?' I ask with a chuckle.

'Well, we all need our space, don't we?'

'I must admit, I've never been in a relationship long enough for a partner to get on my nerves.'

A sip of black coffee sends a wave of warmth through my whole body.

'How did you and Lotta meet?' I ask. 'She told me she didn't grow up here.'

Björn pulls a tin of *snus* from his pocket, takes out a tiny pouch of tobacco and tucks it under his upper lip. Chewing *snus* is second only to golf as a national pastime, and it's the reason why only five percent of Swedes are regular smokers. We love our sacrosanct chewing tobacco so much that we only agreed to join the European Union if we could keep it. It's banned from sale in all the other member countries.

Björn holds the tin out to offer me some. It's a sore reminder of the summer I turned sixteen. I was trying desperately to stop smoking and somehow I thought *snus* would be a good alternative.

'No thanks,' I say, with a shake of my head.

'Lotta was working as a caregiver in Stockholm and living in a shoebox. She came over here to look after my dad, near the end of his life.'

'And you fell in love?'

'She fell in love with the island first,' he explains, before draining the dregs of his coffee.

'And then?'

Lulu calls this my 'little old lady' fascination with love stories. It never wanes. No doubt because I've never known a couple who've loved one another their whole lives.

'And then, she found a way to combine her two passions, for people and the sea, by becoming the captain and unofficial mascot of the route 80 sea bus.'

'Then she noticed you.'

'I did everything I could to make sure she did,' he smiles, shifting the position of the little pouch of tobacco that's deforming his upper lip.

'How about you – do you work for the municipality or for Niklas?'

He snorts a mocking laugh and gets up to fetch a couple of blankets from inside the hut. I wrap myself up warm in the one he hands to me.

'I can't stand that man. You have no idea what he's like. He's so high and mighty, he gets other people to give his orders. For instance, it was his assistant who asked me to come down and meet you on your first day. If I lend a hand around the estate once in a while, it's to honour the memory of his great-grandfather and because I have strong ties to the house his whole life revolved around. It's certainly not to curry favour with that snob, with his hateful manners. Lotta can't fathom why I want nothing to do with him, but this air of mystery around him doesn't sit right with me.'

'What do you mean?'

'We never see them. Him and his family, they keep themselves to themselves. They never show their faces in the community. All he does is sign cheques for the municipality, as if that makes up for it. If you ask me, they've got something to hide.'

He grinds an irate foot into the pebbles, then plucks the *snus* out of his mouth and drops it into his empty mug.

'Old Gustav was nothing like this. My dad was a plumber and an electrician, and he knew the island like the back of his hand. He was hired as a handyman in 1922, right after the manor house was built, to take care of general maintenance and do odd jobs, you know. The Gussmans lived in Stockholm at the time and didn't come over that often.'

Recalling these memories of his father is an obvious pleasure for my friend. I notice how sharply it contrasts with the disgust I feel when I think about my mother.

'My dad adored Gustav,' he continues, unscrewing the lid of the Thermos to pour more coffee for me. 'He was eccentric, and he was a bit of a megalomaniac, but he was a good man. He died far too young, and the way he went was brutal. No time to put his affairs in order or shape his son into a man worthy of the family name.'

'What happened to him?'

'He was in a car accident. And he wasn't even the one driving. Do you know why he decided to buy land on the island?'

I begin shaking my head, and Björn carries on without waiting for a reply:

'Because he loved history. He was obsessed with Charles Emil Lewenhaupt.'

'Wait ... he was the Swedish general who was decapitated for war crimes in the ... eighteenth century, wasn't he?'

'In 1743, to be precise. It's said that when he learned of the fate that awaited him, Lewenhaupt fled to Storholmen and went into hiding in a tunnel the locals had dug to keep their valuables safe from the Danish invaders. Well, Gustav got it into his head to try and find that hiding place. Obviously, he never did.'

I'm not surprised to hear this stuff about secret passages. It seems to be a human trait to dig beneath the earth's surface – to hide from our enemies, protect our property, and to move around in secret.

'When he set his sights on Storholmen,' Björn continues, 'Gustav Gussman sparked quite the craze for the island. His parties during the Roaring Twenties were legendary. And he was on intimate terms with the upper crust of society, all across Europe and even into the Soviet Union. So the manor house was often in the spotlight between the wars. After his death, though, Storholmen gradually slipped back into the shadows, and for more than half a century, the place was a hidden gem in the jewel-studded crown of the Stockholm Archipelago.' He throws his hand out extravagantly as he says these words. Then he moderates his tone once more. 'Until 2012, when it was catapulted back into the spotlight – for all the wrong reasons, as you well know.'

He leans closer to me, then takes my hand and presses it into his, cradling my fingers oh-so tenderly in his warm, calloused palm. If a man of Björn Petterson's calibre had been a part of our childhood, rather than the filthy animals our mother brought home, Sofia might have had a chance to blossom instead of biting the dust. And I might have stayed around instead of running away.

Too many mights, too many maybes.

'I can hardly imagine what you went through,' he says. 'People and their morbid fascination. The media circus that lasted for months.'

And every year, the whole of Sweden reminding me of my sister's birthday. Every year, all those strangers she never knew appropriating my tragedy and my pain.

'That murder made no sense,' Björn says. 'It's not like the site where the manor was built is a traditional place of sacrifice.'

'Sacrifice?' I repeat, not following. 'What are you saying?'

Björn springs up as if he's got a sudden cramp in his leg. He goes into his hut and comes out again a moment later with an earnest look on his face.

'I thought you knew.'

I freeze, then spring to my feet too. My blanket falls to the pebbles.

'What are you talking about? I'm not following you, Björn. Please tell me.'

He slides a hand under his woolly hat to scratch his forehead and scruffs up his eyebrows in the process.

'Your sister ... she was killed on the twenty-ninth of December. A key date in the Viking calendar. And your sister was found hanging from a tree with a pair of scissors around her neck. I don't believe for a second that any of that is a coincidence.'

25
Karl

Arnold rests his jaw on my thigh so I can scratch the top of his head, and responds to my attention with a whimper that sounds like he's purring.

Siv moves her shaker bottle to the side – somehow, I doubt the brown stuff inside is a triple chocolate milkshake – and slides the mouse across her desk. After a few clicks, she leans closer to the screen.

'Maria ... Sjögren,' she reads. 'Sixteen years old. She lived in Näsby Park with her dad.'

Maria Sjögren, sixteen years old, I repeat to myself.

In my mind's eye, I can see the child lying on the stretcher in the tent Alvid and his crew erected on the beach at Sticklinge – her hair wet and her skin frozen. There was something indecent about watching the seawater trickle off her inert body, as if life, imperturbable, were crossing paths with death and continuing on its way.

'I'm meeting with him early this afternoon,' I say.

Arnold gets up and returns to sit at his owner's feet.

'You were right,' Siv continues, pointing at her screen. 'We're looking at the same profile as Sofia Axelsson. I'd like to know why the dad waited so long to report his daughter missing. He went ten days without hearing from her.'

She pauses to take a swig of her gloopy concoction.

'Thank goodness for cacao,' she smiles. 'It does a lovely job of masking the taste of kale.'

Just the thought of mixing chocolate and green vegetables is enough to make me gag.

'With a banana as well, you'd never know it was in there.'

'Honestly, Siv, can't you just make soup like everyone else?'

'Raw foods maximise your vitamin and mineral intake.'

'Eat more salads, then.'

'To tell you the truth, I'd kill for a rare steak instead,' she jokes, fending off a boisterous assault from Arnold.

'No kidding.'

She gets up and announces, 'I need to take him out, otherwise he'll pee right here in my office. His prostate isn't what it used to be.'

'I'll take him.'

Siv passes me the lead. Arnie yelps excitedly as I attach it to his collar.

'Come on, big guy,' I say.

Siv and I take the fire escape down to the back of the building. Arnie relieves himself as soon as I set him free. He dashes off to mark his territory in all four corners of the concrete courtyard, even though I'm pretty sure he's the only representative of his species to ever come here. Instinct is not something we fight.

The cold, combined with a lack of sleep, feels like a helmet squeezing my skull.

'So, the same profile.' Siv carries on where she left off, digging her hands into her pockets. 'A kid from a broken home, a serial runaway for the last eighteen months at least. There must've been a thing or two going on at home. Poor parents.'

'Poor kid, more like,' I snap.

'No, I don't think so, Karl,' she replies in a weary voice, tinged with sadness. 'No matter how much love and attention they get from their parents, who make sure they want for nothing, some kids stray, and some go completely off the rails. Just one person, one bad influence, as people used to say when I was growing up, can be enough to smash years of education to smithereens. When your kids get to the ungrateful age, they seem to forget everything – and not just how to use the washing machine. Sometimes a stranger they've known for five minutes can influence them more than anyone else, even the family that loves them to bits. So yes, my heart goes out to Maria's parents. It's completely possible they did everything they could and more, and now they're going to spend the rest of their lives wondering what they did wrong, when they said the wrong thing, or what they said yes to when they should have said no.'

Arnold comes back to his owner, drooling with delight.

'You know what?' Siv adds. 'We always think about people who've gone, but we should give more thought to those they leave behind.'

She pats her dog on the haunches, and I decide to bite my tongue. I realise this might feel a bit close to home for her. Her daughters have always struck me as model students who have their heads screwed on, but you never know. Anyway, as soon as I dare to open my mouth and share my opinion on such matters, she's always quick to tell me I don't know what I'm talking about because I don't have kids of my own.

'Twenty-ninth of December, 2012; twenty-ninth of December, 2021,' I venture instead.

'Nine years,' Siv replies, seizing the new subject I've put forward. 'That's a long time to wait between two murders. You have to wonder what the killer's been doing all this time. Who knows, maybe they get their kicks out of the anticipation and the foreplay rather than the act itself.'

I shake my head to shoo away the images that immediately spring into my mind.

Arnold groans and stretches with great difficulty.

'In any case,' I say, 'my theory hasn't changed. These crimes were not the work of a beginner. The method has evolved, but the MO and the signature are far too elaborate. It's way too clean.'

'You didn't find anything else back then though, did you?'

'Nothing. Not even by isolating the elements. No other victims who bled to death from scalpel incisions to the femoral arteries, or with scissors around the necks, or with their big toes tied together. Nothing. Nothing at all.'

'How far back did you look?'

'Ten years earlier, at the time, so that's nineteen years ago now.'

'And you cast the net all over Sweden, I imagine.'

I nod. 'Sofia Axelsson lived in the south with her mother, in Kristianstad. That's in the county of Scania, near the Danish border. Considering that her body was found five hundred kilometres from there, I didn't want to leave anything to chance.'

'I'm going to contact Pedro at Europol,' Siv says.

'He's going to tell you that you're wasting his time.'

'And tell me to call him back when I have three similar victims – I know,' she sighs. 'It's a saving grace that we have one hanging and one drowning, though. No journalists have made the connection yet. And nearly a decade is a long time. We're immersed in this, but their databases aren't. And no one else knows about the exsanguination, the scissors and the toes. At least for now.'

I purse my lips and clench my jaw. 'Emma Lindahl isn't privy to those details, but she made the connection herself.'

Siv shrugs and sneezes into her elbow.

'She's the sister of the first victim, Karl. I mean, cataloguing the Gussman manor is the opportunity of a lifetime and the kind of assignment that makes a career, but the fact remains that she took a job at the very place where her sister was found dead, hanging from a tree. Say what you will, but we always have a choice. She could have said no and waved her job goodbye. That would've been a shitty choice, but still, it's a choice. So, whether she's conscious of it or not, she wants to learn more about her sister's death. Fortunately for us, she hasn't been acting like a complete tool. And that doesn't happen too often – which doesn't say much about the state of the world. You asked her not to spill the beans to the press, didn't you?'

'Of course, and she seemed pretty shocked that I would even

have to warn her. She can't stand journalists. I wasn't exactly in her good books already, so that took the biscuit.'

'Shame on you.'

Siv pulls a bag of dog treats out of her pocket, and Arnie lollops towards us.

'Still nothing from the door-to-door enquiries?'

I shake my head slowly, watching Arnie wolf down a handful of bone-shaped biscuits.

'I reached out to those three grannies earlier. I figure they'll have been talking to people and may well have discovered something. I don't know. I'm fishing with my eyes closed really.'

'I saw that the handwriting analysis came back negative as well. Or inconclusive. Hard to say, really. Since when do we need an expert to check what the expert found?' she tuts.

I huff and wag my finger. 'Irregular writing, multiple inter-ruptions in flow, capital letters, it's been one excuse after another but – and I stress the but – it seems doubtful that the writing belongs to Sofia Axelsson. But what am I supposed to do with a report like that?'

Siv rolls her eyes, and my phone starts ringing.

I show her the name on the screen.

'Speak of the devil,' she smiles.

I answer the phone and put the call on speaker.

26
Viktoria

'Do you want a coffee?'

'No thanks.' Björn shakes his head as he takes off his boots and his coat. 'I'll get straight to work.'

'What is it this time?' I ask, picking up the vacuum cleaner and my cleaning bucket.

'Creaky doors.'

'Good luck with the ghost hunting, then,' I wink and disappear upstairs.

When I get there, I go into Madam's room, put down the vacuum cleaner and my supplies in the doorway, grab my feather duster and set about my routine.

When I first started working in hotels, I felt like I was peeping into people's private lives – sensing the stale scent of love and seeing sheets sullied by desire was like spying on them through the keyhole. I've grown used to it as the years have gone by, but I've never quite managed to shake off that first second of uneasiness. Usually, I get straight to work and that's enough to iron out the kink. But here, whenever I go into Madam's bedroom, I have a sense of disquiet, and this keeps me on edge. I take great care not to damage anything, and I put things back in their place with millimetric precision. As a result, it takes me almost as long to clean this room as everywhere else combined.

This morning, I can barely see any dust, so I decide not to bother with the feather duster and fast-forward to the vacuuming instead. I kneel down and pull the two decorative trunks out from under the bed.

I'm horrified to hear a sound like broken china.

Herregud! Oh my God.

Usually these are empty.

My heart's racing. I know it's a complete overreaction, but my instincts are in command now.

I take a deep breath to calm my nerves and decide to check the extent of the damage by opening the trunk on the right, which seems to be heavier than the other one.

I open the lid and find some glass jars – nine of them, to be precise – as well as a bound leather notebook embossed with the initials *GG*.

Not daring to touch anything, I peer anxiously at each of the jars to make sure I haven't broken or made a mess of anything.

'Viktoria! What the hell do you think you're doing?'

Madam's voice turns my blood to ice.

Still on my knees, I stiffen and slowly turn around. Madam is standing in the doorway, baring her teeth at me. I can see the fury in her eyes. She glares at me, exuding arrogance and privilege.

'Close that right now!'

With a hot flush, I do as she says.

'I'm so sorry, I—'

'So now you're poking your nose in my things, are you?'

I shake my head vigorously. 'Not at all, madam. Never. I promise. I ... I pulled out the trunk to clean under the bed and heard a ... a sound. I ... I thought I might have broken something. I just wanted to make sure I hadn't.'

'Get out.'

My neck and back have broken out in a cold sweat.

'I'm sorry, madam. I really didn't mean—'

'Get out, I said!' she screams.

I stand up and leave the room without daring to meet her eye. My heart feels like it's pounding in my throat.

Back on the ground floor, Björn is crouching by a door with black oil all over his fingers and his woolly jumper. He gives me a sympathetic smile.

Incapable of responding, I step around him and set off down the corridor to my apartment, my legs trembling in fear and my chest burning with humiliation.

I got a lift to Ropsten to catch the number 80 sea bus.

It's late morning and the flow of passengers has slowed to a trickle. There are only three of us on board. The driver greets me with a broad smile that makes the corners of her blue eyes wrinkle.

I wait until she's untied the mooring lines and manoeuvred the boat away from the dock before I go and see her at the wheel.

'Lotta Petterson?'

'And you're Karl Rosén,' she replies, as a fresh smile creases her face. She sweeps a long white lock of hair behind her ear. 'You were in charge of the "hanging girl" investigation.'

I nod a slow yes.

Every time I hear that name for her – which wasn't a fabrication by the press, as the rumour goes, but rather a hashtag on Twitter that journalists latched on to, the vision of Sofia strung up from that branch flashes before my eyes. Ironically, hanging was the only form of torture the poor girl didn't suffer.

'I had a word with your friends in the swimming club this morning.'

'I know,' she murmurs.

Her gaze wanders to the horizon for a moment.

'You want to make use of our network and have me do some investigating for you,' she says with a knowing glint in her eye.

'Precisely.' I give her a sly smile. 'Ilse said you have a WhatsApp group for Storholmen and the neighbouring islands.'

'That's right. Just about everyone's on there. And anyone who wants nothing to do with the Facebook empire, we email them. And any digital dinosaurs, we just go and knock on their door.'

'I need to get a message out about the girl whose body was found at Sticklinge.'

'The girl under the ice, right.'

'The girl under the ice,' I repeat.

'Another hashtag, as they say. Nicknames like that stick in your mind.'

She pulls her phone from the pocket of her parka, unlocks it and hands it to me.

'Here, knock yourself out. Find your eyewitnesses, arrest the killer, do what you have to do. It would be nice if this one didn't attract those tour operators that sell cheap thrills.'

'I'll do my best,' I reply, taking her phone. 'Thanks, Lotta.'

'Don't mention it. The group's called "Storholmen",' she adds. 'Original, I know.'

I draft a message asking anyone who saw or noticed anything unusual on the night of 29 December to reach out to us. I sign it with my name and add my contact details.

'Is this all right?' I ask, showing her the screen.

'I'm sure it's fine,' she chuckles, tugging a white woolly hat over her ears. 'Feel free to send it.'

Lotta steps out of her compartment to extend the gangway. 'Looks like you're expected, Detective.'

Emma's waiting for me on the wharf. She gives Lotta a warm smile, which vanishes as soon as she lays eyes on me.

'What a darling that girl is,' Lotta sighs, as if to herself.

Emma's told me she has some crucial information to share with me. When we spoke on the phone, I suggested meeting her at her home in Stockholm, but she preferred that we meet on Storholmen instead. I was happy to oblige. I'd far rather cross a short stretch of the Baltic than sweat for hours in an overheated metal box in a traffic jam.

Emma gets straight to the point as soon as I set foot on dry land. 'Do you mind if we walk?'

I shake my head and follow her lead.

'I found out yesterday,' she begins as we skirt around Ett Glas, 'that my sister was found by someone called Ove Petterson.'

I frown.

'He was the brother of a friend who lives on the island. He used to look after the grounds on the Gussman estate.'

I remember the sad old man with shaggy hair. He couldn't take his eyes off the body. He asked that we not release his name to the press.

'Ove was sixty-six years old at the time and apparently he never got over the shock of ... finding her.' Emma's voice is shaking.

She holds back her words for a moment, and the silence is filled with the sound of the snow crunching beneath our soles.

'He saw the scissors,' she says at last. 'The pair of scissors on the cord around Sofia's neck.'

'Emma...' I grab her by the arm to make her stop and immediately regret my action, because it seems overly rough and too personal, somehow.

But she complies and doesn't wriggle free from my grip.

'I know,' she says. She doesn't seem offended. Determined, rather, in spite of the sadness inside her. 'I can see why you didn't want to release that detail to the public, or even to us, her family. I understand. I don't blame you. I'm glad you didn't tell us, actually. If I'd known, I think I would've lost it. So ... it was better that way. But Björn – Ove's brother – put his finger on something. Something that really freaked Ove out – he was scared to death.'

She stops and exhales a full breath.

'Scared to death,' she whispers to herself.

Then she blinks and turns to look at me.

Despite our difference in height, and the pain and strain on her face, her strength is intimidating. There's nothing vulnerable about her. Quite the opposite, in fact. I'm a giant, but I find her imposing presence reassuring. It's astonishing how much she reminds me of Freyja.

'Those scissors made Björn and Ove think it was some sort of ritual,' she continues. 'A sacrificial ritual.'

Emma shakes her head and starts walking again.

'Sofia was killed and found on the twenty-ninth of December. Nine days after the winter solstice – a crucial time on the Norse pagan calendar. When the night gives way at last and the days start getting longer. That's when the festivities would begin for Yule, the ancestor of our Christmas. To entice the gods to look favourably on them, the Vikings would make offerings...'

She pauses and shakes her head once more.

I give her time to let her thoughts unfold.

'Every nine years, during Yule, the Viking people would organise a *blót*, or a blood sacrifice, which lasted nine days. Nine days during which they killed ... nine times. Mostly animals, but men too. And ... they would hang the bodies from the branches of a tree.'

Emma slows her stride. Suddenly, she looks very pale. She swallows a few times and I suspect she's run out of steam. But she carries on.

'The Vikings would place an open pair of scissors on the chests of the dead to stop them from turning into *draugrs* – or zombies, I suppose we'd say nowadays. And sticking needles into their feet, or tying their big toes together, was thought to stop that from happening as well.' Suddenly, she turns around to face me. 'Listen to me. I must sound like I'm out of my mind. I spent all night researching this stuff and—'

'No needles were stuck in your sister's feet, Emma, but her big toes were tied together with a black thread.'

Emma looks up at me in surprise. Her pale face is glowing with a warrior's energy.

'You knew...'

The way she says the words makes it clear that we've crossed the line of familiarity.

'Yes. The theory of a sacrificial killing seems the most plausible to us, even though the victims were traditionally male. And even though Storholmen has never been a site of worship, so to speak.'

I have to leave it there. I feel winded. The air is heavy in my chest and I'm struggling to catch my breath.

I can see myself now, on 29 December 2012, in the stifling silence of the manor-house grounds. It was as if the whole island were forbidden from making a sound that morning. I can see the crime-scene technician poking his head out from the skirt of tree branches, a mere metre away from Sofia's feet, beckoning for me to join him. There were no words to describe the scene he showed me. Behind the dense foliage, the trunk was glistening with blood. Eight dead mice, birds and hares were hanging from the lowest branches, like morbid Christmas-tree decorations.

The sacrifices of Yule in all their splendour.

Nine offerings, hanging from a tree, to satiate Odin and the gods of Asgard.

28
Emma

I feel drained of all energy, but I'm ravenously hungry.

As Anneli closes the café, I make us a quick bite to eat with some goodies I brought in from Papilles, the deli in Lidingö: slices of rye bread, some crispy *knäckebröd*, charcuterie and French cheeses.

I open a bottle of Amarone, pour us each a glass and start telling her about my conversation with the detective this afternoon. I'm now almost certain that Sofia didn't write the note I found inside the brush at the manor.

'Detective Rosén came across a bit ... aggressive, or tense, the first couple of times I saw him, but I felt like he was more receptive today. More human, somehow,' I say, biting into a chunk of truffled Brie.

'Did you know his wife drowned recently? Over Christmas, apparently.'

'The poor man!' I exclaim, feeling bad for being so quick to judge him.

'It's terrible. Lotta told me this morning. There was a snippet in the paper about it. Such a tragedy.'

I take a cautious sip of my wine. It's only my second glass, but the alcohol feels like a lead weight in my legs already.

And all of a sudden, I picture my sister's legs, dangling above the ground and swaying in the wind. Was there any wind on Storholmen that day? I wonder. And the other days? The nine days she spent here with...

'*Hej.*' Anneli's voice is a tender whisper in my ear. 'You seem like you're miles away, *älskling*. My darling.'

I put my glass down. 'I was thinking about Sofia.'

She interlaces her slender fingers and stretches them out in front of her. She looks like a minister about to make an official declaration.

'You should go and gather your thoughts by the tree, Emma.'

I groan, as if Anneli had just driven her fist into my stomach.

'You work practically every day a stone's throw from where she was found,' she insists. 'There must be a reason for that, Emma. I don't know if you came here to punish yourself or to get some closure, or if you were guided by Sofia's spirit, but you didn't come to Storholmen for the career opportunity. That's what you're telling yourself, *älskling*, but you have to stop lying to yourself. Enough is enough.'

The gentle look in her eyes tempers the harshness of her words. That's what I latch on to as I let this sink in.

'You put on a coat of armour, ready to confront your demons, but it's been nearly two months now, and you're still standing on the edge of the battlefield, paralysed by fear. Go, now. Go and stand by that tree. Say goodbye to your sister. Confide in her. Tell her about your regrets, your nightmares and the guilt that's gnawing away at you even though it shouldn't. Go and cry for her. Cry with her. This is important, Emma. You haven't made all this effort to grieve properly, deal with the pain and look to the future, only to stop short of actually doing it.'

My chest is burning with anger.

I'm angry at Anneli for putting these unspeakable things into words and I'm angry with myself because I know my mother was right. I *did* abandon her and Sofia.

'Anger is just sadness that's been hardened by time, *älskling*,' Anneli says.

I look at her, disarmed.

The tree, Sofia, my mother, Charlotte von Dardel, the heirlooms at the manor, the brush – it's all stacking up like a deck of cards in my mind.

'All right,' I hear myself say after a long silence. 'But please come with me.'

✂

We enter the Gussmans' property through the lower part of the French garden, where I ran into Björn yesterday, and we make our way up to the little mound and its crown of evergreens.

There's next to no chance of us getting caught. The manor grounds are not lit, and it's a bitterly cold night. Anyway, if we do run into someone, I'm sure I'll find something to say.

We're directing the torches on our phones towards the ground, so we can see where we're going without letting too much light escape. I can't feel the cold. All I feel is my heart beating like there's no tomorrow. At the foot of the mound, the trees form a barrier so impenetrable, the beams of our torches get lost in the branches. I know Sofia's immediately when I see it. It's the tallest of them all. The most imposing, the finest-looking, the one with the top that towers over all the others.

The vision of Sofia hanging from these branches comes so clearly to my mind, it feels like she's right there in front of me. I close my eyes to repel the ghost of her. That's a reflex of mine: running away to give myself the illusion that I'm moving forward.

Reluctantly, I call the image back to my mind and contemplate Sofia, in all her pain. I contemplate all that's left of her. An empty shell. A life line, interrupted. I see everything I wish she had become. I see the flower crowns I'll never again braid in her hair to celebrate *Midsommar*, the summer solstice, the festival of plenty. I beg her to forgive me. For not being there. For running away. For thinking only of myself. My sister, my everything. *I'm sorry*. I crouch down and plant my gloved hands in the snow.

'You have to be careful,' a creaky voice suddenly whispers.

I shriek.

Anneli nearly jumps out of her skin.

'That's how you wake them up,' the voice continues.

We sweep the air with our torches, trying to see where it's coming from, our beams of light flashing frantically then fading into the darkness. Anneli's eventually lands on a tall, slender body.

It's the Gussmans' son. The kid I ran into at the manor house.

'Who are you talking about?' I press him, impatiently. 'Who do you think we're waking up?'

'Those who come out of the ground in the garden. When you get down on your knees, that's how you call them. That's how they know you want them to come.'

'We have to go,' Anneli urges, and she means it. 'His parents will probably be out looking for him,' she hisses.

'Will I see you back at the house soon?' he asks me sweetly.

'Soon, yes,' I reply. Then I follow Anneli into the night.

29
Karl

Maria Sjögren's father leads me into the living room of their impressive villa in Näsby Park, where all the windows seem to stare out to sea.

I sit down on a generous black leather sofa, and it strikes me, as I look at the man in the crisp white shirt with the clipped beard, that we all carry our grief in different ways. Some of us cling to our self-control. Others let the sorrow take them over.

Per Sjögren's pain is clear in his lifeless eyes, his gaping mouth, his shaking hands. There's a hint of it on his daughter's coat, which is still hanging in the entryway.

I think about Sofia's mother and how detached she seemed. About her grief, and how it manifested simply as an absence. She lived with her daughter in a tiny two-room apartment. The two of them shared the only bedroom, their beds separated only by a folding screen with clothes draped over it.

I express my condolences to Per Sjögren. He responds with a series of slow movements of his head.

'I need you to tell me about Maria. How she spent her time, who she spent it with.'

He parts his hands and offers his palms to the sky.

'She spent all her time on her phone or her iPad. She didn't do any, er, activities other than that.'

'What did she do on her phone or her tablet?'

'She went online. Girl stuff, I suppose.'

'Do you know if she was active on social media?'

'I'd be surprised if she was. Maria was harassed for months after someone posted a video of her on TikTok that showed her belly.

It became such a concern that her mother and I had to intervene. Shortly after that, my wife was diagnosed with cancer.'

He closes his eyes, then blinks them open again and clasps his hands.

'Your wife died two years ago, as I understand?'

'Yes. It was the day after Christmas, two years ago.'

'I'm terribly sorry for your loss.'

'It was all very sudden. My wife succumbed to an aggressive form of pancreatic cancer. We only had four months between her diagnosis and her ... her death.'

He presses his lips together, making his chin wrinkle. His gaze lands on the only family photo I've seen in the house. The three of them are smiling, a heavenly sunset behind them. Maria must have been about ten years old when the photo was taken. She looks radiant, a child without a care in the world.

'Maria went through a rough time at school when we found out about my wife's illness. Because of the video I told you about. She was a bit overweight and a bunch of morons had a go at her about it. After her mum died, she stopped eating and lost twenty-two kilos in the space of a few months. When she eventually came around, she was very strict about every gram of food she put into her body.'

'Was she seeing a therapist?'

'Of course she was, Inspector,' he sneers. 'Two sessions a week with a psychologist. Either alone or with me present. I didn't see any improvement, though. There was never any improvement,' he repeats, slicing the air with his hand.

'Do you know who was harassing your daughter? Any names you can share with us?'

'Not off the top of my head, no, but the school could tell you. The headteacher kept a close eye on the whole thing.'

'Did Maria have any friends? Was she seeing anyone?'

He shakes his head to both of my questions then clears his throat.

'Maria was a bit of a loner. She never brought anyone home after school, and she never went over to anyone else's place.'

I nod and let a moment of silence go by before I bite the bullet.

'Mr Sjögren, did you know your daughter was self-harming?'

His eyes widen in surprise. His mouth forms a silent 'O'.

'Your daughter had been cutting herself – in the groin, hips and ankles – for several years. You never noticed?'

'Do you have any idea what it's like for a father to raise a teenager on his own?' he cries. 'From the age of twelve, Maria forbade me and my wife from going into the bathroom when she was in there. With her worries about her weight, she'd never let the slightest bit of flesh show, even at the beach, and even when she was nothing but skin and bone. And things only got worse when her mum passed away.'

Suddenly, he brings a fist to his mouth. His eyes redden and then well up. He tries in vain to hold back the tears and ends up having a coughing fit. After a moment, he gets up and takes a swig from a water bottle on the table.

Then he clears his throat again.

'Sorry, I didn't think to offer you anything. Would you like something to drink?'

'It's all right, thanks.'

Bottle still in hand, he sits back down.

'Maria ran away eight times in the last year and a half. This past December, on the anniversary of my wife's death, I was sure she was going to do it again. Maria couldn't stand Christmas without her mum. We weren't a family anymore without her, that's what she told me. So I gave her space. I knew she'd come back. I thought she'd come back. I thought it was just a matter of time. There's no point moving heaven and earth, anyway. There never has been.'

His whole face is collapsing with the weight of the grief. He keeps trying to hold it all together, to maintain the façade, like a sad clown.

'Could your daughter have confided in someone and told them where she was going when she ran away?'

'I don't think so, no.'

'Do you have any idea where she went?'

'She told me she'd sometimes sleep in the metro or in a homeless shelter.'

'Do you think Maria took drugs when she ran away?'

'No idea. I never found anything in her room. No hard drugs, and no soft drugs, either.'

'All right,' I conclude, getting up. 'My forensic colleagues will be in touch to pick up some of her belongings, including her tablet. I understand that her phone isn't here, but she left her iPad and her computer, is that right?'

'Yes.'

'You don't mind if I have a quick look at her room, do you?'

Per Sjögren shakes his head and invites me without a word to follow him down a long corridor filled with abstract paintings.

He opens the last door on the right and steps aside.

I put on a pair of gloves and turn to him in surprise. The room is impeccably neat.

'Maria was an extremely tidy person,' he says.

That's one way to put it. This kid was something of a control freak. Not a single paper or trinket left lying around. A computer sits in pride of place on the desk. A shelf on the wall above it contains a series of books in Swedish and English, arranged by size. The rest of the room is just as spartan and orderly, even the contents of the drawers. A poster of Marilyn Monroe is taped to the back of the door. Above the bed, there are a number of photos of a Swedish actress whose name I forget – Alexia or Alicia or something. Freyja would have known who it was in a heartbeat.

'What comes next?' Per Sjögren asks as I'm taking off my gloves.

'We're going to retrace Maria's steps, and keep going until we cross paths with her killer.'

30
Emma

Sofia's wearing a white gown and a traditional crown of Saint Lucia candles. Sitting at the foot of the tree where she was hanged, fingers and teeth caked in dirt, she's clawing at the ground with her bare hands. And smiling. I tell her she's going to catch cold, she should come inside and go to bed, but she carries on regardless, dark smile and all.

I wake with a start, the sound of my sister's nails scraping the soil in my ears and a taste of blood in my mouth. I take in my surroundings, wondering where I am. Then I feel the warmth of Anneli's body. Her locks caressing my shoulder. I snuggle up to her, trying to put the nightmare behind me.

'What if I stayed right here this morning?' I murmur, stroking Anneli's breast.

'What would you be missing?' she replies sleepily.

'Niklas Gussman's asked me to go to the museum in Lidingö to sort and appraise two boxes of papers his father left him. They've never had the time to go through them.'

'So, in you ride on your trusty steed to make everything right in the world.'

'Close enough. Walking in with my magnifying glass to make sure the grant funding keeps flowing to your little island.'

'Then I fear you have no choice, my dear.'

She kisses me and extricates herself from the sheets.

'Go back to sleep, it's still early,' she says when I sit up too. 'I'm going to put the bread and the buns in the oven.'

'I'll keep you company. I have no desire to slip back into the nightmare I just had.'

The morning is still cloaked in darkness as I sip my first coffee and watch Anneli's flour-dusted hands kneading and braiding the saffron brioche dough.

When the clock strikes seven, I go back upstairs and get ready, then dash to the ferry like a true islander, with two warm buns and hot coffees in hand.

Lotta and I chat and munch on our breakfast, and before long I'm disembarking at Mor Anna, where my taxi is waiting.

✂

Two sweet little old ladies greet me with a *hej* full of vim and vigour when I arrive at Villa Fornboda, the magnificent, yellow turn-of-the-century building that houses the Lidingö town museum.

'Emma Lindahl, representing Von Dardel's. Pleased to meet you.'

'Ooh, we thought it must be you,' one of the women smiles. 'The art expert, I mean. Welcome. We're so happy to see these documents being authenticated at last.'

'Follow us,' the other woman says, adjusting her silk scarf. 'We've had these boxes since ... it must have been before old Mr Gussman died, wasn't it?'

'Just after he died. Three, four years ago. I don't recall. Niklas Gussman had them brought here when they were clearing out his father's study. Let me get us some coffee. Or would you rather have tea?'

'Coffee's perfect. Thank you so much.'

The other woman and I make our way upstairs using the central staircase.

'The history of Lidingö goes hand in hand with the AGA AB gas company and its founder Nils Gustaf Dalén,' my guide tells me as we walk through a room dedicated to the Swedish inventor's memory. 'It must be quite something to be surrounded by so many treasures at the manor house...' She catches herself. 'Wait, what am I saying? You must see that kind of thing every day.'

'Believe me, it really is an honour to be seeing so many unique pieces up close and in such an exceptional place.'

She smiles at me with childlike wonder. 'As I explained to Mr Gussman's secretary, we're all volunteers here at the museum, and there are things we can't do without expert assistance. Here we are,' she adds, opening a door at the end of a series of rooms consecrated to Lidingö's industrial heritage.

The storage room is cramped, and packed with boxes and frames, but features a large window that makes it feel quite pleasant.

'It's hardly palatial, but I cleared this desk for you, and the weather is splendid. Brith will be back shortly with coffee and biscuits for you. Her husband makes a mean almond shortbread. It'd be sinful not to try one. Please don't hesitate if you need anything. No need to come down. Just give us a shout from the top of the stairs. The walls are paper thin, so we'll hear you. I'll leave you to it. Good luck.'

'Here comes your coffee!' her colleague calls, scurrying her way across the parquet floor. 'I put it in a Thermos for you so it'll keep warm. And I brought you some biscuits too,' she winks. 'I suppose you won't know how long this'll take until you open the boxes and see what's what, will you?'

'That's right,' I laugh.

My guide gives me a knowing smile and the two of them leave me to it.

Not a second later, the door opens again.

'I forgot to mention, it's these two right here.' She points to two cardboard boxes standing side by side at the foot of a metal shelving unit.

I nod, thank them, and take off my coat and scarf before pulling on a pair of cotton gloves. I open the first box and lay out the contents on the desk in a number of piles.

I whistle at the sight of the stacks of loose papers, handwritten journals and folders stuffed with more sheets of paper.

It only takes a quick glance for me to realise that nothing is in any sort of order. As far as I can see, there's no rhyme or reason to the dates, subjects and authors. So, I decide to empty the second box as well and start to classify everything. I'll take a closer look at things after that.

Once I've put it all into piles, I decide to tackle the loose sheets of paper first, since they're the most daunting. I take a sip of Brith's fabulous coffee and start reading.

✄

Two hours later, I've found nothing that merits keeping, selling or exhibiting to anyone other than collectors of shopping lists. The papers are mostly an assortment of notes and rough drafts of letters to do with the construction of the manor house and purchases of drapery, paintings and materials, such as Italian marble and Nordic lumber, as well as changes to the plans and complaints about delays on this or that aspect of the work.

Next, I move on to the stack of cardboard folders. There are eight of them in all. After that, I'll have two notebooks to go through, each with about a hundred pages. I expect I'll be done by the end of the afternoon.

At lunchtime, I take a short break and head to the Centrum shopping centre across from the museum and buy a sandwich and a smoothie from Joe & The Juice. Back at the museum, sitting down again at my desk to eat, the storage room seems bright and airy, and I feel comfortable here. I finish my sandwich, then wipe my fingers and put my gloves on again to tackle the last two folders.

One of them contains two folded A3 sheets of paper. The first is a plan of the Gussmans' land on Storholmen. It's dated 1915, seven years before the manor was built. The plan has been divided into a grid resembling a chessboard. The squares are labelled horizontally from A to H and vertically from one to eight. The second sheet is a floor plan of all three levels of the building, dated 1920, with the architect's name in the bottom right corner.

Two documents worth keeping, for sure.

I set them aside and move on to the next folder. This one's thicker and contains thirty or so letters in their original envelopes. I start reading one and am surprised to find myself drawn in, keen to see the others. I smile at the sweet nothings, and at the steamy suggestions Gustav wrote to woo, and also to titillate, his wife, Harriet.

I pour the last of the coffee into my cup and remove one of my gloves to taste one of the shortbread biscuits from Brith, which I'd completely forgotten about. Then I get back to work.

The two notebooks I still have to appraise are leather-bound and embossed with the late great-grandfather's initials: *GG*.

I leaf through the pages quickly to see if there's a chronological order to them. The first one is from 1915. The second is not dated.

'Back to the First World War it is, then,' I say out loud.

This notebook is a real hotchpotch. Far from being about the war, there's all sorts of domestic stuff in here, notes for speeches, scraps of poems, guest lists, names of enemies – what the heck? – and budgets. There's no real substance to the content, but still, this might be of interest to a collector.

I'm about to close the notebook when something jumps out at me. One page contains nothing but three handwritten lines:

DECAPITATION
ALIVE?
1743

There's a line on the opposite page dividing it into two columns.

On the left is a series of capital letters and numbers. On the right, beside each of those letters and numbers, is a cross, or an x:

```
G7 | x
B6 | x
H3 | x
C7 | x
C2 | x
D4 | x
D1 | x
G6 | x
F2 | x
```

The cogs start turning in my mind.

I reach for the folder containing the plans and unfold the one showing the grid of the property before the manor was built.

Suddenly, the penny drops.

I understand what the brilliant Gustav Gussman discovered.

And what that discovery means for us.

For Sofia.

For the girl under the ice.

And for me.

31
Viktoria

I wake even earlier than usual, after a terrible night, during which I tried and failed to shake the horrid feeling I was left with after the altercation with Madam. Never has anyone humiliated me so much. I don't know why I let her speak to me that way.

I ran into her only once yesterday after the incident. And as usual, she ignored me completely. I opened my mouth to say something about what happened, but nothing came out. I felt paralysed. She was in the kitchen for a while – long enough to make herself a cup of tea and a snack – but still, I couldn't muster any words.

That woman scares me. There's something dark and disturbing about her.

I shower and go downstairs to make coffee, hoping it'll clear my head.

I flick the light switch and stifle a scream. Thor is sitting by the window, looking out. He's white as a sheet.

Last night, quite late, I saw him roaming around the French garden.

'*Hej*,' I say. 'Is everything all right?'

It takes him a moment to turn and look at me. The dark rings under his eyes stand out against his delicate features.

'Are you sick?' I ask.

'I don't know.'

'Are you in pain?'

'My back hurts. And my stomach.'

'You're really pale. Maybe you're coming down with something. Are you hungry?'

He shakes his head. 'I feel a bit queasy.'

'I'll make you a black tea. Trust me, it'll do you the world of good.'

He nods, then turns back to the garden.

'What are you looking at?' I ask him as I put the kettle on to boil.

I spoon some loose leaves of Earl Grey into a teapot and take a cup out of the cupboard.

'I'm looking at what might be. And what might not,' he replies as I place his cup on the table.

I crouch down beside him. 'What's going on, Thor?'

He pushes his chair away, opening up the distance I just narrowed.

'I ... I just have a stomach ache.'

He springs to his feet all of a sudden, with a look of bewilderment, then scurries off to his room.

I eat my breakfast with a heavy heart. The kid clearly has a weight on his shoulders. Is it pressure from his father, with his mother a partner in crime? Or is it all coming from his mother, and his father either turns a blind eye or has no idea what's going on under his roof? Or maybe they're just as bad as each other? One thing's for sure, the kid is not doing well. And he needs help.

Three hours later, when Madam and Thor have gone out and Josephine is listening to music in her room, I take the opportunity to go into Thor's. Now's my chance to look for clues as to what's going on with him – anything to give me an idea what's wrong. I doubt that many boys his age keep a diary, but Thor is not like other kids, so I suppose he might.

Gently, I close the door behind me and start digging around. My hands are clammy from the stress. First I check under the bed, then beneath the mattress. I rummage through the desk drawers and look in the back of the wardrobe. I feel the underside of every shelf, where something might have been taped, but I find nothing. Suddenly I find myself wondering if I'm imagining all this, if I'm just getting carried away after the altercation with Madam.

I sigh loudly, telling myself I'd better go and polish the oil lamps instead, like I've been meaning to for ages. That's when I notice a pair of black boxer shorts scrunched up on the floor. I instinctively reach down to pick them up and put them in the wash.

As soon as I touch them, I realise they're damp and sticky, so I put them back where I found them and shake my head with a knowing smile. I don't want to intrude on Thor's privacy. He'd be mortified if he knew I'd seen the evidence.

Then suddenly, I notice my fingers. I stifle a scream.

They're covered in blood.

What the hell? What kind of abuse is this abominable mother subjecting her child to?

32
Karl

I come up from the cellar, put the Côtes-du-Rhône bottle on the kitchen counter and flop back down on the sofa with a sigh.

I close my eyes and pinch the bridge of my nose.

I can't get the thought of Per Sjögren out of my mind.

I don't know how the man's still standing. How can he grieve two huge losses and keep finding the strength to get out of bed in the morning and face a new day of suffering?

Can anyone recover from such devastating blows? First his wife, and then his daughter. He had to watch over that child with two sets of eyes – his own, and his wife's – only for her to slip between his fingers. I had the impression, when I spoke to him, that Maria was like a fish that kept wriggling off the hook. He didn't know her. He doesn't know who she was. I can't fathom how a child you've raised can become a stranger.

How long will it be before he manages to take his daughter's coat down from the hook in the hallway without being wracked by guilt and pain?

And what about me? How long will it take for me to be able to look at the photograph of the pink sky over Stockholm Bay that Freyja took?

Freyja never wanted to have children. She wanted nothing to do with what she called the 'Swedish atavism' that makes every couple pop out two kids – or three if they live in Djursholm, she joked.

What I wanted more than anything was her. So I made her desires my own, because decisions were always hers to make. Whatever you think about the battle of the sexes and genders, some undeniable realities are hard-wired by nature: if you're born female and want kids with your partner, chances are you'll bear the children and give birth to them, so the choice to become a mother is life-changing in more ways than it is for the other parent.

When all is said and done, though, I was never consumed by the desire to become a father. I would've liked to pass things on, of course, but I'm not sure I've ever been ready for the rest, for all the sacrifices fatherhood entails. It's a moot point, anyway, because no one will ever call me 'Dad'.

The door bell chimes, annoyingly.

Do I or don't I answer it? I debate to myself, then decide to see who it is.

Emma Lindahl is standing on the porch, huddled in a white parka.

I'm so surprised, it takes me a second to catch my breath.

'I'm sorry to bother you, Inspector. I tried calling and you didn't pick up. I have to speak to you. It's very important.'

Her cheeks are red from the cold and her eyes are burning with impatience.

'Come in,' I say. Any hint of formality in our dynamic has now completely disappeared.

She takes off her coat and I hang it up in the hallway cupboard. Then she takes off her shoes and follows me through to the living room.

'Want something to drink?'

She shakes her head.

'Are you sure? I'll get you a glass of water.'

I head into the kitchen and come back with two glasses. I hand one to her and she drinks half of it in one gulp before she even sits down.

'I happened upon a notebook of Gustav Gussman's from 1915...'

She pauses, shakes her head.

'Sorry, I don't know where to start.'

Her gaze flits around the room as she gathers her thoughts. Then she takes a seat and begins her story.

'Gustav Gussman – Niklas's great-grandfather – was the man who made the family's fortune. He had the manor house built in 1922 and, in so doing, he put Storholmen on the map. People say he was a big spender, but that wasn't true. I've spent today going through a fair amount of his correspondence and personal papers, so I can tell you, Gustav Gussman would not have paid a penny more than he thought something was worth – for anything. And yet, he chose to build a luxurious estate on an impractical island, and it cost him almost as much to transport the materials over there as the labour and the materials themselves. Why did he do this? For two reasons: the first was his wife, Harriet. He was madly in love with her his whole life. She loved pomp and circumstance and decadent parties, haute couture and high society. And so, her dear husband built a castle for his beautiful princess, where she could dazzle the world.'

She smiles, as if recalling a memory, then carries on.

'But why build on Storholmen, of all places? Back then, there was no attraction there at all. It was just a little island in the Stockholm Archipelago, no more spectacular than the others – especially since its larger neighbour, Lidingö, once used the island as a dumping ground for its rubbish. But I now know the answer to that question, too. If Gustav chose to build the manor his wife so desired on Storholmen, it was because he had an obsession – think of it like Indiana Jones and his quest to find the lost ark. He was looking for a secret hideout – the place where Charles Emil Lewenhaupt, a general who deserted the army, went underground, vanishing without trace. No one has ever even found the entrance to this hiding place, and the legend goes that he stashed a bunch of valuables there during the war.'

She pauses, reaches for her glass and drains the last of the water.

'What I think,' she carries on, wiping the corner of her lips, 'in fact, I'm sure of it, is that Gustav Gussman found that secret underground hideout on Storholmen, and it's on that precise location that he built his property. Why wasn't the manor house built on another plot of land with a nicer view of the bay, for example? Because he wanted to build its basement around Lewenhaupt's hideaway. Gussman was a sneaky character. I think he must have used this underground chamber to hide the artworks he stole from Russia during the war.'

'This sounds like something out of *The Da Vinci Code*, Emma.'

'And the tunnel Dan Brown wrote about really does exist. It's called the Passetto di Borgo, a fortified and raised passageway that connects Saint Peter's Square with the Vatican. The world is full of secret passages and bunkers, every one crazier and more ingenious than the last. In Dracula's Castle, for example, there was a secret passage between the first and third floors, and the entrance was hidden inside a false chimney. There are tunnels in Vietnam used during the war there; the trapdoors to access them were in the middle of the jungle, camouflaged in the forest floor, or under fake termite mounds.'

'What kind of evidence do you have to back this up?'

'The islanders told me the story about Lewenhaupt and his bunker on the island. And the stuff about Gussman looting works of art from Russia – I don't believe that's a myth, not after the number of pieces from that part of the world I've discovered in the Gussman collection.'

'You mentioned a notebook earlier. What did you find, exactly? A plan for an underground bunker?'

Emma starts to laugh. Her cheeks aren't as red now, but her gaze is just as intense.

'Old man Gussman was no idiot. He charted the progress of his research. Seven years before building his manor, he drew a grid of the land it now stands on, in the hope of using it to locate the entrance to the bunker, I believe. And for us to find that now, we just have to decipher his code and compare his notes with the terrain. And that would go much faster with radar.'

She rubs her palms against her jeans without breaking eye contact with me.

'This must be where Sofia and the other victim were held captive for nine days, Karl. It has to be! What better place to lock someone away for so long?'

'A cellar is enough to do the job, Emma. Not to mention, the second victim was found in Lidingö, not Storholmen.'

'It's right next door!' she cries, raising her palms as if to tell me how obvious that is. 'The manor has everything, Karl: the space, the silence, the secluded access to the sea ... Have you seen their private dock? It's hidden in a cove. Since day one of my being there, Niklas Gussman has been acting strangely. He only lets me access the property for a few hours a day. Why's that, do you think? Because he has something to hide.'

I shake my head. 'You do understand that nothing you've told me is enough for me to get a warrant?'

'Not even after two murders? What will it take to get this investigation moving?'

'Emma, the first one happened nine years ago, and the victim of the second was found north of Lidingö. Not at the manor.'

'All right,' she says curtly and stands up. 'I suppose we'll just have to wait nine years for another body to turn up then.'

33
Karl

The clientele at Café Tranan is always cheerful, even on a day like today, when winter makes mid-morning feel more like the middle of the night. It must be because this restaurant in Odenplan is nearly a century young and aging like the fine wines in its cellar. The carefully crafted menu, the attentive service, the pretty red-and-white checked tablecloths, the thick cotton napkins. There's nothing out of place here. Everything feels right. It's hard to tear yourself away from your table when you've polished off the dish of the day. It doesn't feel that way today, though. Today, everything is different. Freyja's shadow is darkening everything.

Arnold yaps when the waitress brings him a bowl of water. She gives him a pat on the head and goes off with a smile.

'Every time I have a coffee it makes me want a cigarette,' Siv says, adding a drop of milk to her cup. 'Isn't that crazy? It's been twenty years since I kicked the habit.'

'You could probably let yourself have just the one, once in a while.'

She rolls her eyes and takes a sip of her coffee.

'Are you kidding? I don't do moderation. When I quit smoking, I started working out, remember? Look at me now,' she says, eyeballing her sculpted torso. 'Every morning I stand on a scale that measures my body fat and water and I drink cocktails made from Peruvian root vegetables. I'm beyond hope, Karl.'

The waitress returns with our cheese omelettes. Arnie lifts his head up from his paws, but a single wag of Siv's finger in front of his inquisitive snout dissuades him from begging for the slightest scrap. He settles down again with a sigh.

'The techs didn't find anything interesting on the kid's computer or iPad,' my boss tells me as she picks up her fork. 'Just some TV series that she downloaded – *Squid Game*, *Game of Thrones*, that sort of thing. Web searches for teenage stuff like periods and masturbation – I'll spare you the details. But no chats or logins to any platforms with a history that might suggest she met her killer online.'

She pauses to take her first bite.

'All that stuff could be on her phone,' I venture. 'Maria certainly didn't have it on her, and we haven't found it yet.'

Siv nods. 'What's new with your side of things?' she asks after a sip of water.

'I've started looking into the killer's pattern, the nine-year thing.'

'And that's a ritual historians have actually written about? Not that I'm condoning the morals of our bloodthirsty ancestors, but still, I'm curious.'

'Absolutely. There's quite a bit of material out there, as it happens. Have you ever heard of the temple at Uppsala?'

'Mmm,' she says with her mouth full.

'Adam of something, an eleventh-century German historian, wrote about the pagan rites people observed every nine years at the Viking site there. Nine sacrifices every nine years, with a feast to follow.'

'There were nine sacrifices in 2012, counting the animals as well as Sofia,' Siv replies. She shakes her head. 'The things I've said in this job that would never cross my mind otherwise. So where are the eight sacrifices to go with Maria Sjögren, then?'

'I have no idea, Siv.'

'Well, our killer must have done something with them.'

'I'm sure you're right.'

'And nine, why was that the Vikings' lucky number? Was that how many wives Odin had, or something?'

'You're not far off the mark. The number nine was sacred. They worked it into everything. There was even a god who had nine mothers.'

'Now that's one way to lighten the load of having kids. Maybe the Vikings were on to something. Sorry. Did you find anything else that might fit the pattern?'

'Only one accident on Storholmen and I can't see how it might be connected to our investigation. In 1994, eighteen years before Sofia was killed, and twenty-seven before Maria, a thirty-nine-year-old Swedish woman named Frigg Bergman died after falling from the roof of the manor house.'

'Did she live there?'

'That's what I'm trying to find out. There wasn't much in the newspapers about it, not even in the local rag. Not long after her death, in early 1995, her husband and their daughter left Sweden and went to Switzerland. No sign of either of them since then.'

'Hmm. Still, I don't see any connection. What's your plan, now?'

'I'm heading over to Storholmen. Apparently a teenager heard something on the night of the twenty-ninth.'

'I'm sure he'll be thrilled to have you ruining what's left of his school holidays. Good luck getting anything useful out of him.'

34
Karl

It's early afternoon by the time I get to Ett Glas. The mother and her son are already there, sitting at a table by the emergency exit, waiting for me. Slouching there with hunched shoulders, he reminds me of Skalman, the turtle in the Bamse cartoon strip who goes into his shell when he wants to be left alone.

'Hello there, I'm Detective Inspector Karl Rosén,' I say, taking a seat so I won't look too intimidating for the kid.

The mother shakes my hand and smiles nervously. 'I saw your message in Lotta's WhatsApp group, and when I mentioned it to my husband at home, Otto here told us he'd heard a boat engine that night when he got up to go to the bathroom.'

Her son is gracing us with nothing but the shock of hair on the top of his head.

'Otto?' His mother tries to rouse him.

No reaction.

'Otto?'

Eventually he looks up at her, then me, and it dawns on me that he's been messing with his phone in his lap.

'Just give it a rest with that thing, will you,' she tuts.

He slowly slides his precious smartphone onto the table and interlaces his fingers. But his shifty eyes are still basically glued to the thing.

'Hello, Otto. I'm Detective Inspector Rosén,' I repeat, sure he hasn't heard a word of my brief conversation with his mother. 'I understand you heard something on the night of the twenty-ninth?'

He nods.

'What did you hear?'

'A boat engine.'

'What time was that?'

'About two in the morning.'

'What did you see?'

He shrugs and hunches his shoulders deeper. 'Nothing. I just heard the sound of it, that's all.'

'And you didn't look out the window? To see what was going on?'

'No.'

'It's not very often you hear boats in the middle of the night in the winter, is it? Weren't you curious to see what was out there?'

He sneaks a look at his phone screen.

'No.'

'Still, you thought it was important enough to contact the police. To contact me and let me know.'

'You wanted to know if anyone had seen anything unusual that night,' he snaps. 'That was unusual.'

'How can you be sure it was the twenty-ninth of December? Don't the days all blend into one another during the school holidays?'

He hesitates for a second before he answers.

'When I looked at the time on my phone when I went to the bathroom, I saw the date.'

'And it said "twenty-nine, December".'

'Yes.'

'So it was actually the night *before* the one we're interested in, Otto – the early hours. We want to know about the night of the twenty-ninth to the thirtieth of December.'

His expression freezes.

I grab his phone and hand it back to him.

He takes it hesitantly and looks at his mother, who gives him a quick smile.

'You did the right thing letting us know, though, Otto,' I carry on, and smile at him in turn. 'That was important. A girl your age is dead. It was brave of you to speak up.'

He puts the phone down in his lap. His chin wrinkles and the corners of his mouth turn downwards.

'I'm sure you won't get in trouble with your mum and dad, Otto.'

He looks up at me suspiciously.

'Now, I'd like you to show me what you saw *that* night. Which I'm sure was the night between the twenty-ninth and the thirtieth of December, wasn't it?'

His mother turns to me, frowning with incomprehension.

'You took a video of something on your phone, am I right?' I say. 'You won't stop looking at the thing. Or you're trying to keep it out of our sight. So, what did you see?'

'Otto?' his mother intervenes, sounding concerned.

'I think your son needs to know that you'll go easy on him, if you don't mind me saying. He'll feel more comfortable talking that way.'

'All right,' she says, still not following.

'Thank you. Otto, I don't think you were at home on the night of the twenty-ninth, were you?'

Otto shakes his head timidly.

From the corner of my eye, I can see his mother looks stunned.

'Your parents aren't going to punish you, Otto,' I hasten to add so he won't clam up. 'What you share with me today could help us make progress in a murder investigation. I'm sure that whatever you did that night, all will be forgiven.'

I smile, hoping his mother isn't about to contradict me.

'Can you show me now, Otto?' I insist.

He unlocks his phone, clicks on the photos icon and scrolls through a few before selecting a video.

'Where were you, Otto?' his mother asks gently, running a hand through her shaggy hair.

'I took the boat out with Pablo, and we went to Lidingö ... to meet up with two girls from school,' he admits, not daring to look at his mother. 'We were on a little beach in Sticklinge. In a cove called Tahiti.'

I know the place well. It's just next to Rödstuguviken Bay, where we found Maria's body.

He hands me his phone and hazards a panicked glance at his mother, who only has eyes for the video I'm about to play.

I make a note of the date and time on the file – 30 December at 2.13 am – then tap play.

The video only lasts sixteen seconds. It shows two teenagers, a girl and a boy, surely the infamous Pablo, dancing to some music on low volume, backs to the sea and beers in hand. Behind them, about fifty metres from the shore a motor boat passes by.

I press pause and zoom in on the image.

It's pitch-black. The sea is illuminated only by the light of the phone's torch and the practically full moon. The person on the boat is wearing a dark puffer jacket with the hood pulled up. There's no way to see who it might be or glean the slightest clue from the boat itself, or tell whether it's transporting anything.

I send the video to Alvid straight from Otto's phone and wrap up our meeting.

I'm about to leave the café when I notice Lotta Petterson sitting across from a man with a head of hair as white as her own. They're each drinking a black coffee and eating a slice of apple tart.

'Hello there, Inspector,' she greets me. 'Did your message do the trick?'

'It looks like it did, yes.'

'Wonderful!'

'You're not at the helm this afternoon?' I nod to the wharf where the water taxi docks.

'No, I've finished my shift. Peter's the one who'll be driving you back. He's almost as good as me,' she says with a friendly smile and a wink.

I return the smile, say goodbye and head for the exit.

I've just opened the door when I have a sudden thought about the islanders' WhatsApp group. I turn around and retrace my steps.

'Inspector!' Lotta greets me once more. 'Back so soon?'

'I'm also looking into something that happened in 1994,' I explain, without further ado, 'and I wonder if I might make use of your network again.'

'Of course. Pull up a chair and tell me everything.'

I grab one from the next table and sit down with her and her companion.

'This is my husband Björn,' Lotta says as I'm unbuttoning my coat.

The man gives me a reluctant nod.

'I'm all ears,' she encourages me. 'Perhaps you'd like a coffee?'

'No, thank you, but it's kind of you to ask. In a nutshell, I'm looking for information about a woman named Frigg Bergman, who died at the manor in 1994.'

'Ah, yes, I remember. What a terrible thing that was. They only stayed a year or two on the estate, I think. They had a son, if I recall.'

'A daughter,' I correct her. 'So, this Frigg Bergman lived at the manor?'

'Yes, why?'

'I haven't found anything to confirm that she or her husband were tenants.'

'It was a bit more complicated than that,' Björn chimes in.

He pushes his plate aside and puts his elbows on the table.

'In the early 1990s, Niklas's father went through some major financial troubles that nearly ruined the empire his grandfather had built. The Gussmans couldn't imagine letting the manor house go. It was a bit like their own Palace of Versailles. The property cost a fortune to run, and they needed cash, so they decided to rent it out for film shoots and fashion shows, that sort of thing. Unfortunately, after a long legal battle with their creditors, it ended up being repossessed, and they had to say goodbye to the manor and its entire contents – furniture, artworks and all.' Björn shakes his head. 'Old Gustav Gussman must have turned in his grave when the bank auctioned the place off.'

He pauses for a sip of coffee.

'The buyer – Bergman – didn't have a chance to get anything valued. He'd barely moved his family in, really, because it was only a few months later, maybe a year, I can't remember, that his wife fell to her death. He sold the manor back to the Gussmans in a hurry. They'd dug themselves out of the hole by that point and ended up buying the place back for a song. They insisted it had lost value because of Frigg Bergman's tragic death. I know, that was a dirty trick for them to play.'

I think this old man must be reading my mind.

'Certain rumours were going around the island,' Lotta adds. 'Bergman knew he was being forced into a bad deal but didn't really have much choice. I don't know who started spreading the rumours, but I know what they were – that maybe his wife's death wasn't accidental. We couldn't help but wonder if he was the one who killed her.'

35
Viktoria

Today is shopping day and I told Josephine she was coming with me, thinking I'd have a chat with her about Thor before I decide the best way to go about protecting the kid. I don't know if anyone will believe a housekeeper over her rich and powerful employers, or even if they'll listen to a word I say, but I have to try and do something.

Taking the captain's hand as I stepped aboard the family's private boat, I felt the same joy I do every time. Josephine didn't say a word during the short crossing to Lidingö. She just turned her back to me and her face to the wind.

Now we're in the back of the car that was waiting at the terminal in Mor Anna to drive us into the centre of Lidingö.

'Do you know what's going on with Thor, *älskling*?' I ask her distractedly.

Josephine turns and looks at me with sadness in her eyes. 'His mum wishes ... that he was different.'

'Different? Are you talking about his – how can I put it – learning difficulties?'

Suddenly I realise how absurd my words sound. When I happened upon him and Josephine talking about Norse mythology in the drawing room, Thor seemed perfectly normal. Of course, he has these absences – sometimes it's like he's come unplugged – but he doesn't seem to have the slightest issue understanding anything.

'Do you know what's stopping him from going to school?'

'His mum says he has ... I forget what she calls it – so he has trouble keeping up in class.'

'And is that true?'

She shrugs. 'How should I know? I've never been in class with him.'

'But what do you think about it?'

'I think Thor's far more intelligent than all of us put together.'

'Do you know what his dad thinks?'

'About what?'

'About his son being home-schooled.'

'He doesn't agree with it. Thor told me his dad's tried to talk to his mum about it a few times. But ... he's afraid of her.'

I can feel my chest tightening.

'She's forcing Thor to change,' Jo says, looking out the car window. 'But we are who we are, it's as simple as that.'

'Do you know if she's hurting him?' I ask, keeping my voice low, thinking about the pair of bloody boxers I found.

My daughter doesn't take her eyes away from the sea, but she nods.

My heart is pounding and my stomach is in knots.

'Has she hurt *you*?'

'No, she doesn't care about me. The only thing that matters to her is her son. That's why she got so angry when you found those nine jars under her bed. All that stuff, it's to transform Thor. And I'm worried she's going to succeed, Mum – because it really works.'

'What are you talking about, Josephine? What are those empty jars supposed to do? What exactly "really works"?'

She rolls her eyes, clearly irritated. 'Nine is the magic number in Norse mythology, Mum. The number that must guide every action. The number nine is the key to everything. For example, there are nine worlds and Thrivaldi, the giant Thor killed, has nine heads. The giant Aegir, who represents the sea, has nine daughters. Heimdall, the guardian of Asgard, has nine mothers. Draupnir, Odin's ring, drips gold every nine nights to make nine new rings. And I could go on. The number nine is everywhere, there's no end to it.'

I'm gobsmacked.

'Where did you learn all this, Jo?'

'Thor told me to read about it. So I'd know how to do it.'

'How to do *what*?'

'How to free him.'

'Free him from what?'

'From his mother.'

'What the heck is all this?' I raise my voice. I'm getting tired of this silliness.

'I'm explaining to you why the number nine is the key to evolving.'

I shake my head. 'This is ridiculous, Jo. You know these are legends, right? They're just stories.'

'Can't you just listen to me for once?' she cries.

I stiffen.

'What I'm saying is important. Do you understand? Just listen to me!'

I glance awkwardly at the rearview mirror and see the driver looking at us. He turns his eyes back to the road straight away.

'The number nine allows you to get whatever you want by making sacrifices.'

My daughter can't hide her anger at me. She's spitting out the words and chopping her hand against her thigh.

'When Odin sacrifices himself, he stays hanging from Yggdrasil, the sacred tree of life, for nine days and nine nights to gain the secret wisdom of the runes. That proves you have to make a sacrifice to achieve something.'

I reach out and cup her hands in mine. And suddenly, it reminds me of when she used to hold my hand to cross the street and kiss my fingers when we made it to the other side, safe and sound.

'Listen to me, Jo, it's not by making sacrifices that you achieve anything. It's by hard work and perseverance. The work we do with pleasure and not in pain. I promise you, we won't let Thor's mother do him any more harm. Don't worry, we'll find a way to help him.'

36
Emma

Yesterday, I emailed Niklas Gussman and asked him to change my schedule, because I'd like to go down to the basement today. I justified my request by referencing the documents of his great-grandfather's that were kept at the museum. Some of the items referred to in those archives might be stored in the cellars, and it seems logical to me to examine them sooner rather than later. If he sees no issue with this, of course.

His response eventually came late this morning, through his secretary: 'Mr Gussman expresses no objection to you taking this initiative.'

This man is never one to mince his words.

I have to admit I was a bit surprised that he'd granted me this privilege so easily. That said, more than eighteen hours passed between the time I wrote to him and the time I received his reply. That would have been ample for him to move, hide or destroy anything he didn't want me to find.

The door to the basement is in the back kitchen.

It opens onto a steep, pale-oak staircase, only the top of which is illuminated by a ceiling light. I walk down the last few steps in darkness. It feels like I'm venturing into the underworld. Feeling around, I eventually locate a switch quite high up on my right, under a light fixture that's attached to the wall.

At the foot of the stairs is a second door, with a round porcelain handle. I open it, and the smell hits my nose immediately – a combination of damp, mould and dust that makes me cough and stings my eyes. I get my water bottle out of my bag and take a few sips before I press another light switch on the wall beside me.

Two large metal lamps blink to life and reveal a corridor that's about a metre and a half wide and looks to be about ten metres long, with two doors on the right and a vast room at the end. It's some sort of storeroom, judging by what I can see from here.

I check the requisition that Niklas gave me: only the property in the storeroom is to be appraised. Next, I unfold the plan of the manor that I've prepared, lay it out on the floor and crouch down to study it.

I was a bag of nerves when I left the inspector's house last night. Honestly, I was expecting more support from him. I knew the man in front of me was paralysed. Paralysed by the grief that's consuming him. On my way home, I realised I hadn't given him my condolences. The evidence to get a warrant might have been lacking, but still, he didn't exactly seem keen on finding a solution to that. Maybe he's doing more than I think, but I refuse to be held back by his inertia.

And so, when I got home, I decided to replicate the plan of the manor and conduct my own investigation.

Using the photos of the documents I took at the museum, I copied Gustav Gussman's grid and layered it over the plan of the manor house and grounds. Then I crossed out some of the squares on my grid to represent those Gussman had marked with an X. I figured the Xs must indicate that he'd explored those areas without finding the entrance to Lewenhaupt's underground passage. This means I can disregard them and start searching where he left off. Obviously, Gussman stopped short of marking the spot where he did find the entrance because he wanted to keep the secret for himself. But still, his grid will have saved me some time.

The basement where I am now corresponds to the square F3.

It's blank and so, if my theory is correct, the entrance to the bunker might be here.

I examine the plaster on the walls of the corridor, but I can't see the slightest gap or join. The floor creaks with my every step.

'Well, at least I'll know if I have company down here,' I say out loud. Then I mock myself, in a lower voice this time, for having this conversation with myself – it tells me I don't feel entirely comfortable here.

After inspecting the floor, I decide to have a go at the two closed doors, even though I'm not supposed to have access to them.

I turn the handle on the first door, and it opens. Inside, a fluorescent light comes on automatically. It's a tiny room with a concrete floor. The only things in here are a water tank, a boiler and a fuse box.

I close the door and move on to the next one. This time, I have to turn a switch with a timer on it to see what's inside. The space is filled with empty wine racks. It seems twice as big as the first one. It has a concrete floor as well. The racks have been screwed to the wall, and I can't see a gap or join anywhere in the walls that would suggest an opening.

I stand up straight and heave a weary sigh. I'm certain that Sofia was held captive somewhere on the Gussman property. Exploring the entire site is going to take forever, but at least, assuming I don't find anything in this basement, I'll be able to mark an X on square F3. I walk down the corridor, fish my cotton gloves out of my pocket and put them on, ready for a closer look at what's waiting for me in the room at the end.

It's much bigger than I thought; it extends into a recess to the right, where there's a heap of rolled-up carpets. It has the same creaky floor as the corridor. Stacked against the wall in front of me are a number of crates filled with old empty bottles that once had lemonade, sparkling water, wine and other alcoholic drinks in them. Now most of them are covered in dust. I examine a few magnificent examples made of blue glass with white lettering spelling out French words; some of these bottles still have their stoppers attached.

For once, I save the least appealing task for last – pushing the heap of dusty and probably spider-infested carpets to one side to make sure they're not concealing a door or covering a trapdoor. First, I have to move a stack of three travel trunks out of the way. They're decorated with stickers from cities and countries all over Europe.

I'm just tall enough to open the one on the top. It's filled with wicker baskets, one of which contains four sets of silver cutlery, four gold-detailed porcelain plates painted with bucolic scenes, just as many stemmed crystal glasses and the same number of cotton napkins, which have yellowed with time. I take this beautiful picnic basket out of the chest and put it to one side.

The chest itself isn't that heavy and I manage to lift it down to the floor, making sure to tense my core to protect my back, the way I learned at Christie's, where I sometimes had to carry objects half my weight. I might have acquired that technique earlier if I'd ever been to a gym. Instead, I learned the hard way and ended up putting my back out. I won't make that mistake again.

Opening the second trunk makes me smile. It contains a gramophone on a wooden stand, which I delicately extricate by sliding my hands under its base. It's a 'Victor V' model, stamped with the name Harriet Gussman and the year it was made: 1907. I set it down beside the picnic basket with a touch of admiration. Then I close the empty trunk and stack it on top of the first.

Now I open the last one. This trunk is made of leather and it's much bigger than the first two. The musty, dusty smell inside is especially pungent. The contents could not be more normal, though. The trunk is filled with clothes: traditional dress, embroidered skirts and blouses, trousers, wool shawls with colourful borders, all devoured by moths, unfortunately. What a shame, I think. The endearing ladies at the Lidingö museum would have loved to showcase these, I'm sure.

I close the trunk and try to push it to one side to make sure there isn't a trapdoor underneath. But it's impossible to shift. I can't move it at all. I try to lift it. But it won't budge. It must be attached to the floor somehow. I open it again and move the old cast-offs out of the way to check that it hasn't been bolted to the floor. But something isn't right. The inside of the trunk looks a lot shallower than its leather shell.

I fumble around in my bag, looking for the tape measure that follows every proper art expert everywhere. Then I measure the inside and outside of the trunk to see if my intuition is correct. As I suspect, this trunk has a false bottom.

The lining is made of a thick, black leather that reminds me of a butcher's apron. I hesitate for a moment before deciding to rip out the staples and carpet nails that hold it in place.

I don't know why I bother looking in my bag, because I already know there isn't anything solid enough in there for me to use. Then, glancing around me, I remember the picnic basket. A silver knife and fork should do the trick. Patiently, I slide the knife between the metal rod and the leather and use the fork to unpick the staples.

Once I've removed about a third of the lining, I stop. My fingertips are red and painful from the effort and I figure I might as well try and pull the rest of the sheet of leather loose. I grab it with both hands, brace myself against the chest and give it one big pull.

Nothing moves.

I try again, harder this time, and now the leather gives way. I instinctively close my eyes at the staccato sound of the staples being ripped out. Then I open them again. I'm holding the lining of the trunk in one hand, except for one bit that's still attached. And I release a scream that empties all the air from my chest.

37

Karl

Emma's sitting in the salon at the manor, on an old teak settle that looks uncomfortable. She's sitting up straight and her expression is just as determined as it was last night, but her face has gone as white as a sheet.

I sit down beside her. 'Would you like us to help you get home? Is there someone you'd like us to call?'

'I need to stop by the café to pick up some things,' she replies without moving a muscle, 'then I'd like to go home, yes.'

'OK. One of our sergeants will accompany you.'

She exhales loudly. 'Thank you, I appreciate it.'

'A psychologist will give you a call tonight to check how you're doing. Will you be alone at home?'

She thinks for a moment, then swallows with difficulty. 'I think so, yes.'

'Will you be all right?'

'I'd rather be on my own.'

She fidgets with the seam of her shirt, then looks up at me.

'Are those bones ... human?'

'Yes.'

She nods her head slowly. 'I suppose this means my assignment at the manor is over,' she sighs. She's still very pale.

'Yes. The Gussmans will have to move out as well, at least until our work at the manor is done.'

'Do you think it might have been another victim – of the killer who went after my sister and that girl?'

'Right now, I have no idea. Examining the body will give us a lot of answers, but not all.'

'Are you going to search the grounds as well?'

'We have a good reason to do that now, yes.'

She stares at me as if she's repeating my answer to herself, either to make sense of it, or to let it sink in.'

'Karl!' It's Alvid calling me from the hallway.

I turn to the man standing guard at the door to the room. 'Would you please take Miss Lindahl home, Sergeant?'

'Of course, Inspector.'

I smile at Emma, who's still sitting there stoically, and walk out to see my friend.

'Paola's here,' Alvid tells me.

I follow him downstairs to the basement, which is illuminated with powerful floodlights.

After pausing at the foot of the stairs to don the regulation coveralls, shoe covers and gloves, we head down the corridor.

'Well, this dressing-up box is charming, isn't it?' Paola quips, leaning over the trunk in her white coveralls.

I say hello to the crime-scene technicians at work around the room and walk over to Paola while Alvid briefs his team.

The skeleton scrunched up in the leather trunk looks like a Halloween decoration. Or a pirate who got trapped inside his own treasure chest.

'I'm not surprised she couldn't move the damn thing. When it decomposed, the corpse literally stuck the leather to the floor. Can you imagine how soupy it must have been in there? Well, it's good we got here when we did. There's nothing left but bones. Lucky us.'

'How long would the ... odorous phase have lasted?'

Paola laughs. 'You can ask "how long did it stink to high hell down here?", you know,' she teases.

She closes the lid of the trunk on the body and shows me a metal disc in the wall, about ten centimetres in diameter.

'That's an air vent – a way for flies to get in. They will have laid their eggs on the body, and then it would have been feasting time for their larvae. Given the temperature in the basement, which must stay cool even in summer, and the size of the trunk, I'd say the body would have taken six months to a year to decompose. And yes, in this confined space, it would have stunk – but not necessarily like something had died down here. Just ... well, you don't want to know.'

I nod.

'When can you give us any information about the victim, do you think?'

'Pretty quickly. I'll get on that tonight. And she didn't touch anything, the woman who found her? Wasn't it her mother who sold strands of her daughter's hair on eBay? Maybe fencing artefacts runs in the family, you never know.'

'No, no, don't worry, she hasn't touched a thing.'

'OK, good.'

'Will you be here a while before you take the body away?'

'I'll be here for a bit, yes. There should be two hundred and six bones, or two hundred and seven if he or she had an extra one in a finger, which does happen sometimes, so that's a heck of a lot of pieces to pick up. But I like jigsaw puzzles, so it's not all bad.'

'What can you tell me at the moment?'

'Besides the fact that shares in the Gussman Group are about to take a dive, not much. Only that the skeleton's been there for a while, like a jack-in-the-box just waiting to pop out.'

'A while?' I repeat, shaking my head. 'Can you be more precise? Ten years. A hundred?'

'More than fifteen.'

'OK.'

'And I get the sense that there's everything I need to give you a full identification, right here in this box.'

'Perfect.'

'And this isn't the body of a child.'

The leather lining of the trunk is lying on the floor like a sheet that's been kicked off the bed during a restless night.

'Well, at least there's that,' I reply, my eyes glued to the smooth surface of the skull.

38
Emma

I step out of the shower, wrap my dressing gown around me and snuggle up on the sofa, where I let my mind wander across the sliver of dark sky my little window looks out on. This couldn't be further from Anneli's living room, above the café, with its sweeping views of the Baltic Sea, so far-reaching you can see the water kissing the sky.

'Here you go,' says Anneli, handing me a hot cup of tea.

I take a cautious sip and the warmth relaxes me in an instant.

Anneli puts her own cup down on the coffee table and sits beside me.

'I already miss the view from Storholmen,' I tell her, letting my head flop back onto the cushion. 'The one you paint in your landscapes.'

'That's not what I paint.' She strokes my cheek and gives me such a sad smile it scares me for a second. 'I paint absence,' she says, as her fingers kiss my ear.

They find their way down my neck, into my damp hair, teasing the stray strands.

She's touching me in silence.

I think about her paintings – the shadows of the forest, that dense, dark green, and the light in the sky barely breaking through the clouds. I think about Lulu's dresses, brimming with the life I can't create for myself.

'I sew, and you paint,' I whisper.

'You find the way forward, and I keep dwelling on the past,' she whispers back.

I find the way forward, I repeat to myself, somewhat unsettled to realise this has never crossed my mind.

I think I'm more resilient than I really am. Maybe I should stop being so hard on myself and ask for help when the burden gets too heavy to bear. I'd better start by learning to ignore the voice inside me that always tells me a call for help is a sign of weakness.

When I went by the café with the sergeant earlier to pick up my things, Anneli was just closing. She could have stayed open for the police but decided to take a bit of time off instead. Without thinking, driven by a sudden urge, or more likely, by the fear of finding myself alone with my toxic thoughts, I asked her to come back to my place with me.

'I lost my sister too,' she admits, breaking my chain of thought. 'Just like you.'

I turn to face her, but she looks away and keeps toying with the damp strands at my neck.

'Oh my God, Anneli…' I take her hand in mine.

I don't ask why she didn't tell me. I know only too well. To keep her pain at bay, to dissociate herself from it, even though it's sticking to her skin. So people won't fawn over her with faux empathy or an unhealthy interest. I kept Sofia's death under wraps too, for as long as I could.

'When?' I ask.

She opens her mouth, then closes it again. Clenches her teeth. 'I can't … I can't talk about it. As soon as I think about her, I fall to pieces. But you … you've eased my pain. The loss is easier to live with when you're by my side. It's like I'm sharing my grief, like you're taking a weight off my shoulders. Because you have the same thing eating away at you from the inside. You're the only person around me who can understand.'

She nestles her head in the hollow of my shoulder. For the first time, I've become her refuge.

'You understand,' she goes on, 'that there's no repairing, no replacing.'

She pauses for a long moment and I think to myself that the

only thing you can do is wait for time to smooth away the edges of the pain. That's it, that's all.

'I wish the memories didn't hurt so much,' she says. 'And it's not even been that long, really. So, when the sadness gets suffocating, I paint. I paint the absence of her.'

I cup her face in my hands and kiss her. Her lips have the salty taste of her tears. We need each other so much.

The sound of my phone jolts us from the moment.

It's Lulu.

'You're not staying at home. It's out of the question.' He can't hide the concern in his voice, even with the music in the background nearly drowning it out. 'Come and see me, Em. I don't want you to be alone. I'm working tonight, so it'll be the middle of the night before I can come to you.'

'I'm with Anneli.'

'Even more reason to come. Both of you. That way I'll get to meet your Anneli and she'll get to meet your Lulu.'

I can just picture him winking at the other end of the line.

I don't say anything.

I look at *my* Anneli. Her chiselled features, her hand stroking my thigh.

'I have absolutely no desire to get dressed up for a night out...'

'Well, just come in your birthday suit then. Natti Natti is probably the only place where no one would bat an eye.'

I smile.

'Come on, Em. I'm wearing your dress, too. It's a sign.'

This time, I laugh. I sew all Lulu's stage dresses.

'Which one?'

'The red diamante. I'm a sexy baby,' he purrs.

I hang up, laughing.

'Did you hear that?' I ask Anneli.

She smiles. 'I'm a sexy baby,' she mimics, getting her wiggle on. And I burst out laughing.

39
Karl

'Good grief, these chia seeds get stuck everywhere, it's intolerable,' Siv complains as she comes into the room beside the interview suite. 'Have I got them all out?' she asks, baring her teeth.

I have a quick look. 'You're all good.'

'I've spent the last ten minutes flossing. If the damned things weren't loaded with omega-threes and sixes, I swear I'd never touch them.'

Siv tips her chin at the two-way mirror.

'Anything to report?'

'Nothing to write home about. Look at him.'

Niklas Gussman is sitting with one leg crossed over the other, hands on his thighs, clenching his jaw. He's leaning slightly towards his lawyer, whose words he's listening to religiously, acknowledging them with minute movements of his head.

'He looks like he's fed up of having his time wasted. Shall we?'

Siv goes first and I follow her into the interview room. Niklas Gussman barely looks up at us. His lawyer gives a brief, artificial smile.

Siv switches on the digital voice recorder and glances at her watch.

'Interview with Niklas Gussman commenced at 8.47 pm in the presence of his legal representative, Mr...?'

'Daniel Hjelm,' his brief replies.

'...in the presence of his legal representative, Mr Daniel Hjelm, Detective Inspector Karl Rosén and myself, Chief Inspector Siv Nord.'

She pauses, leans forward and puts her hands together on the table, as if in prayer.

'As your lawyer has no doubt informed you, Mr Gussman, a body has been found in the basement of your house, in a trunk of old clothes. Do you know the identity of that person?'

'No, of course not.'

'Do you know who that trunk belonged to?'

Niklas Gussman shakes his head.

'For the benefit of the recording, Mr Gussman is shaking his head. Do you know if that trunk had been there for a long time?'

Another silent no.

'Same response from Mr Gussman,' Siv clarifies once more.

'Mr Gussman,' I intervene, 'you do know that this is your home we're talking about, don't you?'

'Listen, Inspector, I moved into the manor only recently. I've barely had a chance to do anything. Managing the group takes up all of my time and we're currently in the midst of a restructuring. I still have my great-grandfather's furniture in my office at the manor. The only thing I've had installed is the Wi-Fi. I've been down to that basement twice since we moved in. The first time was the day we got there almost a year ago, when my wife, my son and I did a tour of the property, and the second was to prepare for the appraisal by Von Dardel's ahead of the manor's centenary—'

He stops abruptly, and we wait for him to elaborate, but he doesn't.

'During these visits to the basement, did you notice the trunks down there?' Siv presses him.

Niklas Gussman puffs his cheeks and exhales slowly. 'I have no specific recollection of that, no. I don't recall noticing anything in particular. Only that there were quite a few things piled up in the open area at the end of the corridor.'

He shakes his head again and stares at the corner of the room.

'I barely remember what's in the other rooms down there. There's an old wine cellar and an electrical room where the fuse boxes are, if my memory serves me well.'

'Did you never spend any time at the manor before you moved

in?' I ask. 'At Christmas, or for birthdays, family celebrations, that sort of thing?'

He sits up and presses his back into his chair. 'Well, of course I did.'

'And in more than forty years, you only went down to the basement ... twice, you say?'

My tone is just as provocative as my words, but Gussman keeps his cool.

'I don't recall the times I played hide-and-seek as a child, Inspector, and I'm sure you don't either.'

'Before you moved in, when had the manor stopped being a permanent residence?'

'It never really was. My great-grandfather used to spend months at a time there, but his principal residence was in Stockholm. When I was a child, we only came in the summer, usually from the midsummer holiday through to the end of July, and sometimes for a few days at Christmas.'

'And the manor was unoccupied for the rest of the year?'

'Yes.'

'And no one would come in and do the cleaning?'

Niklas Gussman frowns almost imperceptibly. 'I don't think so, no. I remember my grandfather used to bring his staff with him for the season, in the summer. The Petterson family would lend a hand with the grounds and some maintenance, I believe – Ove and Björn took over from their father when he died.'

'Who has access to the basement?' Siv asks.

'All the people whose names and contact details you already have: myself, my wife, my son and our housekeeper.'

'Have any keys to the manor ever been lost?'

'Not since we've been living there, no.'

'Have any locks been changed?'

'No.'

'And no one else has the keys, not even the one to the garden gate? A gardener? A cook?'

'Not to my knowledge.'

Siv glances at me and motions for me to take the lead.

'It would be very helpful—' I begin.

'Oh, actually,' Niklas Gussman cuts in, 'Björn Petterson must have a set of keys as well. Yes, I'm sure he does,' he adds, waving a finger in front of his face and shifting in his chair. 'Because he got the manor ready for us when we moved in.'

I avoid looking at Siv so as not to draw the lawyer's attention to the fact that he could use this information to his client's benefit. I simply begin my sentence again:

'It would be very helpful if you could provide us with a list of the occupants of the manor since it was built. For example, if there were any members of the family who spent more time here than others, perhaps some distant cousins or friends of the family.'

'How do you expect my client to know all that?' his lawyer interjects. 'People have been coming and going at the manor for nearly a hundred years,' he adds, smoothing his tie.

'We're not asking your client to conjure up ghosts, just help us flesh out the list of potential suspects.'

Hjelm softens. 'We'll see what we can do.'

'Where were you on the twenty-ninth of December?' asks Siv, changing tack.

This seems to have taken Niklas by surprise.

'What happened on the twenty-ninth of December?' the lawyer asks, extending an arm in front of his client's chest, as much to protect him as to keep him from saying a single word.

'Could you please let your client answer the question, Mr Hjelm?'

The lawyer gives Gussman a quick, irritated nod.

'It depends what time of day you're talking about. I was at home that evening and overnight, because it was during the Christmas holidays, but I might have had some meetings during the day. I don't know. I'll have to check with my assistant.'

'Could you please be a little more precise, Inspector?' the lawyer smirks.

'An individual was seen driving a boat near Rödstuguviken, in Sticklinge, at 2.13 am.'

Hjelm sneers. 'Are you kidding me, Rosén? What connection can there possibly be between the discovery of that girl's body under the ice and the events of today? You might as well try and pin the murder of Olof Palme on my client, while you're at it.'

Siv turns to look at Niklas. 'I'm sure you'll appreciate, Mr Gussman, that this has nothing to do with the assassination of the Swedish prime minister more than thirty years ago. A body was found in the basement of your home. Nine years after a girl was found hanging from a tree on your property. And twenty-seven years after a women died in a fall at the manor. And you, Mr Hjelm,' she turns to him once more, 'will surely understand that we have some questions about this, as misguided and far-fetched as you may think they are.'

Niklas Gussman blinks. His lawyer seems undaunted.

'I fail to see what a fall that happened nearly three decades ago has to do with my client. He wasn't living at the manor at that time. When exactly did this accident happen?'

'In 1994,' I clarify.

'In 1994, I was at boarding school in England,' Gussman volunteers.

'In England? Were you running away from something?'

'As it happens, yes I was, Inspector. I was steering clear of the scandal around the collapse of our group. My father sent me abroad to keep me out of it. The group bounced back quickly enough, but I stayed on to finish my schooling in the UK.'

'Does the name Frigg Bergman mean anything to you?' I go on.

'Not at all, no.'

'Enough with the air of mystery, Inspector. Tell us who this person was, won't you?'

'Frigg Bergman was the thirty-nine-year-old Swedish woman who fell to her death at the manor in 1994. She and her family had lived there just under a year.'

'That was around the time my father lost control of the company and we had to divest ourselves of the property.'

'And so, Mr Gussman, would you please confirm for the record where you were during the night of the twenty-ninth of December?'

'I was at home.'

'Did you hear or see anything strange that night?'

'I have no particular recollection, but nothing in my daily life warrants mention.'

The lawyer looks at his watch with the exaggerated impatience of a B-movie actor.

'Why would you keep your great-grandmother Harriet Gussman's bedroom intact?'

Far from being disarmed by the change of subject, Niklas Gussman relaxes, as if soothed by a fond memory.

'That was my great-grandfather Gustav's wish. More than a wish, in fact. He made it a condition for living in the manor. He had a contract drawn up that all future owners must abide by, to always keep the bedroom of my late great-grandmother as it was. "Until the walls of my castle come down", as he put it. My father used to have flowers put in there, even just for a weekend. My great-grandfather was desperately in love with his wife.'

'Why impose such a precise and restrictive schedule on Emma Lindahl for doing the work you hired her to do?'

His expression darkens and turns to stone.

'So as not to have to deal with the constant presence of a stranger in our home,' he replies curtly.

It looks like I've hit a nerve.

'I very much doubt, Mr Gussman, that you or your advisors would have permitted a stranger, as you call her, to enter your home, no matter how warmly recommended she was by such prestigious institutions as Von Dardel's and Christie's, without first having done your research. But since I don't doubt for a second that you surround yourself with individuals of calibre, I'm certain you knew that Emma Lindahl is the sister of Sofia Axelsson, the girl who was found hanging from a tree on your property in 2012. Am I wrong?'

Niklas squirms in his chair.

His lawyer gives him a discreet nod.

'I was aware of that, yes.' He releases a long sigh. 'But I only found out late in the process, once we'd organised and coordinated the events to celebrate the centenary of the manor this coming October. And by "we", I mean Charlotte von Dardel, the Gussman Group and the Lidingö town hall. I studied with Charlotte at St Andrews, in Scotland, and she knew my wife and I like our peace and quiet. It was unthinkable to allow a team of experts to descend on the manor for weeks. And sending the various collections to the mainland made no sense and would have been rather risky. Indeed, how does one insure treasures without knowing their value? Makes one think of a snake biting its own tail, does it not? Charlotte told me about a brilliant recruit she'd cherry-picked from Christie's, a true prodigy. Young, but scrupulous to the extreme. It only crossed my mind to check her background some weeks before she arrived, on the encouragement of Mr Hjelm, as it happens. That was when we discovered she was the sister of Sofia Axelsson.'

He closes his eyes and releases a breath through his nose, like a bull that's given up on charging and snorting, calming down as rapidly as it saw red.

'I suspected she might have a hidden agenda – that she wanted to investigate her sister's death – so I thought about calling her off. I had no desire for anyone to be poking around left, right and centre. But what reason could I have given? It would have looked suspicious, and people would obviously have wondered if I had something to hide, which is not the case, of course. And who else could we have brought in to replace her? So, Mr Hjelm and I decided to limit her intrusion and control her access to the manor by imposing a schedule, which was admittedly quite restrictive, but would enable us to keep an eye on her.'

Siv and I exchange a glance.

Daniel Hjelm stands and smooths his tie straight. Uninvited, Niklas Gussman does the same.

'Chief Inspector, Inspector, my client has been living in the manor less than a year. He has absolutely no idea of the identity of the person whose body you found in the basement. We have been exceedingly cooperative by answering your questions and we will endeavour to establish the list you have requested. If you have any further requests, please send them my way and we shall do our best to accommodate them. My client and his family will be staying at the Grand Hôtel in Stockholm until you've finished your investigations.'

With this, visibly proud of his final arguments, the lawyer graces us with a subtle, silent nod.

'Duly noted, Mr Hjelm. Thank you both for your time,' Siv smiles. 'In any case, Mr Gussman, you should know that the judge has granted permission to interview your son. His prints are all over the crime scene.'

Niklas shoots a panicked glance at his lawyer, who nods gravely and ushers his client to the way out.

40
Emma

Nestled in the heart of Stockholm, Stureplan is bustling with a crowd that's ready to have a good time – heels braving the snow, hair gelled to the nines, glistening lips just begging to be kissed, legs dancing their way to the bars in anticipation. The square is buzzing like it's a summer's night.

Natti Natti is perched at the top of Danieluska Huset, a towering Renaissance building with all the presence of a chateau in the Loire Valley. It looks like something out of a fairy tale.

Inside, standing heavy in front of a weighty wine-coloured curtain, is a young man with a shaved head, balancing on silver stilettos. Arms rippling with lean dancer's muscles frame his formal waistcoat. I tell him my name, and his official smile softens into one far more genuine.

'Ah, Emma! So *you're* the fairy-fingered seamstress, are you?' He bats his thick, black, sequinned lashes with glee. 'We're all so jealous of Lulu, you simply have no idea. And that dress on New Year's Eve!' He flutters a hand in front of his face and bites his lower lip.

I smile awkwardly, not really knowing how to respond to his compliment.

'He looked like he was wearing a summer sky! You really are quite the artist. Follow me, I'll walk you to your table.'

We leave our coats in the cloakroom in exchange for a golden coin stamped with a number, and as the young man gracefully turns on his heels to pull the curtain aside, I can't help but notice the decorative leather knot on the heel counter of his shoes.

'SJP,' he says, giving me a wink. 'Last autumn's collection. Honey, they're like a pair of slippers!' he gushes.

I doubt Sarah Jessica Parker has ever designed footwear for lounging in, but the spring in this queen's step almost makes me think I'm dreaming as he slaloms between the mahogany tables and midnight-blue velvet armchairs, brushing his fingers oh-so-slightly against their shell-shaped backs. Until we reach a table right in front of the half-moon stage.

'Champagne is on the house,' he says, pulling our chairs out for us. 'Or perhaps you'd prefer something else?'

I look at Anneli, who flashes me a ravenous smile.

'Champagne it is, then!' the young man sparkles and gives us another wink. 'I'll let Lulu know you're here and have those bubbles with you in a heartbeat. Any preference?'

We shake our heads politely.

Looking around, I notice my friend chatting with some clients across the room, corseted in his red sheath dress that makes him look to die for.

He sees me, excuses himself from his groupies and struts his way over to us.

'Oh, how fabulous,' he purrs. 'If it isn't the little black dress squared! You're both ravishing. Delighted to meet you, Anneli. I shan't kiss you, or else we might never tear ourselves apart,' he flutters, exaggerating with his eyelashes. 'I mustn't sit down, either, or it'll take a crane to get me back on these heels. Did you see that, Em, I just had a group of students try to sway me. They'd love me to come to campus in an *L.A. Confidential* dress. I told them I love my three-piece suit far too much for that, and I have no intention of putting my poor feet through any more hell than I already do.' He shows us the stilts he's wearing. 'A few hours in the evening are just peachy, but for anyone to squeeze their feet into these things twenty-four-seven, they must be desperate. Or a total masochist.'

'Does the university know, then?' I'm a bit surprised.

'Didn't I tell you? I saw a couple of my students here one night. They didn't recognise me, but I thought I'd better take the lead and let the chancellor know about my little sideline – professor by day, drag queen by night. You should have seen her face! At first she burst out laughing. She thought I was joking. Then her voice did the whole up-and-down thing when she realised I wasn't. Priceless.'

'What did she say?'

'What *could* she say, in times like these when we defend gender expression like hallowed ground? That a papyrologist who can rattle off the names of all the pharaohs of the thirty-one dynasties faster than he can recite the alphabet has no right to cram his family jewels into a cocktail dress? No, of course not. She just said how *de-light-ful* that was,' he mimics, chanting the syllables with a wave of his hand.

'Gender is a territory, you know,' Anneli speaks up. 'A personal territory. It's sexual, it's carnal. It's all about identity. It's a territory that can take years to understand and embrace. I didn't come out until after a failed marriage. I don't know when you realised who you were, though?'

'Oh, honey, the first time I found myself looking at a mound of Venus I wondered what on earth I was supposed to do with that wilted orchid.'

We all burst out laughing.

The champagne arrives and Lulu raises a glass with us.

'So, what do you think?' he asks, opening the whole room to us with a sweep of his arm. 'Classy, isn't it? Not flashy. Can you believe, Anneli, that Emma has never set foot in here before? She's never wanted to come.'

'You must be joking?' Anneli says in surprise.

'No, she never has. Not before tonight.'

He knocks back a shocking mouthful of champagne, the glass barely touching his lips to save his lipstick.

'So, you're kidnapping my sweet Emma and keeping her on Storholmen forever, are you?'

Anneli laughs. 'Apparently so,' she says, reaching for my hand and interlacing our fingers.

'But what about our French 75s on your balcony?' Lulu makes a show of moping.

'We'll have them on the patio at Ett Glas,' Anneli smiles. 'I promise.'

Lulu looks at her for a second. Then he reaches out to her, takes a stray lock that's escaped from her bun, and sweeps it back behind her ear.

'If you can get her to come back here once in a while, Anneli, then honey, I think we have ourselves a deal.'

41
Karl

I stop on the front steps. I'm exhausted.

The day has taken an unexpected turn. I hope the evening will be a bit more restful, though I doubt it will be.

In the sky, a sliver of moon pierces the clouds like a flash of milky-white leg through a slit in a long black dress. If the wind hadn't picked up, I'd be going out paddling in the dark. But it's whipping up the sea and the swell is rolling too high, even for me.

I have no desire to go inside. I don't want to be in the house Freyja still inhabits, in spite of myself. And yet I find myself opening the door, wondering what I'm going to make for dinner.

The Côtes-du-Rhône bottle is still waiting for me on the kitchen counter. I put it there when Emma paid me that impromptu evening visit and didn't put it away. I pick up the pieces I brought upstairs last night and put them in the bin, mindful of the rest of the shards strewn around the cellar. I'll clean those up now, before I shower and eat.

Reluctantly, I make my way down the stairs, carrying a bowl of hot, soapy water and a bucket. The fatigue, weariness and sadness seem to get heavier with every step.

I unlock the cellar door.

The wine has dried and left a big, dark stain on the waxed concrete floor. Streaks radiate from the centre like rays from a black sun. The glass is sticking to the floor; I'm going to have to use gloves and a brush to clean this mess up.

I head back upstairs to fetch what I need, fill a second bowl with hot water and return to the cellar.

On my knees, I scrub and I rub at the stain until the floor is grey again.

'Right, now that's done,' I say out loud.

I cross the room, replace the full bucket with the empty one I brought down earlier and leave the bowl of soapy water beside the chair.

This time, I have no choice but to look at my wife.

'Don't you ever do that again, Freyja, do you hear me?' I growl, and point to the stain I've just cleaned up.

She doesn't even try to say anything through the gag in her mouth. She sits up on her mattress, places her cuffed hands on her thighs and stares at me defiantly.

She's a far cry from the Freyja I knew. The one who would step into heels to show off the shape of her calves and rouge her lips so you couldn't take your eyes off them. Her dirty hair is caked to her forehead and nose. She reeks. I've only tended to her hygiene twice since she's been locked up down here. And I can't have emptied her bucket more often than that.

'I'm going to give your rope some slack so I can clean you up a bit, all right?'

She lifts her chin and lowers it halfway, interrupting the movement as if changing her mind. She won't give in. She won't say yes.

'If you stay calm, you'll get something to drink and something to eat. Is that clear?'

She hesitates.

But refuses to concede.

She won't surrender. And yet she's thirsty, she's hungry and she must long to feel clean.

Nearly two weeks now, she's been resisting.

After fifteen years in my arms and in my bed, she should know me better. I'm not about to concede, either.

42
Karl

I walk into the morgue carrying a coffee.

Leaning against the autopsy table, Paola's guarding the skeleton we found at the manor with a completely inappropriate look of pride and jubilation on her face.

'You have no idea how happy it makes me to be doing forensic anthropology again,' she tells me as I join her. 'My first love!'

She takes the cup from my hand without taking her eyes off the table.

'*Tack snälla*. Thanks. I'm so tired I can't see straight.'

I daren't tell her I had a bad night's sleep as well. Freyja fought like a wild animal so I had to give up on the sponge-bath plan.

'Did you lose Alvid?' Paola asks.

'He stayed back at the lab. They've got too much to do.'

'He's obsessed – if not possessed – by this case. It's like trying to tear our teenager away from Fortnite.'

She raises the coffee to her lips, then lowers it again.

'For the record, I treated this post mortem independently of the Axelsson and Sjögren cases, to stay impartial – insofar as possible, anyway – and avoid being influenced by them. Before you ask, I have no way of knowing when your victim went into the trunk. It was made in 1908, so it could be a long time ago. I don't have a cause of death for you, either. A nice, big head trauma would have made life easier for us, but not this time. There's no visible trauma to this skeleton.'

Now she does take a sip of coffee, followed by another longer one, and puts the cup down behind her, on the edge of the stainless-steel sink.

'Right, let's start by determining the sex. A mere examination of the skull could be enough with a margin of error less than fifteen percent. Because men literally have bigger heads than women. But because I'm a perfectionist, I also examined the pubis. This is broader in members of the so-called "weaker" sex to allow for childbirth. Bingo! Your bag of bones is female.'

She pauses and gives me a sheepish look.

'Sorry. That was horrible, what I just said. It sounded better in my head.'

She carries on, forcing a smile.

'In childbirth, the pubic bones separate to let babies out and sometimes – *snap!* – the ligaments break and cause bleeding around the bone. When the bones realign, little circular or linear grooves can form on the inner surface. You can see these child-bearing marks here,' she points to some small nicks in the bone with a purple-gloved index finger. 'Which means our skeleton here...' She draws a circle in the air with her fingers, inviting me to finish her sentence.

'...Was a mother.'

'No, Karl. She gave birth vaginally. Believe me, you're not born a mother. You become one. And it takes much more than the act of childbirth. Anyway, on to her age. Now, a part of the hip bone, or the iliac crest to be precise, fuses in a person's early twenties. The collarbone, or clavicle, reaches the peak of its development around the same time, sometime two or three years later. And the very end of the spinal cord, the sacrum, stops growing around the age of thirty. So, once you've established that your skeleton is more than twenty-five to thirty years old, you start looking at the degenerative changes to the bones. It's pretty depressing, when you think about it. At last you become a responsible adult, then everything starts to go downhill. Our evolution is really messed up. Oh crap, where was I?'

'Degenerative markers, you were saying.'

'Ah, yes. To the pubic symphysis here, for example.' Paola

touches a finger to the pelvis at the top of two bones forming a triangle. 'The extremities of the ribs are also a good indicator of age. Their surfaces change over time – anthropologists have tables and moulds to refer to on this. So, with all these tools in my arsenal, I'd say she was in her early forties.'

She turns to pick up her coffee, savours another sip and resumes her explanation.

'As for ancestry – we don't say "race" anymore, thank goodness – we determine this by examining the morphology of the skull. People of European ancestry tend to have narrower faces with sloping eye sockets and prominent nasal bones, with a sharp inferior nasal border and a larger nasal spine, here, here and here.'

I smile at her.

'I'm not finished. Our victim was a metre and sixty-eight centimetres tall.'

'Well, that's precise.'

'Indeed. We use something mathematical called the regression equation – don't ask me why, because you probably couldn't care less. Anyway, we apply this equation to the length of the femur – that's the longest bone in the body – and the length of the tibia, and *ta-da!*' she announces, raising her arms to the sky, 'that gives you a person's height to within a centimetre. Isn't it amazing what you can gather from a bag of ... sorry, a collection of bones?'

'Fabulous. Have you been able to get any DNA?'

'I thought you'd never ask. This victim of yours went by the name of Bernadette Johansson. No, I'm just pulling your leg. I have no idea yet. But I was able to extract DNA from the tooth pulp, so with that and her dental profile, you should have everything you need to ID her soon enough.'

I lean in and plant a kiss on her forehead.

'Paola, you're amazing.'

43
Karl

I walk into Siv's office. It's eerily quiet.

'Where's Arnie?'

'At the vet's,' she replies, tipping some green powder into her hand-held blender. 'For his rheumatism,' she assures me, adding a handful of blueberries before closing the lid.

'Bon appétit.'

'After the kebab and the beers I had on my way home last night, it's a liquid lunch for me.'

'Did your blender get banished from the kitchen, or something?'

She switches it on and holds the lid, shaking as it blends for ten seconds or so, before switching it off again.

'Every time I go into the break room, I get fed up with having to explain what I'm putting in there and with touting the benefits of every superfood under the sun. And if it's not that, then someone's always going on at me about some email I haven't replied to or some paperwork I have to sign so the office can buy some bloody ballpoint pens. If you want to live a quiet life, you have to fly under the radar. So, here I am, camping out with *my* blender in *my* office.'

She unscrews the motor base from the blender, replaces it with a cap, pops off the lid and chugs a mouthful of what looks like molasses.

'I saw Paola's findings came in overnight,' she says with a smile of approval. 'That woman is incredible.'

'I went by the morgue this morning.'

'Now we can only hope that this Jane Doe was reported

missing. That would help us identify her. I've also received the lab report on the video taken by that teenager on Storholmen, er...'

'Otto Andersson.'

'Yes. It's completely unusable. By which I mean, we won't get any leads from it. It shows an individual on a boat in the dark, wearing a dark coat with a hood hiding their face. The colour and the make of the boat are indistinguishable. This person isn't doing anything suspicious per se. We don't see them dumping anything overboard, for example. So there's nothing to prove it's our killer. It could well just be a night owl who likes freezing their tits or balls off. People are strange, you know.'

I lean back in my chair and grip the armrests to resist the urge to scratch my arms. Freyja's claw marks are stinging and itching like mad. I should have taken the time to disinfect them.

'This whole thing is turning into a bit of a shit show,' Siv goes on, wiping her mouth. 'We've got a deadly fall in 1994, a death by hanging in 2012, a body dumped at sea in 2021, and a trunk full of bones that's been there since who knows when. Two forty-somethings and two teens. All four of them female, of course, but still. We're running all over the place.'

I tip my head to one side and pout.

'The manor's the common denominator, of course,' she concedes. 'But not for the girl under the ice.' She takes a long, brown swig of her shake.

'Not to our knowledge.'

'True,' she admits.

'If we give any weight to the theory about sacrificial killings every nine years, our skeleton could well have been there eighteen years – since 2003. That would complete the pattern: 1994 for the fall, 2003 for the trunk, 2012 for Sofia and 2021 for Maria.'

'Well, we can always hope.'

'We could start by trying to figure out why the Gussman kid's prints are all around that trunk.'

'That's going to be fun, with his mum and the lawyer putting up roadblocks. You know what Hjelm's going to say, don't you?'

'That the kid's prints are all over the place because he lives there.'

Siv nods at me. 'Have you spoken to the old gent who looks after the grounds about the keys?' she asks.

'Björn Petterson. Yes, I've asked him to come down to the station. We'll see what—'

I'm interrupted by two sharp raps on the door, which opens immediately.

Siv scowls and looks like she's ready to give whoever dares enter without being invited a stern talking to.

Alvid pokes his head around the door. 'We've got an ID on the skeleton,' he announces in a high voice. 'Viktoria Wallin.'

'Who's that?' I ask, shaking my head.

'A housekeeper who worked at the manor.'

'For the Gussman family?'

'No, for the Bergman family.'

'Bergman?' I repeat. 'As in Frigg Bergman? The woman who fell to her death at the manor in 1994?'

'Yes. Viktoria Wallin worked for Frigg and Kristian Bergman. Her husband, Pontus Wallin, reported her missing in 1994.'

44
Viktoria

I pry *The Poetic Edda* out of Josephine's hands, place a bookmark at the page she was reading when she fell asleep and put the book down on her bedside table.

I stand there for a moment, watching her sleep, missing the times when I used to dream she'd gain weight, sleep through the night, eat her own food and stop wearing nappies. The times when I used to wish she wasn't stuck to me like glue. These days, all I'm good for is the comfort my money gives her. Nothing else seems to connect her to me. I can see it gives her no pleasure to be in my company anymore.

In the space of a few weeks, my daughter has changed dramatically. Her bedroom has become a shrine to Norse mythology. She consumes nothing but Viking rites, at all hours, all the time. This has become an unhealthy, all-consuming obsession. Thor, or 'T', as she calls him, has hypnotised her completely. He's cast a spell on her.

I first tried to steer her away from those stories by reminding her that nowadays, in 1994, no one believes in a world of gods and giants anymore. She finds the idea of a 'saviour' coming back to life and walking on water just as absurd, and frankly, she's right. Tired of my efforts to undermine her, she's just stopped talking to me. She'll say only the bare minimum to me to get through the day. So, I've decided to change tactics and play along. I pretend that she's managed to convert me and tell her I'm interested in the topic – fascinated by it, even. My constant questions have succeeded in defrosting our conversations a little.

But I haven't kept my promise to do everything to save Thor

from his mother's claws. I'm ashamed to say it, but that kid horrifies me. He's brainwashed my child to the extent that she's praying to Odin every night. She's the one who's in danger, not him.

For a few weeks now, I've been pulling out all the stops to find a new job. It's an incredibly difficult thing to do when you're not free to come and go for interviews. It would be easier if I quit my job at the manor first, but that would mean asking Pontus for help so we could have a roof over our heads, because I don't have enough savings to tide us over. To be honest, though, I'm not sure he'd take us in.

I switch off the bedside lamp and carry my cup of tea through to my room. Then, true to habit, I open my window and bask in the cool night air.

The moon is so full, it looks portly. How could I have let Josephine slip so far away from me? Was there something I should have done? Something that would have prevented my opinions, my wisdom, my outlook on life losing all value in her eyes? I also wonder whether I missed something important when we were living with Pontus. Whether something happened – something more than what I'd long suspected. But the man took us both in when we had nowhere else to go. He put a roof over our heads and food on our table. Surely he can't be that bad, can he?

Suddenly, I see a shadow moving across the grounds, carrying a torch. It's Madam, off on one of her mysterious nocturnal expeditions A second beam dances along behind, flashing off her blonde hair. I immediately recognise Thor's slender silhouette.

I close the window and without giving the decision I've just made a second thought, I pull on my coat and shoes and step outside. If I want to know what this abominable Frigg Bergman and her son are up to, it's now or never.

45
Karl

Niklas Gussman's wife, Alice, walks into the interview room preceded by her son, Jens. He's nearly as tall as her, but she's placed both her hands protectively on his shoulders.

Their lawyer, Hjelm, is right behind them, a notepad pinned under his arm and tapping away at his phone. He switches off the device as his clients take a seat and nods to me in greeting.

I sit down in turn, across from Jens.

So as not to intimidate him, Siv and I agreed that I'd conduct the interview alone. She'll be watching from the viewing room.

Jens scans the room as if he's tracking a bird that's trapped and trying to find a way out.

'Hello, Mrs Gussman,' I begin. 'Hello, Jens. I apologise for making you come all the way here. For you, Jens, I imagine it must feel quite daunting to be in a police station, but the gravity of the case we're examining means we have no choice but to take a statement from you. I promise I'll make it quick.'

'Yes, all right, you've made your point,' Hjelm interjects. 'Unless I'm mistaken, you're not the resident shrink from the support unit. Just get on with it, Inspector.'

Mrs Gussman furrows her brow, looking like she'd rather be somewhere else.

'As we agreed, we're going to have a chat with you first, Jens, then I'll talk to your mum.'

'Yes, I know. And I'll go and sit with my dad in the waiting room.'

I nod, watching his body language. The kid's fourteen, but he looks a lot younger. He nods back, and keeps looking at me.

'We've found a skeleton in your basement,' I say. 'That's why it's important for us to talk to everyone who lives at the manor.'

Jens gives his mother a worried glance.

Alice Gussman gives him a tense smile in return.

'My parents told me you found a skeleton in our house. In a trunk. Next to the music bottles.'

'The music bottles?' I ask.

Alice Gussman sits up straight, parts her lips, then changes her mind, places her palms on her thighs and lets her son say what he has to say.

'Yes. You can make music with bottles. Haven't you ever tried it?'

'No,' I admit with a smile.

Alice Gussman's face relaxes and her expression softens.

'You have to fill them up, some a bit more than others. Then you blow across the top, like you're playing panpipes,' Jens explains.

'Ah, I see. And you've played music with these bottles?'

'Of course. But I had to clean them first because they were covered in dust.'

'Do you often go down to the basement?'

Jens tilts his head from side to side. 'It depends.'

I wait a moment for him to elaborate, but he stops there, squinting slightly as if this is a game of chess and it's my turn to move a pawn.

The lawyer sighs dramatically, even though he has no reason to interrupt our conversation right now.

'It depends on what, Jens?' I ask.

The kid hesitates and looks at his mother. She responds with a frown.

'It depends what I hear,' he replies after a short silence.

'My son has an overactive imagination,' Alice Gussman adds, with an awkward laugh.

'What do you mean?' I carry on, undeterred.

'Noises.'

He pauses again, like he's lost his train of thought.

'What kinds of noises, Jens?'

'Noises like...' He puts the fingers of his right hand on the table and starts scratching at the surface with his nails. 'A creaking sound, and some sort of squeaking too. Whispering, as well. And sighs, but big ones, like this.' Jens starts panting.

His mother blushes.

Hjelm's eyes widen.

'So, I went downstairs to see what it was—'

'Jens, I think that's enough,' his mother says sternly. 'Do you remember what your father and I said? The inspector's not interested in that stuff from your video games and science-fiction books,' she adds in a gentler tone, tilting her head at him as if she's talking to a four-year-old. 'You know why we're here.'

'Well, I was scared,' he continues as if he hasn't heard a word she said.

'Jens,' Hjelm growls.

'And then I realised they weren't interested in me,' the kid carries on, regardless.

'Who are you talking about, Jens?'

He shrugs. 'I don't know why. Maybe because I'm a boy.'

His mother reaches for his hand.

He pulls it away from her immediately.

She glances at Hjelm in a panic.

'I know what we said, Mum, but this is important. I have to tell him the truth. He's with the police. He's an inspector.'

Alice Gussman scrunches up her face as if she's about to start crying. But she lowers her eyes, clears her throat and looks at her hands.

'Let's call it a day,' Hjelm decides, standing up.

'And you thought those noises were coming from the basement?' I continue.

'I couldn't tell, so I went down there to see.'

'So, you followed them?'

'Inspector!' the lawyer intervenes, slamming his fist on the table.

'I want to answer!' Jens spits and sputters. 'You can't stop me from answering the question, do you hear me?'

Hjelm sighs deeply.

Alice Gussman clamps her hand over her mouth.

'We always think that monsters come from beneath,' Jens goes on as if we hadn't been interrupted. 'From under the bed, or under the ground. In the beginning, I thought they came through the mirror in Harriet's room. Harriet, she's my great-great-grandmother. That's why I blocked the way. Then, when I saw them coming out from under the ground, I wondered if they had to come through the garden and into the basement before they came through the mirror.'

'Who did you see coming out of the ground?'

'I've seen a few of them.'

'Girls? Boys?'

'I don't know. They had coats with hoods on. And then ... everything gets muddled in my mind. But I recognised one of them. It was the girl who works for Dad.'

I shake my head. 'What girl?'

'The one who's going through the artworks in the house.'

'Emma?'

'That's enough, Inspector. Enough!' Alice Gussman cries.

'But, Mum...'

'Jens, I think the inspector has everything he needs,' she says in a shaky voice, taming her temper.

She smiles and strokes his cheek.

'Now go and find your dad.'

Hjelm gets up.

I know there's no point pushing it. Extricating information from a minor won't get me anywhere in court.

'Thank you, Jens,' I say. 'Your mother's right. I have everything I need.'

I put on my parka, my scarf, my gloves and a hat, ready to brave the cold, and sling my bag over my padded shoulder as I walk out of Ett Glas.

Anneli and I came back from Natti Natti at an indecent hour. Still, in spite of the fatigue crippling my body, I couldn't manage to sleep.

All I could think about was the poor person whose remains I discovered at the manor. Did Sofia's killer put them through hell too? How old were they? Were they dead before they were stuffed into that trunk? Who did they think about when they drew their last breath – their mother, their husband, their child ... their sister?

My phone rings as I'm passing the sauna.

It's Karl. Detective Inspector Rosén.

'Have you identified the victim?' I ask before he's even said hello.

'Yes. She was a thirty-nine-year-old woman who worked at the manor in the 1990s.'

'For the Gussmans?'

'No. At the time, the manor belonged to another family. Her name was Viktoria Wallin,' he adds, anticipating my next question.

'Do you know if she died the same way as Sofia?'

'No, not yet.'

'Do you think it's the same killer?'

'I have no idea, Emma.'

'Did you get the warrant?'

'We should have it by this evening. The search will be under way first thing tomorrow morning.'

'OK,' I reply, deciding not to tell him I'm on my way to the manor right now with every intention to continue where I left off yesterday before my chilling discovery got in the way.

'I have a question, Emma.'

'Go ahead.'

'I'd like to know if you've seen the Gussmans' son, Jens, since you ran into him at the manor, in the room where you found the brush.'

'Yes,' I reply without hesitation.

If he's asking me the question, he already knows the answer.

'I went to gather my thoughts by the tree where Sofia was found.'

'O–K,' he replies. By the way he stretches out the word, he must assume the Gussmans aren't aware of this. 'When was that?'

'Two, three days ago. It was late in the evening,' I add.

'And the Gussman kid was roaming around in the middle of the night ... all by himself, was he?'

'Yes. He was hiding. He said we mustn't make a sound so as not to alert those who come out of the ground.'

Karl doesn't say anything for a moment.

'All right, thanks. How are you feeling?' he eventually asks.

'I'm OK.' It's the answer that will bring the conversation to an end quickest.

'Good. Don't hesitate to call me if you need anything at all.'

I doubt his offer is anything more than a formality, but I thank him and hang up, then start walking faster. I'd like to have two good hours before night falls and complicates my search.

Björn told me the police have left the premises and the Gussmans are at a hotel. That means the coast is clear.

✂

I enter the estate through the French formal garden and walk up through the grounds to the main house. My plan is to start by exploring one of the two outbuildings that are connected to it by a solarium. As far as I can gather, they're often left open. I hope the Gussmans didn't lock them before they left.

I notice Sofia's tree over by the pools and stop in my tracks. All of a sudden, everything starts to make sense.

I was so sure that Gustav Gussman had built the manor over the entrance to Lewenhaupt's bunker. But it's just dawned on me that he likely found another way to conceal the secret passage. That's what Jens Gussman must have meant when he talked about 'those who come out of the ground'. He must have seen someone emerging at ground level, carrying something – probably the body of the girl under the ice.

I'm shaking with fear and anticipation.

Gussman built two types of features in his French formal garden: pools and fountains. That's where I have to look.

I drop my bag, crouch down and pull out the grid I drew. I've been so obsessed with the manor house, so sure the entrance to the bunker was inside, that I only saw what I wanted to see.

Now I'm finally starting to see this chessboard with fresh eyes. The series of squares that Gustav Gussman crossed out form an arc from east to south around an area that looks untouched, like an empty cup.

And that corresponds to the area between the two fountains. A shoulder-height retaining wall covered in ivy runs for four, maybe five metres between the two, connecting this level to the one above. There are two staircases, one on either end, leading up to the second pool.

My heart is pounding as I approach the wall.

If Jens is right, that people do come out of the ground, there must be some sort of door or trapdoor. I get down on my knees and start searching the greenery for a hidden ring or stone that might open something. I search the entire length of the wall, and find nothing.

Next, I go up the staircase on the right and find myself by the upper pool, on a strip of grass between the water and a paved pathway.

From the top down, I search the whole length of the wall once more, pulling aside the stems of ivy, looking for a gap or some loose mortar in the stonework.

And still, I find nothing.

The sun is starting to go down. It'll be a lot harder to keep searching by torchlight. So I decide to move on from this area and take a closer look at the edges of the pools before it gets dark.

It ends up taking me two hours to inspect every inch, on all fours, in the pitch-black, with a torch in my hand.

When I eventually get up, my back is killing me, the knees of my jeans are soaked and my toes and face are numb with cold. I open and close my mouth a few times, jump up and down to get the blood flowing and unfold my map again.

Shining a beam of light on the grid forces me to take a more critical look at it. If this is a game of chess, I'm losing. For now, at least. But no matter how I look at it, I keep reaching the same conclusion as before. The bunker must be here. In the garden. I have to start again.

From the beginning.

I take the staircase on the left side this time, down towards the lower pool, and with a sigh I stand in front of the retaining wall and its curtain of ivy.

'I'm going to find you this time,' I say out loud.

Holding the torch in my right hand, I use my left, like I did before, to lift away the ivy stems, like I'm combing a head of hair one strand at a time.

It's not an easy task with one hand.

I lower my torch and try to balance it on my bag so it shines on the wall and I'll have both hands free. Unsurprisingly, my makeshift solution only works for a few seconds before the torch falls to the ground.

I pick it up again, and I swear as my back protests.

Despite wearing gloves, the cold's setting into my fingers. I jam the torch between my thighs and rub my palms together to warm them up. The beam shines a circle of light on the paving slabs beside the wall.

Suddenly, I narrow my eyes. The low angle of the light is making something stand out on one of the slabs. I walk closer and crouch down. And there it is. A short, narrow groove in the shape of an arc.

My heart lurches into my mouth.

I eyeball the distance between the wall and the mark on the ground. Then I try to picture the trajectory of the door that must have carved that groove in the stone. I look at the wall again and lift aside the curtain of ivy once more. And, practically right at the foot of the staircase, I finally find what I'm looking for. A gap so narrow, it's easy to mistake for a join between the stones. I place my palm over it. I can feel a very slight draught coming from within.

A mix of anxiety and elation takes my breath away and I have to open my mouth wide to get some air.

I place my palms flat against the wall and push with all my might.

Nothing happens.

I shift along the wall a bit and push again.

This time, a section of wall swings to one side and opens.

When I step back into the interview room after making a quick call to Emma, Alice Gussman has not moved an inch. She tugs at the edges of her beige blazer, smooths a shaky hand through her blonde hair and eventually looks up at me.

She opens her mouth and closes it again, like she doesn't know what to say. Then her face contorts with grief and she breaks down in tears, shaking.

I lower my eyes and give her the space to feel her pain, despite the desperate urge I feel to cry as well – to come to terms with the man I've become.

I only look up again once her breathing calms down. I wonder what's taking Daniel Hjelm so long. I thought he'd be back by now.

'He's persuading your boss to sign a confidentiality agreement,' Alice Gussman sniffles, as if I've thought that out loud. 'Welcome to a day in my life, Inspector. It's been like this since Jens was six years old. Shutting my son away in a golden cage my husband built and Hjelm locked up.' She presses her lips together. 'Hiding away my only boy. Disguising what makes him different. So as not to sully the Gussman name. So no one will know his son and heir is a maniac who's good for nothing.'

'What does Jens suffer from?'

'It depends which specialist you ask. Psychosis, schizophrenia, personality disorder, possession, hallucinations, you name it. They all find their own diagnosis and prescribe their own remedy. Olanzapine, diazepam, ziprasidone, brexpiprazole. Sometimes in a cocktail. We don't know. Nobody knows. And we spend ... *I* spend all my time taking my child from one doctor, clinic and therapy session to the next. I have to do it all in silence, having people sign confidentiality agreements wherever I go, under penalty of colossal damages, just to give my husband peace of mind – so he knows that no one will go around saying his son is mad. Or possessed by the devil. Take your pick.'

'What happened when your son was six years old? Did he have some sort of emotional upset? Was there a traumatic event?'

She looks up at the grey wall, as if there's a window there.

'You know, I used to tell myself Jens was just a spoiled child, a bit more temperamental and deceptive than the norm – I was trying to explain his whims, how difficult and angry he could be. But one evening, at the manor, he lashed out at Daniel Hjelm and his wife quite violently. That was just before he turned six.' She shakes her head. 'We were having dessert when suddenly he started screaming at them to take off their masks. He kept repeating it wasn't polite to keep your mask on at the table. I was stunned. We all were.' She clenches her jaw. 'Then he threw himself at Linda, Daniel's wife, and started scratching at her face. He was in a blind rage.' Her lips start trembling. 'Niklas had to march him off to the bathroom and hold him under a cold shower to calm him down. He was like a wild animal.'

She falls silent for a few seconds, and I can almost see a film of the events that evening playing out in her eyes.

'We spent a long time this morning preparing for his interview,' she carries on, smoothing her fingertips across her forehead. 'Daniel sat with him all morning practising for it.' She toys nervously with one of her rings. 'All that to protect the famous family firm. If word gets out that Niklas, the sole heir to the great Gustav Gussman's fortune, has a son who's batshit crazy, investor confidence will tank. That's what my husband says every time I beg him to stop being ashamed of our son.'

She closes her eyes and wipes her nose with the back of her hand.

'If you're wondering why he made Emma Lindahl stick to such a nonsensical schedule, you need look no further. She can only work when we're not there. Still, that didn't stop Jens from crossing paths with her. Me neither, for that matter.'

She pauses.

'I don't know where the line between reality and imagination lies for my son, Inspector, but I believe him when he said he saw Ms Lindahl in the grounds of the property. That's what he meant earlier when he said she "came out of the ground".'

She takes a deep breath.

'This bloody family name. I can't stand it anymore. I can't stand living and hiding behind it. If only you knew...'

Hjelm opens the door to the interview room and freezes when he senses the tension in the air.

'Well, this makes a change, Daniel,' Alice Gussman says as she gets up. 'For once, you've arrived too late.'

48
Karl

I'm about to leave the office. I just gave Siv a quick update before she went to pick Arnold up from the vet's. I'm going to Rinkeby, to the northwest of Stockholm, to pay a visit to Pontus Wallin – the husband of Viktoria Wallin, our 1994 victim. Driving across the city in the middle of the afternoon is going to take forever.

'DI Rosén!'

I turn around. It's the sergeant at the front desk.

'Some guy named Petterson is waiting for you,' she says. 'I put him in room two.'

Bloody hell. I'd completely forgotten about the old guy from Storholmen. I go back the way I just came and walk into the interview room.

Björn Petterson is sitting at the table, spinning an empty paper cup like a top.

'I'm sorry to have kept you waiting so long,' I say as I take off my jacket. 'You must have heard that we've found human remains at the manor, in a trunk in the basement.'

He nods.

'The victim is the housekeeper who worked for Mr and Mrs Bergman in 1994, Viktoria Wallin. Did you know her?'

'The poor soul,' he replies, shaking his head.

'Did you know her well?'

He nods again. 'Our paths crossed a few times.'

'When, exactly?'

'Whenever there was something to fix at the manor.'

'What kinds of things?'

'Blown fuses, water leaks, blocked toilets. All kinds of things.'

'What can you tell me about her?'

Björn Petterson puckers his lips. 'She was quite a ... cheerful woman. A nice person.'

'Conscientious? Trustworthy?'

'Yes, she seemed so. You could see it in her eyes. She had a genuine smile.'

'Did she ever complain to you about the Bergmans?'

'No, not that I recall.'

'Did you ever witness an altercation, or any tension between Viktoria and her employers?'

He frowns, and his bushy eyebrows meet in the middle. 'Just the once. I was oiling the hinges on the doors on the ground floor. I remember because I got a stain on a jumper my wife had just bought me. I heard Frigg Bergman yelling at Viktoria. It made me jump and I knocked the oil over. Frigg didn't see me, but Viktoria did.'

'What was she yelling about?'

He puffs up his cheeks then blows out the air, shaking his head. 'I can't recall.'

'How did Viktoria react?'

'She was frightened. I remember her saying she was sorry a lot.'

'Did she say anything when she saw you?'

He shakes his head again, and closes his eyes this time. 'I don't remember. It was all so long ago.'

'Did the Bergmans ever complain about her?'

'Not to me, and not that I heard.'

'Do you know how the rumours on the island about Frigg Bergman's death started?'

'No, like my wife explained, I've no idea.'

I nod. 'Niklas Gussman told us yesterday that you have a set of keys for the manor.'

'Yes. It's the same set Gustav Gussman gave to my father. The locks at the manor have never been changed.'

'Not even after the Bergmans left, in 1994?'

'No,' he replies, shaking his head. 'They had an alarm installed after Sofia Axelsson was murdered, that's all.' Petterson runs his fingertip around the rim of the paper cup.

'Do you often use those keys?' I ask him.

'Whenever there's something to fix at the manor and the Gussmans aren't there,' he replies, gazing into space. 'I can't begin to think how many times I've used them.'

'But never when the Bergmans owned the place?'

'No, never.'

'I imagine you've been down to the basement before?'

He looks up at me. 'Of course. That's where the boiler and the fuse box are.'

'Did you happen to notice anything out of the ordinary after the Bergmans left? A lock that had been forced? A strange odour?'

'I didn't set foot in the manor for more than a year after they went – the time it took for the Gussmans to get it back. It was a complicated process, that's all I know.'

He puts the cup down slowly, like he's trying to balance it on a tightrope.

'Do you know if Viktoria's husband lived at the manor too?'

'No, I don't think he did.'

'Did you ever meet him?'

'Not very often. Actually, I remember the first time I saw him, I thought he was her brother.'

'Her brother? Why? Did they look alike?'

'Not at all. I just misunderstood the situation.'

'What do you mean?'

'I saw Viktoria giving him some money. The fact that they were married never crossed my mind.'

'In your opinion, could she have stolen that money from the Bergmans?'

'No idea. But I doubt it. Viktoria struck me as a loyal, honest person.'

'What makes you say that?'

He shrugs. 'I don't know. Just the impression I got. A feeling.'

'When did you see Pontus Wallin again after that?'

'I remember bumping into him on the ferry dock. We were waiting for a while because the boat was delayed. I struck up a conversation with him. He wasn't the chatty type. It was a bit like getting blood out of a stone. I remember, because when she got there, Lotta had to wait for the police boat to move out of the way...'

Björn frowns. Then his eyes go as wide as dinner plates.

'That was the day Frigg Bergman died.'

49
Emma

The opening in the wall is about a metre wide and a metre and forty centimetres high.

I make myself take a deep breath to get my head straight, then point my torch into what looks very much like a tunnel carved out of the rock.

A nervous laugh sends shivers through me. Then I feel like I'm on the verge of tears. Lewenhaupt's bunker. It really exists. Gustav Gussman found it, after all.

I jam the torch into my armpit and force my way inside. Now the beam is lighting the whole circumference of a passage just wide and tall enough for me to hunch over and crawl through in my parka. I sling my bag over my shoulder and venture into the depths.

About two metres along the passage, the ceiling gets high enough for me to stand. I straighten up, one hand on my stiff back and the other shining the torch in front of me. The tunnel is comfortably over head height now.

The smell is changing in here too. The fresh, crisp scent of the snow has been replaced by the unpleasant waft of damp earth.

The beam lights the way only a few metres ahead, and there's no way of knowing how far the tunnel goes. I can't see anywhere on the bare walls to put a candle or a torch. Anyone coming through here must have used a headlamp, especially if they had their arms full.

Another shiver runs through me.

The darkness all around suddenly gives me the sense that I'm walking into the lion's den.

I stop for a moment and tell myself that I haven't made it this far only to turn around. If I am walking into the lion's den, at least I'm conscious of it.

And so, on tenterhooks, I keep going. My throat is dry and I'm sweating with fear.

Soon the passage opens into a cavernous room carved out of the rock. Not that I can see a great deal of it, though. There's only so much the beam of the torch can illuminate at once.

With a trembling hand, I sweep the torch from side to side to get a sense of the size of this place. Suddenly, the beam of light lands on a circular metal candleholder, hanging from a chain overhead. And in it I count nine candles with blackened wicks. I notice the space smells different again. Probably because the volume of air in here is greater.

I angle the torch downwards, and two wooden legs fill the beam.

Table legs.

I step backwards to take in more of the scene, but still can't see everything. I sweep the light up the legs to one end of a table top. Deep gouges streak across the wood.

My whole body tenses with horror. I grip the torch so tightly the plastic casing makes a cracking sound. And the echo that makes is terrifying.

50
Karl

The stairwell of the building reeks of urine and deep-fried food, and the chemical odour of insecticide hangs in the corridor that leads to Pontus Wallin's apartment.

I wonder if I've left too much slack in Freyja's rope. And that makes me realise I haven't thought about her at all since lunchtime.

On the way here, I kept pondering what the link could be between Viktoria and the others. Who was the first to die? Who was the original victim? Frigg Bergman? Did she fall ... or was she pushed? Or did Viktoria die first? She doesn't fit the same profile as Sofia and Maria, though. She was older. She was working, and seemed well balanced. I can't see any logical connection between their deaths and those of the two teenagers. What if there were other victims before them? It would be a great help to know whether Viktoria's death was accidental or not.

I knock twice, sharply, on the door that says *WALLIN* in bold capital letters on a white sticker.

A clean-shaven man with close-cropped hair and a cigarillo between his lips opens up.

'Rosén, yeah?' he growls, scratching a forehead creased with wrinkles.

I nod and follow him into a narrow hallway with smoke-yellowed walls. The intolerable stench of stale tobacco is already permeating my hair and clothes.

The hallway opens into an impeccably tidy room with a kitchenette, a shabby black leather sofa made for two and a square, pale wooden table.

Wallin pulls out a chair and invites me to take a seat.

'I can't believe you've found Viktoria,' he says, stubbing out his cigarillo in the ashtray. 'I told the detective – or the inspector, I don't know who – at the time, that she was dead. Everyone was so sure she'd packed up and left me. Turns out to be the opposite, though, if someone packed her up instead, eh?' He breaks into a hearty laugh that soon becomes a coughing fit. His cheeks go hollow, making his already gaunt face look even more skeletal.

'When was the last time you spoke to Viktoria?' I ask, ignoring his sick joke.

'Now that's a question and a half. I haven't got the foggiest. It was nearly thirty years ago, mate.'

'You don't remember the last time you saw your wife?'

He laughs again, and this time his body shakes. 'Too right I don't. Things are getting a bit mixed up in here in my old age, you know,' he says, tapping an index finger to his right temple.

'When you called the police, how long had it been since you last heard from her?'

'Probably a few months, I'd say.'

'You were separated?'

He shifts his torso side to side. 'She went off to be an old-fashioned housekeeper at that castle place on Storholmen. She always worked in luxury hotels, so that's how she got the job. Gave me a break, it did, not to have her here under my feet. Always telling me what to do, when and how, she was. Always moaning 'cos I never brought home enough money. So I said to her: well, if you're not happy, then you know where the front door is, love.'

He whistles and sweeps away the air with his hand.

'And that's what she did. So yeah, we were separated, but we used to help each other out all the same.'

'Meaning?'

He shrugs. 'We weren't mad at each other or anything.'

'Were you in frequent contact?'

'Nah. Not at all.'

'What made you decide to call the police?'

'Well, y'know, whenever I needed something, I could just give her a call, so long as it was during the times she said. I forget when they were exactly, but there were two periods when she had the place to herself, when the people she worked for weren't home. One day, I called and she didn't pick up. So I went over there. I knocked on the door. And no one answered. That was when I knew something was up. Obviously, the cops wouldn't hear a word I had to say. We weren't divorced, but we weren't living together either, and she was a grown adult free to do as she pleased. I reported her missing but they didn't exactly send out a search party.'

'Would you go and visit her on Storholmen, or would she come here?'

Wallin opens a box of cigarillos, jams one between his lips and sparks it up with a lighter he pulls from his shirt pocket.

'No, she never came back here again.'

He blows the smoke upwards, making a grey cloud that disperses in a few seconds.

'Did you often visit her on Storholmen?'

'Only once or twice.'

'For what reason?'

'Well, to see her. To see if she was doing all right.'

'I've been told she gave you money.'

He freezes. His expression darkens. 'Yeah, I'd lost my job and needed a bit of help making ends meet. Who told you that? Was it that daughter of hers?'

'She had a daughter?'

'Yeah, Josephine.'

'Josephine Wallin?'

'No, Magnusson or Magnussen, something like that. That was her dad's name. *Herregud!* She was a difficult one, that kid,' he says, waving a hand in front of his face. 'Even worse than her mother. Viktoria had her with a Danish or a Norwegian guy, I think, and he walked out on the both of them. Then I took 'em under my wing. But Jo was a real pain. She never warmed to me.'

He sticks out his tongue, plucks a piece of tobacco from it, drops it in the ashtray, then wipes his finger on the edge.

'It's because of her that Viktoria left, in the end. No sense tempting fate, is there? First, my wife won't let me touch her,' he lifts a finger. 'Then her daughter comes home with a friend and the two of them prance around the house in front of me wearing next to nothing.' He lifts another. 'After a while, enough is enough. What's a man supposed to do?'

He puts his fingers away, perhaps forgetting what number comes next.

I clench my teeth and count to ten. To stop myself from doing something I'd later regret. Apparently some parents like to take things out on their kids. I prefer to channel that kind of energy into sleazy bastards like this.

'How old was Josephine when she went to live at the manor?'

He twists his mouth into a dubious pout and tilts his head to one side. 'I'd say ... somewhere between fourteen and sixteen. A teenager, y'know.'

'And you don't know what became of her?'

'No idea.'

'When did you last see her?'

'The day when she and her mother packed their bags for Storholmen and shut that door behind them.'

'And you haven't heard from her since?'

'Not a sausage. Not even a postcard. It's not like we used to talk a lot. But even less in the end. And that was all fine by me.'

Frigg Bergman, Viktoria Wallin and now Josephine, Viktoria's daughter. Three women who lived together at the manor in 1994. Two dead, and one disappeared. What the hell happened there on the Bergmans' watch?'

'And you don't know where she might be now?'

'How am I supposed to know? Do I look like a fortune-teller?

Maybe she went off to find her old man in Norway, or wherever. Or maybe she's pushing up the daisies somewhere.'

He takes a drag of his cigarillo and grimaces.

'If you ask me, you should keep on looking around that castle place. Chances are, that kid ended up not far from where her mother did.'

51
Emma

I bend forward, digging my fingers into my knees like claws.

I'm suffocating.

I suck in a breath. It whistles into my lungs, but all I want to do is throw up. Something bangs into my stomach and I shriek. It echoes all around this cavernous place. Then I realise that leaning over, my bag slipped from my shoulder and bumped against me.

I stand up again. I have to see it. I have to muster the courage to look. I have to know.

I'm shaking, and so is the torch. It's making the light dance around creepily and I have to hold it with both hands to keep it still.

I point the beam back to where it was before and force myself to look at the heavy, bloodstained ropes knotted around the legs of the table and coiled on the top.

There's some sort of rim around the tabletop. I move closer and see that it's actually a channel carved into the wood. It leads to a hollow with a small hole at the bottom. Underneath, there's a metal bowl on the floor.

I feel sick to my stomach and bend over double once more. Then I groan and straighten up, spitting and wiping away the saliva that came rushing up.

I sweep the light across to the adjacent wall. It's covered in a spatter of black droplets.

I groan and let the beam of the torch fall to the ground.

I have to breathe calmly. One breath in. One breath out.

I wipe the beads of sweat from my forehead. With that

movement, the torch sends an arc of light streaking across the cavern.

I freeze.

Slowly, I guide the beam back to where I accidentally flashed it.

'No. No no no no no...' I gasp.

I close my eyes to try and unsee what I just saw, and open them again, in spite of myself. It's Sofia. Picture after picture of her face, covered in blood, up on the wall.

The pain comes on sharply. It shoots right through me. Like an arrow. It's killing me.

I bend forward once again and throw up, until the spasms turn to tears.

My legs are about to give out, but I find the strength to stand up and plunge a shaking hand into my bag for my phone. I pull it out, try, and fail, to use facial recognition to unlock it in the dark. I desperately tap in my passcode instead.

Fy fan! For fuck's sake.

There's no signal.

I have to get out of here and call the police. I have to call Karl.

Still crying, I spit out what I can of the bile coating my throat and my tongue. Then I turn around and head back the way I came in.

I have to get out, I keep telling myself with every step.

I have to get out of this place.

52
Viktoria

When I get out into the garden, there's no sign of Madam and Thor. There's no more light, no more whispering – only the dark silence of Storholmen.

I'm walking towards the mound of trees when I hear a creaking noise. I follow the sound. I can't tell exactly where it's coming from, but it must be somewhere near the fountains. Walking down the little staircase to the lower pool, I can see that part of the wall has come away from the rest of it. It's like a door that's been left ajar.

And that door opens into some sort of cave. Or rather, a tunnel, because I can't see the end of it.

I creep into the opening and tiptoe forwards with outstretched arms, feeling my way ahead, touching the walls of the tunnel and the void in front of me. My eyes are just getting used to the darkness, when suddenly I hear Madam's voice. Guided by her chanting, I keep going, towards a weak, flickering light. The outline of a cave begins to take shape. I'm moving in slow motion, not wanting to make a sound, though I doubt Madam would hear me.

I crouch down to get a better look.

The space is illuminated by a circle of candles hanging from the roof. Madam is wearing a long, pale tunic, chanting some kind of a spell as she places some glass jars – like the ones I found in the chest under her bed – around the edge of a wooden table. They're full of something, but I can't tell what. Beside that, on a smaller table, there's a vase with a bouquet of dead branches.

At that moment, Thor enters my field of vision. His mother

comes towards him and starts to undress him. He just stands there like a rag doll while she takes off his jumper, first the right sleeve, then the left, and his undershirt – to reveal a wide bandage.

My stomach is in knots. What *has* this witch done to her son?

She struggles for a moment to unpin the bandage around his torso. Then Thor raises his arms and turns on the spot while his mother unravels the fabric.

As the last few inches of the bandage fall away, I clamp my hands over my mouth to stifle a scream.

Madam pulls Thor's trousers down, then his boxers, to reveal her child's ... vulva.

'Mum, no, please ... Mum, I don't want...'

'That's enough!' Madam barks, before pulling the poor child towards the wooden table.

Thor lies down naked, sobbing silently.

I stand up slowly, still hidden in the shadows at the end of the tunnel, thinking about the bloody boxers I found and the stomach pains Thor was complaining about. That poor child was having a period, I realise.

Repeating her litany, Mrs Bergman opens the first jar and plucks a branch from the vase. She dips the end of the twig in the jar like a paintbrush and taps it rhythmically over her daughter's body.

Streaks of a dark liquid drizzle over the child's pale skin, pearling into teardrops of blood on her legs, breasts, belly and vulva.

'No, Mum, no,' she pleads, her whole body shaking with the cold and her tears.

53
Emma

'Karl, I'm at the manor! You have to come!'

I'm screaming into the night, the phone shaking against my ear.

'I found the place where Sofia was held prisoner. In the bunker under the pools. In the French garden. There's blood everywhere! And photos ... Oh my God, Karl. Oh my God...'

I hiccough. My breath is caught in the bottom of my chest. I can't breathe.

'Where are you?' His cool voice prompts me to calm down.

'In the grounds. At the manor. By the fountains.'

'I'm on my way. I'm coming by boat from Djursholm. Give me a quarter of an hour.'

He hangs up.

I can see that Anneli has been trying to reach me. I'll call her back later.

I keep my phone in my hand, in case Karl tries to reach me. I switch off the torch and bend forwards, searching for the deep breath that won't come.

I should have asked Karl to bring a more powerful torch than mine. But I don't want to call him back. I don't want to slow him down. I just want him to get here.

The cold is becoming intolerable. My feet, my legs, my fingers are frozen. The pain is numbing everything though, so I let it wash over me. I don't want to think. Imagine. Or speculate.

Yet my mind ventures to that place. It ventures deep into that cavern. And onto that table. Sofia must have screamed to be set free. Screaming, pleading, then silently surrendering when she understood there would be no way out of there.

I'm sure she must have thought about me. About the memories we made. Unless nothing of her at all was left, in the end.

✂

At last, I can hear the sound of an engine approaching.

The rumbling quells, then dies, and I can't hear anything.

Two minutes later, a silhouette emerges from the trees. An imposing figure. Karl walks like Lulu. With determination and confidence.

As he approaches the lower pool where I'm standing, he picks up the pace. He's carrying a heavy torch. It must be three times as big as mine.

He looks me up and down for a second, then directs the beam of light towards the entrance to the bunker. The weapon at his waist is sticking out of its holster.

Suddenly I realise the danger I was in. I was inside the lair of Sofia's killer, who's still on the loose. And who killed another girl, maybe even the woman whose body was in that trunk, too.

My heart is pounding.

'Go and see your friend at the café. Is she home?'

I nod.

'I threw up,' I whisper. 'Sorry ... maybe I...'

'It doesn't matter, Emma, don't worry. Go, I don't want you to stay here. I'll come and see you at the café when I'm finished, all right? And don't say a word to anyone. We still don't know who's behind all this.'

I nod but stay rooted to the spot, stunned. I watch him stoop and disappear into the tunnel. Finally, I turn on my heels and head towards Ett Glas.

My body protests every step of the way. If it wasn't so cold, I'd sit down right here, in the middle of the path, because I've completely lost all strength.

✂

When at long last I push the door to the café open, my head is spinning and my heart is in my mouth.

The heat in the room is both soothing and stifling.

'Emma!' Anneli cries, dashing over and wrapping her arms around me. 'What's happened? Where were you?' she asks, stepping back to look me in the eye. 'You had me worried to death. I don't know how many times I called you, and you didn't pick up.'

She draws me into her embrace again.

But I need air.

I need space.

I need a break.

I need silence.

I don't want to talk about what I saw and wish I could forget.

'Sit down,' she says. 'Just sit down, *min älskling.*'

Anneli pulls up a chair; the legs screech across the floor. I collapse onto it. I'm completely drained.

'Good grief, your hands are like blocks of ice and your jeans are soaked. You must be freezing. I'll go and get you a change of clothes and make you some tea.'

She disappears down the corridor and returns a minute later with some dry clothes, then heads for the kitchen.

I take off my wet jeans and socks, put on the clean clothes and sit down again. My legs are shaking. Lost in my thoughts, I don't hear Anneli coming.

'Here you go,' she says, placing a mug of steaming tea on the table.

She puts a hot water bottle on my thighs and sits by my side, not taking her eyes off me.

I reach my hand towards hers and she takes hold of it, kisses it, cradles it. She draws me into her arms and I seek refuge there, snuggling my face into the warmth of her neck until I find solace. At last I heave a shaking, healing sigh.

'What happened, Emma?' she murmurs as I detach myself from her.

She scans me with her eyes, searching for answers.

'I found the place where Sofia was tortured.'

54
Karl

The tunnel opens into a cavernous room where I can finally stand up straight. There's a strong smell of vomit. It's too cold for me to put on a pair of latex gloves. The leather ones I'm already wearing will do the job.

I sweep the beam of my torch around me to get a sense of the space.

The room is circular with a vaulted ceiling. It must be about four metres across. A table stands against the wall to the left, with a bowl on the floor beneath it.

That's where Sofia and Maria were drained of their blood.

I clench my teeth and fend off the thoughts bombarding me, then sweep the light to the wall on the right, where dozens of photos have been pinned up seemingly at random. I walk closer, stepping over a pool of vomit. They're all Polaroids of Sofia and Maria. Close-ups of their terrified, bleeding, sleeping – maybe even dead – faces. Photos of the scissors strung around their necks. Of their big toes lashed together.

I need some air. It was one thing to imagine this horrific place; it's another thing entirely to be standing inside it.

I put the torch down at my feet and suck in a draught of foul air, then another, and suddenly my chest is shaking with an onslaught of dry sobbing.

I stay there, bending forwards with my hands on my thighs, gripping them harder and harder as the pain, the grief and the shame barrel through me.

Families and loved ones of victims always talk about the moment they find out their dearly beloved has died – the triviality of that minute when everything turns upside down.

I'll never forget that minute, either. That moment when my life mirrored those of the people I see every day as a police officer.

The moment when I came home to surprise my wife on our wedding anniversary and found her sitting at her computer with headphones on, watching a video that chilled me to the bone. Freyja was watching herself slicing into Sofia Axelsson's flesh.

Everything – absolutely everything – instantly fell apart. Myself, my life, my career, my future, everything I've ever been sure about. All that remained were the remnants of a reality that had never existed, because I'd only ever lived one half of my story. A cop for nearly three decades, for the past fifteen years I'd been going to bed and waking up beside a monster. I had desired a monster like no other woman. I had loved her to the point of putting her above all else.

I stood there, petrified, unable to say a word, until the Freyja on the screen turned and spoke to the camera, Sofia gagged and fighting for her life in the background.

I broke down and wailed in pain and horror. That was the moment my life ended.

✂

I pick up the torch again, stand up and close my eyes to force myself to breathe as calmly as possible. I have to keep looking around.

Blinking my eyes open again, I can picture Sofia swaying gently from that branch, rocked by the wind. The tree where she was found hanging is only about thirty metres from the entrance to the passage, and the manor's private dock, where I tied up my boat, is two hundred metres away. It would only have taken five minutes to carry Maria's body down to the jetty, judging by her weight. Perhaps just a minute or two if the body was transported on a sledge. It would have been easy enough to slide it down the hill from the garden to the dock. It was snowing on the night of

29 December, so any tracks would have quickly been covered. Then it would only have been a matter of loading the body into the boat and dumping it in the bay at Sticklinge.

Jens Gussman must have witnessed that scene. He must have seen Freyja's accomplice leaving the tunnel through the hidden door between the two pools.

I back up towards the entrance to the cavern and point my torch at the wall in front of me.

Just to my right, the beam illuminates a panel of grey cloth that's suspended from a rod. It blends in with the colour of the rock. I step closer, hand on the butt of my Sig Sauer. Then I use my torch to move the curtain to one side and point my pistol behind it. A pungent smell of decay assaults my nostrils and stings my tongue. I reflexively shake my head, then step into the alcove. A strange series of shadows emerges on the walls.

I look up. On the upper part of the wall, in a recess, I can see mice, gerbils and birds hanging from hooks. There are eight of them in all.

Eight dead animals – the missing pieces my wife and her accomplice needed to complete their nine sacrifices.

55
Emma

The café's doorbell rings.

Anneli jumps. She's still reeling from the shock of what I just told her.

'That must be Karl,' I say, getting up.

She blinks, as if she's just been jolted awake from a dream.

'I'll go,' I add, walking around the side of the sofa.

Anneli nods, then gets up too. 'I'll put some coffee on,' she says as I head downstairs.

The light on the porch showers Karl in a yellow light that makes his grey, tired skin look tanned.

'*Hej*,' I automatically greet him.

He gives me a sad, thin smile and takes off his shoes.

'Come upstairs. Anneli's just putting the coffee on.'

'I can't stay long. I'd like to go home and ... change before my colleagues get to the scene.'

'When will they be here?'

'They told me two and a half, three hours, so that means at least four. You should get some sleep and wait for me to call you.'

'Three hours? That's a bit long, isn't it?' I say as we get to the living room.

'Alvid, who's in charge of the crime-scene team, is on his way to another scene in Täby,' Karl explains as he sits down. 'There's no body here, so we're not a priority.'

Anneli puts a tray with three steaming cups and a pitcher of milk in the middle of the coffee table.

'What are you hoping to glean from the place, besides fingerprints?' I ask, reaching for one of the cups.

'DNA,' Karl replies, helping himself too. 'To determine if your sister and Maria were the only ones held captive in there, or if other victims were as well. Viktoria Wallin, for example.'

He takes a sip of his coffee and his gaze wanders to our reflections in the bay window. His shoulders are hunched, and his thoughts seem to drift out to sea.

'Are you all right?' I ask him.

He turns to face me, surprised by my concern.

'I was so sorry to hear about your wife,' I add. 'Perhaps you should just stay home when you get there and let someone else take over?'

'Our sincerest condolences, Inspector, for losing Freyja,' Anneli interjects, placing her hand on mine briefly.

He gives us a weary smile. 'When I told you I'd stop by, the idea was for me to check how you're doing, not the other way round.'

He gets up, unfolding his full height so it towers over us.

'I'll be on my way. Do you mind if I use the bathroom before I leave?'

'Of course not,' Anneli replies. 'It's at the end of the hallway, third door on your right.'

I watch Karl walk away, thinking about the day I met him. He was so certain he could climb the mountains in his way instead of skirting around them. I could see the fire in his eyes. But now that fire's gone out. He seems detached from everything. Unless he's just become tired and weary now that we're seeing the light at the end of the tunnel, so to speak. He reminds me of the colossus with feet of clay in the King of Babylon's premonitory dream – a fragile giant ready to collapse at any moment.

I turn and look out of the bay window.

The night is as dense, and the sea is as black, as a piece of coal.

I wonder what Karl is feeling and what it's like to lose a partner. Love is everlasting in the void, as is grief, but the absence of the other weighs so heavy on everyday things. The life you wove, sewed and mended over the years you shared dies as well. All that's left in the end is half of everything.

'*Hej*,' Anneli whispers, touching my thigh. 'Are you OK?'

My gaze slides from the dark sky to her eyes. 'I thou—'

I stop, leaving the words hanging from the tip of my tongue.

Karl is standing in the hallway. Pointing his gun at us.

'Show me your hands,' he barks. 'Both of you. Hands up.'

I'm speechless. Well, almost.

'Bloody hell, Karl! What's got into you?'

'Hands in the air, where I can see them,' he insists, and he means it.

Anneli slowly raises her hands to her head.

I do the same.

'Now listen to me. And do as I say. If you don't, and if either of you tries anything, you'll get a bullet in the head. Is that understood?'

We nod silently.

'Get up. Keep your hands in the air.'

'Karl, what the hell are you doing?'

'On your feet, Emma.'

We do as he says.

'Where are your coats?'

'Downstairs,' I reply. 'By the café entrance.'

He glances at our phones on the coffee table.

'Right. My gun is pointing at Anneli's head, Emma. If you try anything at all, I pull the trigger.'

Judging by the way he's holding his weapon, he means it. My heart is racing like I'm running away from something. And that's exactly what I wish I could do right now.

'Down you go, then. Emma, you first. Slowly.'

I walk down the stairs ahead of Anneli.

'Now Emma, I want you to get Anneli's coat and put it on her, one arm first, then the other.'

I grab Anneli's parka from the coat rack and do as Karl says.

'Keep your hands in the air,' he insists when she doesn't raise them again. 'Now it's your turn, Anneli. You help Emma with her coat.'

She bundles me up and looks at me as if she's expecting me to say something, but I don't see what I could possibly do or say with a gun pointed at us.

'Now put your shoes on. We're going to the manor. Emma, you're going to walk in front. Same rule again: you speak, you scream, you try anything on with me, it's a bullet to the head.'

I moisten my lips. It feels like I'm running my tongue over thorns.

'You're going to walk us to the French garden.'

Oh, my God. Is he going to shut us up in the bunker and block the way out?

'Pull up your hoods. Now out you go,' he barks. 'You lead the way, Emma.'

With a trembling hand, I open the door and follow the path I've taken dozens of times. I know we won't bump into anyone at this time of night. I've barely seen a soul here during the daytime. Even if we did, I'd never dare try anything.

Anneli doesn't say a word. All I can hear is the sound of our boots creaking in the cold.

I enter the grounds through the side gate.

'Now walk across the garden,' Karl commands.

But when we draw near the entrance of the tunnel, he adds: 'Keep going. Down to the jetty.'

I turn to look at him, wondering if I've misunderstood. Anneli's eyes are glued to her feet as they crunch through the snow.

'Keep looking ahead.'

I do as I'm told and head down the slope I saw him walking up earlier this evening.

There's only one boat by the jetty, and that's Karl's.

'Show me your hands. Again, it's the same rule as before,' he warns us, pulling a pair of handcuffs from his pocket. He slaps one of the cuffs on my right hand and the other on Anneli's, then takes her by the arm and helps her aboard.

He sits us down, one facing the other.

Anneli gives me a desperate look.

I try to read Karl's expression, but he won't look at me.

'Needless to say, if you get any ideas about jumping overboard, you're going to have a hard time swimming with those cuffs on,' he growls and starts the boat's engine.

56
Viktoria

I emerge from the tunnel, draw a deep breath of air that stings my throat, and run back to the house, troubled by the images of Thor that are streaming through my mind – those delicate features, that willowy figure, the gentleness of her ways with Josephine.

Herregud... Does my sweet Jo have any idea that Thor's really a girl?

Oh. My. God.

I have to catch my breath and wrap my head around this. I need to figure out what to do.

Should I call the police? Talk to the Duke? Or is it enough for us to just leave this house and this island? Should I go and wake up Jo so we can leave right now? Or do I give notice and pretend I haven't seen anything?

The woman is out of her mind. That child. That poor child.

If I call the police, will they even believe me? It'll be my word against hers. Me, the housekeeper, against her, the heiress. Thor is suffering, and she's completely at Madam's mercy. If no one believes me and I get fired, what will happen to the child? I can't just leave that woman to inflict her wicked ways on her. I can't do that.

No, I need proof.

Suddenly, I remember the notebook Madam keeps in her chest, under her bed, with those glass jars. There must be a reason why she tucks it away there. Perhaps she hasn't taken it with her into her secret bunker. Maybe it's her diary. Photos would be solid proof of what she's putting her daughter through.

I enter the manor through the veranda on the side.

The lights are out in Mr Bergman's study. He must have gone up to bed. I doubt he'll be trying to find his wife at this time of night, but if I bump into him, I'll just tell him what a monster she is.

I tiptoe up the stairs, thinking about Thor's body turning red earlier. If that really was blood, where did her crazy mother get it from? And whose blood was it?

I open the door to Madam's room. My heart is on fire, and it doesn't know which way to run. I have no idea where to even start looking, I realise, as I shut the door behind me. Or what I'm looking for. Besides the notebook, of course.

I switch on the bedside lamp and draw the curtains. Even if I do get caught, I'm not exactly planning to spend the rest of my life here, with this family.

I decide to start with the trunks. After the almighty dressing-down she gave me, Madam must have moved her papers, but you never know.

One by one, I open them. They're all empty.

I lift the mattress and inspect the boxspring, then crouch down and check the bedside tables. Nothing.

Surely Madam must keep her diary somewhere accessible. She's caught me on all fours, rummaging through her things before, so she probably doesn't suspect I'll do it again. As for the Duke, he isn't the type to go sniffing around.

I stand up again and move over to the chest of drawers. If there's nothing in there, I'll try the two wardrobes. I go through the drawers, through Madam's underwear and linens, when at last I find the leather-bound notebook I've been looking for – it's between some blouses.

I sit down on the floor, by the bedside lamp, to read it.

The cover is stamped with the initials *GG*. It didn't really jump out at me first, because everything in the manor house is engraved with *GG* and *HG*. Gustav and Harriet Gussman marked their territory all over the place. Their initials are on everything from the silverware to the door handles. Perhaps it was a sign of nobility or a way of asserting their caste. How should I know?

The pages are crammed with lines of narrow handwriting in blue ink. There are two hundred and six of them, all numbered by hand. I start by reading the first few lines of page one.

> *All great destinies and accomplishments are born from tireless work and determination.*
> *My manor is no different. It is the offspring of perseverance and a love of history.*
> *It is the proof that no pursuit is impossible, if one allows oneself the time and the means.*
> *Gustav Gussman*
> *Storholmen, 16 January 1922*

Madam must have found this journal among the belongings the previous owners left behind. But why hide it?

Suddenly, I hear the front door slamming shut.

Fan. Oh, hell.

A few seconds later, there's a swishing of light steps on the stairs. The sound stops abruptly. Silence. Then a gasp of surprise and the frightful crash of something falling, followed by screams of pain.

A brief moan – and then nothing.

57
Karl

I'm about to open the cellar door at home.

I know what's going to happen. There's no doubt in my mind anymore.

I uncuff the two of them. Emma is standing bolt upright. Rooted to the spot.

I unlock the door and send Anneli down there first.

She squeals with joy. And Freyja does the same.

Tears stream down their faces as they're reunited. I let Anneli throw herself into my wife's arms.

Freyja blissfully closes her eyes and runs her fingers through the hair of this woman whose path I've crossed on Storholmen time after time, without ever really looking at her. She served me coffee the day of Sofia's death, and Maria's too. And now again, just this evening, with the same hands that carved into the flesh of those children to drain them of their blood.

Emma's still standing there mesmerised, blinking without comprehending what's unfolding in front of her.

At Anneli's, I went to the bathroom with the uneasy feeling that I'd missed something. Something I'd filed away and hadn't yet got around to analysing. I washed my hands and splashed some water on my face. Then when I was looking for a towel, I noticed a little frame on the wall, in an alcove. A painting of a mountain and a woman, truncated along the right edge.

For a few seconds, I stood there in shock. The painting is the other half of the canvas that sits on Freyja's bedside table. My wife's painting starts where that one ends. It's the other half of the mountain and the woman. The second part of a diptych.

Suddenly, everything was clear and I realised what I'd missed. When Anneli expressed her condolences earlier, she didn't say 'your wife' or 'your partner'. She said Freyja's name, as if she knew her.

I thought, or rather I hoped, there was a man in this horrifying equation. A man who manipulated my wife, perverted her, preying on her weaknesses to turn her into a monster.

But the missing part of that equation was a woman: Anneli Lund.

58
Viktoria

I've added two boxes, the trunks that were under Madam's bed and a blue porcelain bowl to the list of objects I need to ask Mr Bergman about. I need to know if they belong to the family or if they were part of the collection at the manor.

I tuck my notepad and my pencil into the pocket of my apron, and I keep going through Madam's room.

I'm helping the Duke put the house in order before he goes. He and his daughter are leaving the country and moving to Switzerland, far away from the traumatic events that have happened here – especially the hateful rumours going around that he pushed his wife on purpose. I don't believe it for a second. The poor man is in pieces. He's asked me not to add to the drama of his wife's sudden death, and not to say anything to the police about what Freyja was subjected to. Because that's their daughter's name: Freyja. I'll have learned some things from this whole experience, if nothing else.

From what he discreetly explained, I gather that Frigg Bergman fell into a deep depression two years ago, when Freyja 'became a woman'. After that, he noticed his daughter was looking and dressing in a more masculine way, and he figured she was exploring her adolescent identity – not knowing that his wife was orchestrating the transformation. Transitioning from the goddess of love to the god of all gods, Freyja suddenly asked her father to start calling her Thor. As she put it, 'only men are truly the masters of destiny'. That's the nonsense he told me about.

The Duke bought the manor in the hope of giving his family a fresh start. Unfortunately, his frequent absences gave his lunatic of a wife free rein so she completely lost touch with reality.

So, I've said nothing to the police. What's the point? Frigg is dead and her daughter is going to Switzerland for a new start, with her father's family.

I pick up the three tarnished silver brushes from Harriet Gussman's old bedroom and go downstairs. I've been meaning to give these a polish for a while. They look like they're covered in soot.

I can't use the central staircase anymore. Not since I saw Madam's twisted body sprawled on the bottom four steps, in a position that had nothing human about it. Her knee was touching her hip, and one of her arms was bent back on itself. Her neck was twisted so far, you could see the sticky mess of hair and blood at the back of her skull.

When I heard her dreadful fall that night, I ran out of the room where I'd been hiding and, without thinking, went straight to the top of the stairs, forgetting that I wasn't supposed to be up on that floor in the middle of the night. I leaned over the balustrade and saw the Duke crouched next to his wife's body. Freyja was sitting hunched on the floor alongside, staring at her mother with empty eyes.

Thank goodness Josephine was asleep in our apartment in the other wing of the manor, because this was the kind of sight you can never unsee.

I called an ambulance right away. The police weren't far behind. They concluded that Madam had tripped and fallen to her death.

It's horrible to say, but since she died, the atmosphere at the manor has been lighter. The weighted blanket that used to smother everything has been lifted.

I walk down the corridor and head straight for the basement.

To the nook in the big room at the end, where I keep the big basin I use to give things a good soak and a scrub. I tip a cupful of bicarbonate of sofa into the basin from the big eight-kilo box Björn brought me. I keep that down here too so it won't clutter the back kitchen.

'Mum!' Josephine tears down the stairs, calling my name.

She's holding Gustav Gussman's leather notebook and gasping for breath as she runs up to me.

'I can't find my silk scarf. The one Freyja bought for me.'

'I washed it,' I reply, adding some apple cider vinegar to the basin. 'I laid it flat to dry on the windowsill in my room. What are you doing?'

'I'm helping Freyja sort through her things.'

'That has to stay here,' I say, pointing to the notebook.

'Freyja wants to keep it.'

'She can't keep it, *älskling*, it belongs at the manor. It's part of the manor's history. She has to leave it here.'

'But she's the one who found it. It was hidden behind a shelf of old books at the top of the bookcase in the big study. Pretty cool, isn't it?'

'Very cool,' I reply, watching the bicarbonate of soda frothing with the vinegar, before gently placing the brushes into the basin.

'She wouldn't have found the secret tunnel without this notebook. Old Gustav wrote about his searches in here, and all kinds of things.'

I nod and reach for the old toothbrush I leave in my cleaning box.

My daughter suddenly changes the subject completely: 'Freyja's dad called. He said he'd be back in just over a week.'

'Yes, that's the plan.'

'Freyja and her dad have invited me to go to Switzerland with them.'

'Now's really not the best time, *älskling*,' I reply, gently brushing the silver. 'We'll move back to Stockholm and let them get settled. Then you can go and see Freyja during the holidays, all right?'

'No, I meant they've invited me to go and live with them there, in Switzerland.'

I look up at my daughter. 'What?' I ask, as if her words weren't clear enough. 'But *älskling*, our life is here, in Sweden.'

'I'm not talking about you, Mum, I'm talking about me.'

'Do you really think I'm going to let you move abroad with a couple of strangers, Jo, at your age?'

'They're not strangers.'

'It's up to me, your mother, to raise you. And believe me, I still have my work cut out.'

'But I don't want to be apart from Freyja.'

'I understand, *min hjärta*. I know, sweetheart.'

'Can you imagine the life I could have with the Bergmans?' she argues. 'You could never give me that kind of education.'

'Jo, that's enough,' I tell her, still brushing away at the silver. 'You're right, I could never give you the life Mr Bergman gives his daughter. We're not cut from the same cloth, them and us. That's just the way it is. Not everyone is born with a silver spoon in their mouth.'

'So, what's my future supposed to look like, then?' She starts crying. 'You don't expect me to spend my life cleaning up other people's shit like you, do you?'

She shoves the basin and knocks it over, covering the floor in a white, frothy paste and sending the brushes flying. There's a clink as the casing of one of them cracks.

'I don't want to end up like you, eating out of rich people's hands,' she goes on. She's out of her mind. 'Do you really think that's what I dream of doing with my life?'

'Josephine, that's enough!' I hear myself shouting. 'Have you gone mad? What's got into you? You do not speak to me like that, do you hear me? I'm your mother, for heaven's sake. Show me some respect. Eating out of rich people's hands is what I have to do to put food on your plate, I'll have you know!'

Freyja appears in the corridor.

My daughter turns to her in an instant.

'She won't let me,' she tells Freyja. Her voice is now as calm as can be.

I look at my daughter and suddenly I know that our bond has

broken. That child, Freyja, has made it vanish into thin air. I feel sick to my stomach. And scared.

'I told you she wouldn't,' Freyja coolly replies, looking me up and down with an arrogance that only fuels my anger and my anguish. 'She wants to control you. She doesn't want you to become somebody. She doesn't want you to do better than her. Can't you see? She's jealous of you.'

'What the hell, Freyja? You watch your language,' I fume.

'Do you want to end up like her?' Freyja goes on.

'That's enough!' I put my foot down. 'Just stop it, both of you. Josephine, go to your room.'

My daughter doesn't budge. She doesn't take her eyes off Freyja. She seems to be waiting for a signal or an order.

'Josephine, did you hear me? Go to your room. Now!'

'How about you, Viktoria, do you want to end up like her as well?'

I shake my head, not comprehending what this hateful child is saying to me.

'Do you want to end up like my mother, Viktoria?'

Her words both incense me and chill me to the bone.

'Surely you don't think she fell down the stairs all by herself, do you?'

59
Emma

Anneli throws herself into the arms of a woman who's tied up like an animal. They're melting into one another, locked in an embrace as if they were the only ones here.

Karl puts his weapon back in its holster without a word. His lips are quivering. He's holding back his tears. Or his anger, I don't know.

Anneli cups the woman's face in her hands and kisses her forehead. It's a long, tender kiss. The kiss of two soul mates reunited. The woman smiles with ease and pleasure.

'I gave them Maria,' Anneli whispers. 'I put her out there on the ninth day, in the bay, across from Djursholm, where the sea had taken you away, just across from your home.'

I step back, my mouth agape, gasping for the air that won't come. I feel like I've been punched in the stomach.

'I offered them her body so that yours would come back to me. I had to say goodbye to you,' Anneli goes on, clearly enamoured with this woman. 'Never, never did I think that ... you'd be here ... that you were alive. Oh, my sweet Freyja.'

Karl places a hand on my shoulder.

'That's my wife,' he barely whispers.

I turn to him, but he can't tear himself away from the sight of his prisoner and Anneli. Their bodies still entwined. The indecent intimacy of their embrace.

Are monsters really capable of love?

'This is my sister,' Anneli suddenly looks up and tells me, her face glowing with an ecstatic smile. 'See, she's not dead after all.'

60
Viktoria

I need to send a message in a bottle.

To let someone know I'm here. To let someone know they've tied me up.

I've started writing an SOS on a page of my notepad, but I have to do something with it. I have to find somewhere to put it. I'm afraid Freyja or Josephine might get their hands on it.

In the position I'm in, with my wrists bound together, I end up practically poking holes through the paper as I'm writing. I don't have much time so I've kept it as simple as I can:

HELP ME I'M TRAPPED.

I have to hide the piece of paper and the pencil in my pocket every time Freyja or Josephine comes down to ask me the same question, time after time.

I start crying again. In fear, and from the cold, but most of all with a sadness so deep it pains my heart. It stings my skin and makes my muscles ache.

I need to send a message in a bottle.

I look around me to see what I can reach. The only things that jump out at me aren't things that might travel: crates of empty bottles, a gramophone, some old carpets, the box of bicarbonate of soda and the basin, which I now have to use to do my business. But then the brushes come to mind. Josephine picked up the two that were intact and took them away. But where's the other one? The one with the casing that broke when she shoved the basin to the floor? I get down on all fours and lower my face to the floor. Maybe it's slid below the sink. I spot the part that broke off, poking out from beneath a crate of glass milk bottles. I slide my hand under there, stretching my fingers as far as the rope around my wrists will let me. Eventually I manage to reach it with my middle finger and bring it close enough to pick up.

Now I need to find the rest of the brush. I scour the floor, trying to remember what colour the bristles are, when I see it at last, over by the pile of carpets. I lie down and manage to bring it towards me with my foot.

This is my message in a bottle. It's my only chance.

I don't see where else I could put my call for help. It's this, or nothing.

I'm going to put my name on there, where I am and today's date. You never know. Then I'll squeeze my piece of paper inside the brush and snap the casing back into place.

But how can I make sure the brush makes it out of the cellar so someone will find it? So that it falls and breaks open again? It won't take much of an impact to do that, but no one will think to pry it open otherwise.

I could try and get closer to Björn's toolbox. Then kick the brush towards it so it's just alongside. That's how we let him know something needs repairing. We put it by his toolbox.

Suddenly, I hear the door to the basement opening at the top of the stairs.

I only have a second. There's no more time to think. I slide my SOS message into the brush, snap the casing back into place and tuck it all out of sight behind me.

As Josephine comes down the corridor, I realise I've made the wrong choice. I have to finish my message. If Björn comes to fix something, what will they do with me? Where will they hold me prisoner?

'I came to see if you'd changed your mind,' my daughter stands in front of me and says.

I beckon for her to come closer.

All I want is to hold her in my arms, for her to reconnect with me.

'Mum, let me go with Freyja,' she persists, cocking her head to one side.

Is that a hint of softening I see in her eyes?

'No, sweetheart, you know I can't. Just come here, will you? Please.'

Her body moves towards me ever so slightly.

'I'm your mother, *min hjärta*. You're my daughter. I carried you right here, in my belly. I've seen you grow up and blossom like a flower. My sweet, sweet Jo.'

'I don't want you to call me Jo anymore. It's Anneli now. Josephine comes from Joseph. I'm fed up with women having to follow in the footsteps of men. Because it's really the other way around. They're the ones who come from us.'

'Anneli? All right. All right, my love.'

'She won't let you go, Anneli,' Freyja calls from the end of the corridor.

She walks towards us slowly, like she wants to draw out the pleasure.

'Just look at my mother: she held me prisoner. If I hadn't pushed her, she'd never have stopped.'

She positions herself between me and my daughter and grasps Josephine's chin between her fingers and thumb.

'Listen to me. When Dad gets back, we'll tell him she just walked out on you. She abandoned you.'

'No, Josephine, no!' I cry, trying to drown out the sound of Freyja's words, the ideas she's putting in my daughter's head, her wicked plan. 'I'll never abandon you Jo, never. Do you hear me? You're the flesh of my flesh,' I tell her. I'm pounding my chest with my fists as the tears stream down my cheeks.

'She's already abandoned you,' Freyja shrugs. 'She wasn't there to keep that disgusting pig's hands off you. And she still gives him money, can you imagine? It's like she's paying him for hurting you.'

'No, nooo,' I sob. 'I'm your mother. I love you. I want to take care of you. Can't you see?'

But my daughter only has eyes and ears for Freyja.

'What kind of life do you want to lead, Anneli? Do you want to go back to living in a dingy apartment and have another one of your mum's lovers touching you up as soon as she turns her back? Or do you want to come and live in Switzerland with Dad and me? He even said he could be your legal guardian.'

I rush forwards and start screaming for help.

But I know no one can hear me. There's no one else in the manor.

Freyja suddenly comes towards me, and I instinctively raise my hands in front of my face to protect myself. But she's seen the brush now, and she grabs it.

'That belongs in the room with the four-poster bed, doesn't it?' she asks my daughter.

Josephine nods absently. She looks like she's miles away. I seize my chance to get through to her.

'Jo, *min älskling*, just untie me, will you? Please, darling, we'll talk about it. We'll find a solution that makes you happy, all right?'

'Anneli, look at me,' Freyja insists. 'She won't protect you the way I'll protect you. I'm your sister. You know that. We've been sisters for thousands of years. I would never have had the courage to break free from my mother if you hadn't come into my life. Now it's my turn to help you find your freedom.'

'Jo! Josephine!' I gasp. I'm begging her now.

'Are you ready?' Freyja continues.

My daughter nods silently. She locks eyes with me.

And I look at her. I look into her eyes to see inside her, the way I have every day since she was born. I'm looking for her love, and mine. I'm looking for the life we created together, the weight of the years, of my presence. I'm looking for everything I thought I'd built. And I realise there's nothing left.

I'm petrified.

'Hold her feet,' Freyja commands.

I begin to shake uncontrollably. I cling to the hope that when my daughter touches my skin, she'll remember her motherland, she'll come to her senses.

But she does it without batting an eye.

And I scream in desperation.

My cry releases all the sadness and the unbearable pain she's provoked.

She's my child. My. Child.

Freyja creeps up behind me and I hear an unpleasant ripping sound. Then she pulls something cold over my head.

Helvete. It's a bag.

And that's the sound of duct tape being ripped off the roll.

The smell of it sticks to the back of my throat.

I try to lift my hands to my face, but someone stops me. It's Josephine. It's her hand. I know it from the texture.

With every panicked in-breath, I suck some of the bag into my mouth.

'Take it ... off ... can't ... brea...'

So I cling to my daughter's hand.

And I think of nothing else.

But the softness of her skin. Just her hand in mine. Our fingers intertwined.

61
Emma

Anneli turns away from me.

I look at her fingers, intertwined with Freyja's filthy nails.

I picture them caked with black, dried blood.

I see them slipping the noose around Sofia's neck. Then I feel them clasping mine, in front of the tree where she hanged my sister.

I feel her cool hand on the warmth between my legs.

I feel her skin when we wake, and I sense Sofia's, forever filled with sunshine.

Then I see her fingers digging into my sister's flesh.

I see her taking those photos. Pulling them out of the Polaroid slot. Shaking them so Sofia's face appears, twisted with pain, then sticking them up on the wall of their cave like holiday snapshots.

I see her fingers painting, spattered with blue and green – then spattered with blood.

I hear the music of her words, of her love, then the silence inflicted on Sofia.

Then suddenly, I launch myself at them, screaming with a rage that rises up from my belly. I lash out at their hands, their forearms, their shoulders. I don't give them a chance to fight back. I just keep balling my fists and laying into them. Their shrieks of pain jolt through me, charging me up, and I wail right back at them with my mouth wide open. Then my fist stops in mid-flight as Karl scoops his arm around my waist and yanks me back.

I shout and I struggle, kick my feet every which way, but he doesn't loosen his grip.

Then in the space of a second, as if someone has flipped a

switch, my rage melts into an immense flood of grief, and I'm submerged. I feel like I'm just letting myself sink, like I've given up fighting to keep my head above the surface.

But Karl keeps me from going under. And he holds me tight as I break down and cry, like a marionette with my strings cut.

62
Karl

1 October 2022

I woke up this morning with a raging urge to go out to sea. I downed a coffee, then got into my kayak to watch the sun rise. I paddled to the dock at Mor Anna, in Lidingö, watching the forest blushing with autumn kisses. I changed my clothes at the little terminal and now I'm waiting for the route 80 sea bus, sipping my second coffee and savouring the cinnamony goodness of a fresh, warm *kanelbulle*.

Lotta ties the boat up at the dock and waves.

'*Hej*, if it isn't Detective Inspector Rosén himself!'

I step onto the gangway and she opens her arms wide to draw me into the most caring of embraces.

'So, are you managing to keep your head above water?' she asks me. 'No one's talked about anything else these whole nine months.'

'I've stopped listening,' I reply with a smile.

I spent seven months listening, in spite of Alvid and Siv telling me not to. When I read the article in *Aftonbladet* that said Freyja and Anneli had enticed Sofia and Maria into their trap by promising them a ludicrous sum of money for a modelling shoot – and driven them to the manor in *our* boat, enough was enough. I didn't want to know anymore.

How many innocent souls did they lure into their web? Siv is still moving heaven and earth to trace any potential victims before 2012. Because Sofia Axelsson might not have been the first.

'I suppose with the trial starting in ten days, we're not out of the woods yet,' Lotta says. 'It's going to be hell. We'll be glad when it all blows over. Anyway,' she changes tack, realising the topic's irritating me, 'it looks like the whole of Sweden is on your side. Hashtag Batman&Rosén, Hashtag FreeRosén and ... what's that other one? Emma told me ... Ah yes. Hashtag DexterRosén! People are extraordinary.'

They are, and so are the times we're living in. Everything that drives me mad about social media has been working in my favour since I was arrested. Here I was, thinking my home was going to be vandalised by vigilantes and there'd be petitions going around to drive me out of the sleepy little village of Djursholm, and quite the opposite has happened. My neighbours have brought food over for me and invited me to dinner. I even received some indecent propositions – including one from a married woman.

'I hope you won't have to wear that thing on your ankle much longer,' Lotta adds.

'I won't get away without doing at least some hard time, you know.'

'Emma told me that Gussman's paying for your defence. He's got that heavy of his representing you, hasn't he?'

I laugh and nod. That moniker suits Hjelm to a T.

'So, like I always say, anything is possible.' Lotta gives me a solar smile – too bright for even the darkest of moods to resist.

The boat docks on Storholmen and the passengers disembark. Lotta heads back to sea, and I venture forth to face my demons.

✄

Ett Glas is right there in front of me, empty and inanimate. As my therapist predicted, everything's coming back to me, all at once. It's like there are a thousand voices whispering my story.

So, I do as she suggested and stand there in front of the café, feeling like I'm preparing myself for a duel. Even after six months of therapy, the same thing keeps slapping me in the face – that I was complicit in what Freyja inflicted on innocent people. It's my job to see through the masks people wear and expose them. And yet I saw nothing.

When I walked in on her that night, Freyja switched off her computer immediately and refused to give me the passwords she used to lock her morbid memories away.

So I picked her up and carried her down to the cellar, kicking and biting, to tie her up and interview her like I would any other suspect. How long had she been killing people? How many children had she killed? And most of all, who was she with? Who was holding the camera? Who was her accomplice?

I bombarded her with questions all night. I deprived her of food, water and the bathroom. But she said nothing. Not a word. Instead, she subjected me to silence, and it was terrifying. There was no remorse in her eyes whatsoever. It was as if, all of a sudden, someone else was living inside her body.

I couldn't stand her silence, or how powerless I was to get her to talk. It was because I hadn't seen her true face that Sofia died. And Maria too. While I was holding Freyja captive in our cellar, Maria was kidnapped and taken to the manor on the island to be tortured to death in an underground bunker by my wife's accomplice.

I didn't want to call Siv. I couldn't ask her to clean up the blood I'd allowed to be spilled. I just couldn't. If I'd called her that night, I would have been sidelined, suspected of aiding and abetting, kicked off the force. The career and life I knew, and had patiently and painstakingly built, were over, anyway. What had happened bulldozed through it all, burned it to the ground. It was a death I'd have to come to terms with. I'd have to rebuild everything, learn it all over again, start from scratch. All that was left of me was the desire to repair the damage my ignorance had done.

I could only think of one way to redeem myself. For the victims, for myself, for Siv, Alvid, Paola and all my colleagues. And that was to find my wife's accomplice, by investigating or by getting

Freyja to talk. Once I'd found that person, I would arrest them and take them in with Freyja. I knew I'd be arrested myself for kidnapping and imprisonment, and I'd lose my job, but that was a price I was willing to pay.

So, I tied Freyja up and locked her in our cellar, to treat her the way she treated her victims. And, to explain her absence, I invented the most plausible scenario – drowning. Freyja is an excellent swimmer, but she's always taken senseless risks, such as venturing out to sea after nightfall.

Three days after my surprise-gone-wrong and that horrific discovery, I went for dinner in town with Alvid to fabricate an alibi for myself. When I came home, I put Freyja's clothes in a pile on our jetty, where she always leaves them when she goes for a swim. That was when all the unbearable lies began. When I said Freyja was nowhere to be found when I got home – not in our bedroom, nor in her office, so I'd gone outside to see if she was waiting for me by the fire pit. And found her things. 'Freyja didn't come back from her swim,' I kept repeating, before throwing up the anxiety that was tying my stomach in knots.

The only thing I didn't have to fake was my never-ending sadness at having lost the woman I loved. Freyja Rosén was just a figment of my imagination, a projection of my desires and almost certainly my fantasies.

I had to get used to our horrific routine. Every morning and every night, I tried to get her to talk. I tried starving her and taunting her so she'd tell me who the person holding the camera was – the person she killed with, or for. So she'd tell me if she had killed any other children.

But she wouldn't say a word.

In spite of the hatred and the disgust her presence provoked in me, I was incapable of any other form of violence. Maybe my psychologist was right in the end, at least about that. Maybe I don't have anything in common with my wife.

One question is still nagging at me, though. Why did she

choose me as her life partner? Or why did she let me choose her? Did she detect a sliver of darkness in me that she secretly hoped to bring to light? My psychologist tells me I'm taking things too far, I'm punishing myself, but the urge to know is stronger than me. Why?

For the thrill of living with someone who was hunting her without knowing it? Was it some sort of sick role play? Or did she do it for the information she knew she could glean from me about the investigation? My work gave her long stretches of time alone – or 'solitude', as she called it. And she filled that time with Anneli. How did I live under the illusion of a happy marriage? These questions will all go unanswered, and I will keep asking myself them for the rest of my life.

I sigh, exhausted by these few minutes in the company of myself, and I walk around the back of the café, up towards the manor.

The island is bustling with life, as if the ghosts have finally passed into the hereafter so those they've left behind can flourish.

I enter the property through the French formal garden and see two marquees standing in the lower section, facing out to sea. Tonight is the opening ceremony of the manor's centenary celebrations, and Emma has asked me to come. The place has changed, she tells me.

She's chatting with Björn, pointing at the lectern that's been set up by the lower pool. She waves to me, finishes her conversation and comes over to greet me.

We draw each other into a warm embrace. Then, with a grand *ta-da!* and a sweep of her arm, she gestures to the house like a lady of the manor proudly showing off her estate.

'Does it feel like this place is ready for a party, or what?' she beams.

'Absolutely. What time does everything start?'

'In six hours.'

I feign a look of panic.

'I don't think you know me well enough, Inspector. Everything is under control. Come with me,' she adds, slipping her arm into mine.

'Hjelm told me he'd managed to get you out of giving evidence at the trial,' I say as we're walking up towards the house.

'Thank goodness,' she replies. 'I still can't get over how fucked up it was, what they did. Maybe they were trying to keep the cycle of perversion going, like they were passing the poison down from mother to daughter or something.'

Emma's hand squeezes my arm.

It was more likely the opposite, I reflect. With every girl they murdered, Freyja and Anneli were desperately trying to break the maternal chain. To kill a reflection of themselves still under the spell and control of their mothers. Because every new victim they offered to the gods was a chance to detach themselves a little more from their past, my psychologist has explained.

I decide to spare Emma the analysis.

'Anneli wants to see you,' I tell her instead.

'To gloat in the morbid glory of it all – looking her victim's sister in the eye after she lured her into her bed?'

'I don't know. Maybe ... but maybe it's not that simple. Maybe she really did enjoy your company.'

'I swear, it makes me sick to my stomach. I really don't know what drew me to her. How could I not have seen the evil in her? The madness, the perversion. I can't wrap my head around it.'

'You were swept up in your own drama, Emma. There was no space for anything else.'

'Look,' she says as we walk up to Sofia's tree.

I smile.

The evergreen is covered with wreaths of pastel-toned fabric flowers. It looks like it's decked out for the celebration of a fresh season, and now it has a whole new story to tell.

I lean closer to Emma and plant a kiss on her forehead.

'Lulu and I sewed them all,' she says. 'They're the crowns of midsummer festival flowers I never got to weave into Sofia's hair.'

Acknowledgements

Yule Island will always have a special place in my heart, because it's the first novel I dreamed up in this part of the world I moved to with my family in the summer of 2021. As Galabru in the classic French comedy film *Bienvenue chez les Ch'tis* famously said, 'C'est le NOOOOORD.' Sweden really does feel like the Far North for a girl from the South of France like me!

The seed for this story was planted when my friend Anna Winqvist, who came to visit before we'd even finished unpacking our moving boxes on the island of Lidingö, said to me: 'Johana, you do know there's a haunted manor on Storholmen, that little islet just across the water from you, don't you?'

That seed was watered by something my sister from another mister, Eva Senge, said when she came to lend a hand with our little dragons later that summer. I had bought an eighteenth-century dressing table from our house's previous owner, and it came with a number of silver hairbrushes. 'Imagine if there was an SOS hidden inside one of those!' Eva said.

And so, *Yule Island* began to take shape in my mind, in the most gruesome of ways, of course.

I wrote it in the dead of winter during those oh-so-short, snowy days Emma, Viktoria and Karl describe in the book. They were actually the first three friends I made in Sweden. Moving up here was – and still is – quite the adventure for a Mediterranean girl.

First of all, I'd like to thank my family, the Lagunas clan. My parents, Odile and Jean-Louis, and my sister, Elsa, are always by my side, and their infectious energy, their kindness and their unconditional love help to make the distance more doable. Thank you for our bloodthirsty, criminal conversations, the things we read, and for being those second pairs of eyes. I can't do this without you.

Thank you to my four Vikings and their laughs like rays of sunshine, their sweet nothings and the love that makes up for everything, even the nights when they come and get me to find a teddy lost in the bed covers or chase away a monster hiding in the wardrobe.

Heartfelt thanks to the stellar team at my French publisher, Calmann-Lévy – Caroline Lépée, Camille Lucet, Philippe Robinet, Anne Sitruk, Valérie Taillefer, Mélanie Rousset, Patricia Roussel, Adélaïde Sorel, Mélanie Trapateau, Doriane Auvray and Antoine de La Burgade, to name but a few of those I've so enjoyed working and growing alongside.

Lilas Seewald, my agent, my writing fairy godmother, this tandem of ours is ten years old now but I still love riding it with you. I'm raising my glass (of red wine) to you and toasting our next decade!

A thousand thanks to Karen Sullivan and the team at Orenda Books for carrying my books across the channel and across the pond with the energy only they can, and to David Warriner, my terrific translator, my pen and my voice in English, for his talent and keen eye.

Tremendous thanks to Caroline Vallat, my evil twin, whose unconditional love for stories and characters gives me strength with every book and makes me want to tie my readers' hearts in knots, and to Bruno Lamarque, my bro with the southern lilt in his voice who joined me on this trip to the frozen north with his signature passion and sunny spirit.

Thank you to the brilliant Alexandre Beaudoin, doctor of forensic science, for answering all my twisted questions without ever losing patience, and for planting ideas in my mind even wilder than my own.

Huge thanks to Delphine Lamarque-Curan for her words and the pathways they opened up and shed light on, and to Sussi Louise Smith, my rock 'n' roll fairy godmother, for her caring presence and the things we share.

Dear booksellers and avid readers, thank you again and again for bringing my words, my characters and my stories to life. Your passion is what feeds mine. Nothing, absolutely nothing, lifts me up more than your enthusiasm. Our interactions are the reasons why I write.